THE ELEVENTH GRIEVE

THE ELEVENTH GRIEVE

a climate-change novel by

GARTH HALLBERG

The Reason for Everything Press
New York

For the planet

"The terror of the ordinary, Jake.

My job is to show you the terror of the ordinary."

— *Rita Ten Grieve*

CHAPTER 1

THERE WERE NO OYSTERS. THAT WAS HOW IT ALL BEGAN. THERE COULD be no doubt about it, none whatsoever, according to the boyish waiter who had come to take Jake Krimmer's lunch order. In the stuffy dining room of the Athenaeum Club, where high ceilings, thick carpets, and well-spaced tables conspired to muffle errant sounds, the adamant declaration bordered on rudeness, if not outright incivility.

"Hah! Since when?" Krimmer asked amiably, humoring the young man. He wasn't about to risk a scene in the home away from home of so many of Washington, DC's self-important movers and shakers, where stern portraits of presidents past—*club* and *country* and in one case, both—stared down from all four walls. Instead, he kept his eyes fixed on the captivating gloom-and-doom headlines rolling by on his brand-new toy, an iPhone 23X with a supersized, foldout, paper-thin screen.

ARIZONA HEAT WAVE SENDS COST OF GALLON OF DRINKING WATER SOARING, NOW TWICE AS MUCH AS GALLON OF GAS

RISING SEA LEVEL BREACHES PRIVATE HAMPTONS LEVEE; HIGH TIDE SWEEPS AWAY $200 MILLION HOME

FOREST FIRES IN DROUGHT-PLAGUED MICHIGAN ONLY 40% CONTAINED

"I repeat, there are no oysters," the waiter said, even louder and more insistently as he stood stiffly at attention, his hands firmly attached to his sides, as if the satin stripes of his tuxedo pants were made of Velcro.

Krimmer glanced around to make sure no gray and balding heads were turned. "I repeat, too—since when?" he asked, less agreeably this time, as he resumed his preoccupation with the streaming news. Happily, a day rarely went by without a meteorological disaster of one kind or another in some part of the country—extremes of temperature, violent storms, too much precipitation or too little. To Krimmer's unending satisfaction, what was calamitous for those citizens affected by the aerodynamics of an atmosphere gone haywire—"weird weather" was what he was always careful to call it—was exceedingly good for his bank account.

"I say again, there are no oysters," the waiter proclaimed for the third time, amping up the volume as if he failed to grasp that Krimmer, unlike the other diners, hadn't yet seen forty—*Not even close!*—what with his full head of wavy brown hair, and lean, mean, six-foot frame—*OK, five-ten and a half*—attesting to his devotion to his squash game and his treadmill, except on weekends or summer Fridays, when golf was his preferred sport. Hence, it was highly unlikely he was hard of hearing or pre-senile.

Krimmer's eyes finally rose to meet the source of his annoyance. The waiter's lips were parted as he inclined his head over the table, suggesting further explanation might be forthcoming, but all he managed to say was, "Sir."

The young man—the boy really—did look vaguely familiar: a slender, almost willowy frame; wheat-colored, streaky blond hair slicked back into a stubby man bun; cheeks pale and shadowless, not even fuzzed. For one disconcerting moment, Krimmer imagined he was seeing the face of a pretty girl. Not any pretty girl, but a particular pretty girl who was hovering just out of range of conscious recall.

Rather than dwell on that transgressive notion, he targeted his tormentor with his smartphone. The facial recognition app was still in beta test, but it was better than resorting to a fake, "big-fella" hello while you were mentally running through your contact list. Unfortunately, FaceFinder came up empty. Despite his flash of recollection, maybe his memory was playing tricks on him. Or perhaps the lovely lady had refused to be captured on his phone with a twosie.

As Krimmer dismissed the uncanny resemblance, he had no inkling that the waiter's unrelenting assertions were merely an opening salvo by a formidable adversary, intent on waging a bloodless but life-changing battle whose full extent and outcome would not be evident for days. And even if he had had some premonition of what lay ahead, he would never have imagined how difficult it would be to keep his emotions in check and his sanity intact while living through the struggle. For Jake Krimmer was about to undergo a trial by fire in an alternate future, orchestrated by a person of unknown origin, with a technology so advanced, even for early in the fourth decade of the twenty-first century, that at times it seemed supernatural—and perhaps it was. In either case, the imminent ordeal was meant to change Krimmer's entire personal philosophy and world view in a profound and heretofore unimaginable way. But still unsuspecting of what was to come, and habitually skeptical and self-assured, he refused to take the waiter's troubling words literally.

"Help me understand why there are no oysters if they're listed on the menu?" Krimmer asked, polite and formal to a fault.

The enigmatic waiter snapped to attention again. "There are no oysters because the oysters are all dead," he began in a shrill, ominous monotone, as though his monkey suit had morphed into a military uniform and he was a nervous lieutenant, duty-bound to be the bearer of bad news to his commanding officer. "The Blue Points are dead, and the Cotuits and the Wellfleets—all dead. Even the Chesapeakes are—"

Krimmer bristled at the waiter's alarming report. He cut him short, letting out a sharp, guttural sound, half gasp, half growl. "Hah! Since when?"

He loved all oysters, but *Crassostrea virginica* from Chesapeake Bay were at the top of the list. In fact, the experts generally acknowledged that in the original Algonquian dialect, *Chesepiuk* meant Great Shellfish Bay. It wasn't just that Chesapeakes were the truffles of the sea; they were a token of a vanished time, when everything was right with his world, when life was simpler and more innocent. Plump and mineral-sweet and not too briny, a half-dozen Chesapeakes transported Krimmer back to the gauzy memories of his boyhood summers, swimming and sailing and fishing in the fertile, deep-blue waters off the Maryland coast. It had been a rite of passage, the day his father taught him how to pry open their fiercely clenched, corrugated shells and slurp in the slippery meat and salty juice with a single, greedy gulp.

The waiter noticed his customer's anguish, barely. He raised his voice another agonizing notch to offer a perfunctory expression of sympathy. "I'm sorry to be the one to tell you, and I grieve for them myself, but the Chesapeakes are dead, too." Once more, deference came grudgingly. "Sir."

Krimmer glanced around again, his apprehension mounting, but all the members were engrossed in their lunches and their discreet, well-modulated horse-trading. The joke around town was that given the perennially sclerotic Congress, the Athenaeum was where the vital bread-and-butter business of government got done—brokering connections, lobbying votes, and cozying up to wealthy donors. The only reason Krimmer found himself dining alone was that the senior-most assistant secretary of energy had to cancel at the last minute to help his boss deal with a situation that was of special interest to Krimmer: the latest blow to the nation's overloaded electrical grid brought on by weird weather.

Perhaps sensing he had gone too far, the waiter finally relaxed his military posture. Instead, his body curved provocatively over the table, his features dissolving into an almost feminine pout, revealing eyes that loomed large and sorrowful and deep above his transfixed quarry—indigo eyes, that mysterious, mutable blend of violet and navy blue that suffused the eastern sky at end of day, opposite the dying sun. When he spoke, the monotone was gone, replaced by a more natural intonation and a barely noticeable accent, still high-pitched but with a teasing, throaty hum that once again put Krimmer's memory on alert. He was hearing that pretty girl's voice, and now he was certain he had heard it before, maybe flirting at a cocktail party in Georgetown, maybe another man's wandering wife. But before he could place it more precisely, the waiter was pouring poison in his ear. "Why can't I make you understand? The oysters are all dead because the ocean is too warm."

Holy Christmas, that's why he's so effing obnoxious. The waiter was a goddamned Green, the progressive Democrats' answer to the unwavering America Firsters with their sainted relics: Blue Lives Matter flags, Sharpie pens, and fiery-red MAGA baseball caps. Bad enough that the Greens' environmental rants had started to sway sober-minded mainstream politicians. But the thought of being served by a love child of Gaia and the Sierra Club positively ruined his appetite.

"Would you please ask the maître d' to step over here." It was not a question.

"He doesn't have any oysters either. Sir."

The bottomless sorrow of the indigo eyes finally kicked into place. A cocktail party in Georgetown, yes, but it wasn't another man's wife, it was a twenty-something Washington newbie who'd come on to him a week ago, or so he thought—fresh blood in the press corps maybe, or a political operative or PR flack. Her name was Rita; that much was coming back to him. That and a foreign-sounding last name to go with her vaguely foreign accent. But when he suggested escaping for a quiet dinner, she must have thought he was too old for her, or too tipsy. Rita what's-her-name not only brushed him off but also refused to give him her email or her cell.

Once again confused and embarrassed by the gender-bending image, Krimmer buried his head in his wide-screen smartphone. "How many times do I have to ask? Please get me Marcus," he said. *That's that,* he told himself, as he resumed scrolling through the Pollyanna-challenged news stories, permitting himself a secretive, self-satisfied smile when he finally found what he was searching for: WIDESPREAD BROWNOUT IN MIAMI AREA ENTERS FOURTH DAY.

Just as Krimmer had hoped, the Erector-Set towers that criss-crossed the flat Florida landscape with high-voltage transmission lines had toppled like toys in the face of a violent line of thunder-storms. Meanwhile, the transformers had exploded like cherry bombs trying to keep up with the surging demand for electricity from the air conditioning–obsessed, short-tempered citizenry. The final body count for Sunshine Energy, the local electrical utility, was half-a-dozen substations, along with about thirty miles of overhead lines. Demand was down—who needed electricity if the Intracoastal Waterway was meandering through your living room?—but supply was down even more, creating a bottleneck in the flow of power. In industry terms, the grid was "congested."

In order to keep Sunshine's customers happy, the SPC or South-east Power Combine, the regional grid operator in six southeastern states, had to send in reinforcements—more expensive electricity from utilities in Georgia and the Carolinas. The first dirty little secret was that, adhering to Generally Accepted Accounting Principles, Sun-shine's customers were charged the higher rate for *all* the electricity they used during the congestion period, not just a prorated amount. The second was that this so-called *congestion revenue*, the difference between the "normal" rate and the higher rate actually paid by cus-tomers, didn't go to the utility or SPC, but to Krimmer.

Neither inspired scam nor sharp business practice, the entire scheme was perfectly legitimate and aboveboard. Krimmer had bid on Financial Transmission Rights, or FTRs, auctioned off by the Southeast Power Combine, the grid operator, to hedge against unforeseen increases in demand or reduced supply. FTRs were complex financial instruments that jumped in value anytime the grid was congested—as it was currently, battered by weird weather. These futures contracts entitled the holder to collect any congestion revenue generated between two specified points during a specified time period—e.g. from the Carolinas to Miami for several days this week. Krimmer's successful bids would earn him an impressive return per megawatt hour, or a couple-hundred g's when the congestion period ended tomorrow or the next day. Sunshine Energy's customers could scream—assuming they ever found out about it or could understand it, both of which were highly unlikely—but in a deregulated energy market, financial engineering was king.

"Is something wrong, sir?" Marcus, the always reliable, gray-haired maître d' was by his side. He had a confused, faraway expression, as if he wasn't sure who Krimmer was, as if FaceFinder was failing him, too.

It took Krimmer a moment to realize that the waiter was nowhere in sight. He got right to the point. "Why are there no oysters?"

"No oysters? Who told you that?"

"The new waiter."

Marcus made a quick survey of the dining room. "You mean Henry? He's hardly new. He's been with us for six months."

"No, not Henry." Henry was an ex-defensive back for the Washington Commanders. After five years in the NFL, he was lucky that his only disability was a permanent stoop. "The young one. Kind of blond, with bluish eyes?" When Marcus didn't seem to understand, Krimmer added, "The boy with the big mouth." When that didn't do the trick either, he supplied the clincher—"The fucking Green."

The maître d' looked profoundly pained, as if Krimmer had discovered a bug floating in his soup. Not electronic, of course—never in the Athenaeum—but a bug of the six-legged variety. "You know we wouldn't hire that kind, sir," Marcus reassured him.

"Then who told you I wanted to see you?"

"Why, no one told me. If I may say so, sir, you had a very distressed expression on your face. I thought I'd better check if everything was OK."

Krimmer took another look around, but he was no more successful than the maître d'. "You mean to say that we don't have a new waiter here, who . . . who kind of looks like a girl?" *A girl named Rita who I had high hopes for, in fact.*

Marcus's patient smile was born of years of service. "No sir, but I can assure you, we do have oysters. They're getting harder to come by, and at the price we must charge, they don't exactly fly out of the kitchen."

"Are they local?" Despite the waiter's apocalyptic tidings, Krimmer was eternally grateful that wild oysters from Chesapeake Bay were at least surviving, if not exactly thriving, pushing back against the rising water temperature, parasites, residential and industrial pollution, and a century and a half of mechanical overharvesting. And in a pinch, there were good ones to be had from the aquaculture farms down in Virginia.

"Sorry, sir. All we have today are Malpeques from Canada."

Krimmer had enough presence of mind to return Marcus's smile, not only to conceal his disappointment but also his growing uneasiness about the entire incident. Inexplicably, the mention of Malpeques had triggered the names of their now dearly departed brethren, at least according to the nonexistent, boyish-girlish waiter. They were merrily tripping through his brain like annoying background music.

"You know, sir, the ocean's not so warm up in Nova Scotia," Marcus said.

For some reason, Krimmer felt an explanation was in order. "It's not so much the temperature as the acid water that gets them," he clarified. "It eats away the shells of the young oysters so they can't harden."

"Of course, you're the expert, sir," Marcus allowed with just a hint of smugness, bestowing on Krimmer a pang of guilt to accompany the litany of endangered bivalves, and transforming the background music into a clod-footed march. *As if I should take the reason for the oysters' reported demise personally—as if it's my fault that there's big money to be made from the consequences of weird weather.* Krimmer grabbed his smartphone, tapping the link to the video of the press conference where the senior-most assistant's boss, the secretary himself, was facing down the customary phalanx of microphones and cameras.

"I'm terribly sorry for the confusion. May I bring you a half-dozen Malpeques to start, sir?"

The sound was muted, but on the big screen Krimmer couldn't miss how Mr. Secretary's lips were uncannily flapping in perfect time with the marching oysters. The scrolling text across the bottom told the story: ENERGY CZAR ASSURES FLORIDA CRISIS WILL END SHORTLY; BAN ON DAYTIME AIR CONDITIONERS TO BE LIFTED TOMORROW.

Krimmer tried to tune out the music with the thought of how well his FTRs would be performing.

"May I, Mr. Krimmer?"

"No, that's all right," he replied without looking up. "I've changed my mind about the oysters." *What seems to be left of it*, he added silently, as the noisy procession snaked from his left hemisphere to the right, abandoning any pretense of being rational, much less quieting down.

"Very good, sir. I'll have someone bring the rest of your lunch immediately. What else did you order?"

Every marching band needs a drum major, or was it a majorette? "Someone" immediately conjured up the image of indigo-eyes—the waiter or the cocktail-party newbie, it wasn't at all clear—heading up the parade. "What else did I order?" Krimmer mumbled.

"I can check with the kitchen, of course," he heard Marcus say, as the rhythmic pounding found its way into the deepest, most intimate recesses of his beleaguered gray matter, and happily took on a more familiar, more benign aspect. The merry band of oysters was now splashing along a strip of pristine Chesapeake beach, followed by a prancing, towheaded little boy, clapping and cheering to his watching parents that the oysters were alive after all. Not just the Chesapeakes and Blue Points and Wellfleets and Cotuits, but the Duxburys from Cape Cod, and the Chincoteagues from Maryland's Eastern Shore, and the Hog Islands from the north coast of California, and the Moonstones from Rhode Island, and the Peconic Golds from Long Island Sound, and the Bodie Islands from North Carolina's Outer Banks, and the Apalachicolas from the bulge in the Florida Panhandle. All of them were joyously and defiantly alive, oysters from all across America, from anywhere the brackish, intertidal edges of the ocean kissed the land.

For a few brief moments, until an indigo shadow fell across the scene, this dizzying mash-up of memory and anxiety was undeniably real to Krimmer, as real as the concerned gaze of Marcus, and the hand he was extending toward Krimmer's shoulder as if to steady him. "Are you all right, sir?" the maître d' asked.

Krimmer shook his head, meaning to agree.

"I think you need to eat something, sir."

"That's all right," Krimmer said, frightened he might be completely losing it at such an early age. "I've changed my mind about lunch, too."

He rose slowly from his chair, making a point of staring straight ahead. Marcus stepped aside with the kind of deferential nod that the waiter, real or imaginary, could never have mustered. With the Athenaeum's amply separated tables, no dodging or weaving was necessary to reach the entrance to the dining room. The ancient elevator was creaking slowly toward the rooftop gym, so Krimmer headed for the fire stairs, effortlessly taking them two at a time, down all three flights without an extra gasp for breath. Before opening the door to the lobby, he stopped and took a moment to adjust his tie as he tried to make sense of what had just happened.

Nothing has changed, he told himself. *Nothing is different despite the increasing regularity and severity of weird weather.* Hadn't he just read somewhere that some Silicon Valley bro was offering $100 million to anyone who could prove beyond a shadow of a doubt that the gradual rise in global temperature, a measly average of one-quarter degree Fahrenheit per decade since 1970, was something other than the same kind of natural variation that the planet had experienced for tens of thousands of years? What idiotic geek, even one who was a zillionaire, would risk that kind of money if there was any chance it was true—if it really was an abnormally warming climate, and not just an unfortunate stretch of weird weather, that was causing all the trouble?

So why couldn't he stop himself from imagining the worst? Why couldn't he shake the feeling that his shadowy nemesis was still standing stiffly at his side, a ghostly subaltern insisting on the oysters' doom, calling out a mournful cadence as they marched on by, ratcheting up his incipient guilt with each new name of the fallen or battle now lost?

CHAPTER 2

KRIMMER STARTED TO FEEL MORE LIKE HIMSELF THE MINUTE HE stepped outside. He ripped off his tie, slung his suit jacket over his shoulder, and quickly concluded that his brush with an oyster-happy apparition could be safely explained away by the enigmatic waiter's doppelgänger-resemblance to the cocktail-party newbie, the mysterious Rita. As for Marcus's head scratching, Jake decided the maître d' must be getting forgetful in his old age.

Lunch hour in Washington on an unusually warm and sunny autumn afternoon could have that kind of therapeutic effect. The same dome of high pressure stifling Florida was bringing springtime in October to the entire National Capital Region. On days like this, the buds were blooming—not the cherry blossoms, but the multitude of female federal workers who kept the nation's bureaucracy functioning, if not exactly humming. The short skirts and flimsy blouses made the brief walk back to his office down Pennsylvania Avenue highly scenic. Several times, a slender, flaxen-haired beauty reminded him of the indigo-eyed temptress, and how alluring she was before she blew him off. *Rita, Rita Ten-something . . . Dutch maybe . . . that's it. Hey, what the hell, Connie just bailed on our get-away plans for the long Columbus Day weekend. Why not try to track Rita down this afternoon?*

Caught up in this cloudless mood, Krimmer wondered how he'd ever allowed himself to be the least bit remorseful about how he earned his livelihood. Why apologize, just because the Chicken Littles referred to the somewhat sordid and sometimes socially embarrassing source of his outrageous income as "climate change"—a.k.a. anthropogenic, or man-made, global warming? Personally, he'd rather be confined for life in a sweltering Arizona tract house with a brood of bawling rug rats than dignify any of those exaggerated, high-minded monikers by letting them pass his lips. Hence, his preference for the more descriptive phrase—"weird weather."

Whatever you called it, or whether you ascribed it to mankind's selfish shortsightedness or to a fickle Mother Nature or even to a moody judgmental deity, weird weather was an undeniable fact of life. And like any other fact of life that lent itself to making money, such as spurious blockchain currencies or crop failure or a space-weapons race, it presented an enticing opportunity for a savvy, ideology-adverse entrepreneur.

In a capitalist economy, the supply of electricity was not an inalienable right, like life, liberty, or the pursuit of happiness. Electrical power was no different than soybeans or copper, a commodity that could be bought and sold to help satisfy the voracious appetite of the free market. And like any commodity, its fundamental value was only determined by the law of supply and demand, expertly modulated by the push and pull of self-interested speculators. The trick was to identify the weak links so that the system could be legally gamed, profitably and repeatedly. That's where the regional grid operators, like the Southeast Power Combine, came in handy.

About 75 percent of the country's Rube Goldberg–style electrical grid—200,000-odd miles of high-voltage transmission lines,

5.5 million miles of local lines, 500-plus utility companies—was coordinated by a congressionally sanctioned, jerry-rigged network of eight nonprofit Independent System Operators and Regional Transmission Organizations—or ISOs and RTOs. These regional grid operators were charged with dealing with the inevitable disconnects between supply and demand brought on by aging equipment, burdensome environmental requirements, the occasional terrorist threat, the more frequent Russian or third-world hacker, and—oh yes—weird weather.

Hence, the periodic auctions of Financial Transmission Rights by the grid operators to smooth out the costs and lessen the financial risks of transferring power from the haves to the have-nots. But if an astute speculator like Krimmer could accurately forecast that weird weather was on the way, he could snap up any FTR that was mispriced and make a handsome profit.

More better yet, a Financial Transmission Right was nothing but another form of the smart money's favorite potato chip: a derivative. The more you eat, the more you want. And like any derivative, it was a naked monetary instrument. It didn't obligate the holder to *physically* transmit electricity from one system to another. The electricity would still flow as needed, but the successful bidder for an FTR could sit back and collect the congestion revenue between one location and another without the unnecessary complication of having to dirty their hands with the operation of the business. What could be simpler or more efficient, as long as you could foresee the future—who needed power and when?

"Hey, Sam," Krimmer yelled as he burst through the office door, searching for his number one fortune-teller: the thirtysomething, chestnut-haired, broad-shouldered, lacrosse-playing, Rhodes Scholar finalist from the University of Oklahoma, the state where she was born and bred. No babushka or gypsy getup for this sexy seer; she looked like a million bucks.

Of course, that didn't matter anymore, Krimmer quickly admonished himself. *It was over, six months ago, but who was counting?* No more than it mattered how simpatico they'd been in every way, how first-time–long-time he'd found someone with whom he could envision sharing his life, maybe even plan for the future. It didn't even matter that the breakup was a self-inflicted wound, or that she was a dissertation short of a PhD in atmospheric sciences. The only thing that mattered was that Sam was still his crack meteorologist and secret weapon.

"There you are," he said cheerily as he stuck his head over the half-wall of her cubicle. Krimmer was well aware his triumph today was actually Samantha's. She had put out an early call on the extreme conditions in Florida, so when the temperature in Miami soared above 105 degrees for three straight days, Krimmer made a killing with his FTRs. But his real coup—thanks to Sam—was doubling down on his bet in the aftermath of the heat wave, correctly anticipating that once the cold front rolled in from the west, the thunderstorms would break the spike in temperature with commensurate fury, taking another big bite out of Sunshine Energy's remaining supply.

Krimmer's good humor didn't seem to be catching. Samantha kept her eyes glued on her trusty crystal ball—the array of screens, three high, four wide, on which she depended for her unerringly accurate predictions.

"You hear the latest from Florida?" he finally asked. "Looks like we've got another day of easy money."

Sam seemed in no hurry to respond. When she did turn to face him, she fixed him with those big, brown, soulful eyes—eyes that were known to have made him melt in a way indigo never would. "That's old news," she said.

He hesitated. "Drinks on me, tonight. Whaddaya say?"

"Did you forget we don't do that anymore, Krims?" Samantha asked in a dreary, downbeat tone he'd heard more than once, usually when she was feeling blue about missing out on Oxford or never completing her doctorate. Krimmer wondered what was up with her now, considering how well things were going.

"Oh, yeah, just kidding," he said as he quickly retreated, skipping over to his in-house quant's cube. In Wall Street parlance, *quant* was short for *quantitative*—a computer geek schooled in the dark arts of statistical analysis. "Hey, Robert, did ya hear? We scored big in Miami."

"Two standard deviations," the quant conceded.

Krimmer started to frown, then realized that was a big win, statistically. "Hey, have you grabbed lunch yet? How about pizza to celebrate?"

"Slice is on your desk, chief."

Krimmer didn't blink. Quants were paid to stay one step ahead of the pack.

"Anchovies and mushrooms, just the way you like it."

"Way to go," Krimmer said, as he made a beeline for his corner cube and the exhilarating panorama of the National Mall outside his window. He could see all the way from the Washington Monument on his right to the Capitol building on his left—*politically speaking, it would be a distinct improvement the other way around.* The view cost him a small fortune every month, thanks to the absurd Height of Buildings Act of 1910, which basically put a lid on the Washington skyline—think Paris, rather than New York or London—while jacking the price of commercial office space into the stratosphere. Krimmer's penthouse-level perch was a rare exception to the law. It only existed because Congress got its act together long enough to pass an amendment that permitted human occupancy on the roofs of existing buildings, shoehorned in around all the HVAC machinery. Still, at moments like this, the expense was worth it for the high it gave him, being able to look down on the beautiful heart of the dysfunctional nation.

Krimmer tapped his desktop computer screen to get his calls. Jared Mortenson's face popped up first, looking every inch the straitlaced

Beltway attorney. Blue suit, white shirt, red tie, grim lips, crossed arms, spine bent uncomfortably straight—more painful than a portrait in a high school yearbook. Mortenson was the firm's lawyer and, optics aside, he was a damned fine legal beagle, making sure Krimmer stayed out of regulatory trouble. He was also an ace fixer, smoothing over any misunderstandings about who owed what to whom, and running interference with the pesky media. Those stalwart defenders of the little guy never stopped sniffing around for their next tiresomely routine, greedy finance–guy exposé.

Sadly, Mortenson's personal life was less buttoned up. In fact, it wasn't buttoned up at all, thanks to an injudicious early marriage that lasted until he had acquired an enviable asset base and then ended tragically—he was left with peanuts. His ex-wife was even awarded the BMW Spyder i9 plug-in hybrid with the swan-wing doors and shark-nose front end, a vehicle that Krimmer had heard so much about but never seen that he had concluded it was as mythical as Pegasus or the Phoenix. As a result, even though Jared was a couple of years older, he looked up to Jake: for his style, his money, and especially his success with the ladies, although he went to great pains to hide his hero-worship behind an endless barrage of chippy banter. He had shamelessly adopted Krimmer like a lost dog adopts a soft-touch stranger. Or maybe it was the other way around: maybe Jake had felt sorry and adopted him. In the end, it didn't matter. You needed either a dog or a friend in Washington, and Jared was a little of both.

Krimmer reminded himself that Mortenson only called on his office line when there was an issue. If Jared had just wanted to meet up for a drink or a game of squash, he would use his smartphone or text. Hell, trouble could always wait; first things first.

Krimmer took a bite of pizza and Googled *Rita Ten Holland*—typing the name in the old-fashioned way—the AI chatbot would probably come up with hotels in Amsterdam. He scanned the first couple pages of the millions of results and clicked off. *Not to worry.*

The sweeping view of the city from his window was as illusory as the gender-bending waiter. In reality, Washington was a small town, and the social circuit Krimmer traveled was even smaller. He would see the cocktail-party newbie again and there would be a different outcome this time, he was certain. Why, he wouldn't be the least bit surprised if after thinking it over, she was the one who reached out to reconnect with the charming and engaging fellow she had so hastily rebuffed. For a second, he even imagined it might be Ms. Indigo-Eyes herself who was calling his name.

"Got a minute, Krims?"

He swung around in his chair. Samantha and Robert were standing at the entrance to his cubicle. Krimmer was not much for formality—hence the open office plan, although his cubicle was twice the size of theirs combined, and the walls were half again as high. Robert wore faded jeans, a ratty-looking T-shirt from the Baltimore zoo, and a pair of black-and-white sneakers that predated Nikes, if not all of basketball. Samantha was always perfectly groomed and coiffed, in a classic, conservative but office-casual way, but today she was over the top. Her navy-blue suit and snow-white, pleated blouse was accented by an antique cameo brooch, the ivory-skinned Victorian *grande dame* securing the ruffle collar not half as elegant as she was.

"Hey, you got a job interview or something?"

Samantha scowled at his wisecrack. "I had a conference this morning at Timmy's school." Timmy was her manifestly ungovernable six-year-old, maybe even something more serious—Sam had never said, but Krimmer had his suspicions. Nonetheless, she loved Timmy more than life, even if he was the spitting image of her ex-husband, a blue-eyed, blond-haired, master-race type, to hear Samantha describe him.

"So what's up, doc?" he asked, an old in-joke from the days he and Sam did have drinks after work, and he didn't have to warn himself to stay in all-business mode.

Samantha was still scowling. "Oklahoma."

Robert jumped in. "We've got another hot one, chief," he said, flashing a thumbs-up in a vain attempt to act businesslike.

"No pun intended?"

The beginnings of a grin froze on Robert's face, as though he was unsure whether to expand it further or beat a fast retreat. Despite their math skills, quants were always a little slow on the uptake.

Samantha had apparently decided to forgive him for his earlier lack of sensitivity. "What would you say, Krims, to tornadoes?" she exclaimed, one eyebrow arched knowingly, an inverse wink.

"Tornadoes, huh? I should have guessed."

"How about an EF5?"

Krimmer's eyes widened. EF5s were rare, but they could be gold mines. With wind speeds in excess of 200 miles per hour and a ground track up to a mile wide, they pretty much devastated anything in their path. What would make Krimmer's day would be a lucky strike on a power plant or high-voltage transmission line, compromising supply for days.

"An EF5? Are you sure?"

"I'd say it's fifty-fifty whether it's rated an EF5," Samantha said. "There have only been three, nationally, in the past five years. But an EF4 is no walk in the park."

Krimmer stroked his chin. "When?" he asked.

"Sunday. Day after tomorrow."

"That doesn't give us much time."

"It's not like predicting the tide, Krims, or a solar eclipse."

"That's why we pay you the big bucks, Sam," he said, and instantly regretted it when Robert's face fell, and Samantha threatened to scowl again.

As Samantha explained it, a bubble of warm, moist air was making its way north from the Gulf of Mexico, while the frigid polar vortex was putting in an early appearance over the Great Lakes, thanks to the record low level of summer sea ice in the Arctic. The impending collision would create an exceptionally large thermal imbalance that would hang around for days and spawn severe weather throughout the Great Plains.

"Gotta love that melting Arctic sea ice," Krimmer exclaimed.

Sam's enthusiasm deflated. "Not good news for Tornado Alley."

"I though Tornado Alley shifted east into Missouri and Arkansas."

"Nope, it just got wider. Now it's a six-lane highway."

"But shouldn't less sea ice mean less cold and a weaker vortex?" Krimmer asked.

"Less ice means less jet stream, too," Sam replied. "So neither party is going anywhere anytime soon."

"What do the models have to say, Robert?"

"Let's have a look at the grid," the quant said enthusiastically.

Krimmer pushed the magic button on his desk. The pool table–sized screen on the interior wall lit up to display the entire dendritic US electrical grid, an anatomical illustration of the central nervous system of the nation. The flashing, color-coded high-voltage lines, interconnecting the utilities within the ISOs and RTOs, were updated in real time to show where congestion pricing was in effect.

"Samantha can't identify a datum for the atmospheric disruptions with any precision," Robert said, using a laser pointer to make a large circle in central and eastern Oklahoma. "So we need to employ a Bayesian probability distribution to locate the areas most likely to experience outages. I want to check the numbers again, but based on the hyper-parameters of previous storms, the probabilistic path goes right through the territory of the CSPP, with GPG&E as the bull's-eye."

Translated into English, Robert was recommending the purchase of Financial Transmission Rights that would lock in any congestion revenue generated in the next few days, if and when Great Plains Gas & Electric had to import more expensive electricity from any number of utilities in the fourteen-state Regional Transmission Organization, the Central States Power Pool.

"What's the upside?" Krimmer asked.

"That's up to you," Robert said, handing Krimmer a printout crawling with figures; a half dozen lines were highlighted in yellow. "Those are my optimal predictions for the expected value of the FTRs between GPG&E and the utilities the CSPP is most likely to employ to provide power." The greater the portfolio of Financial Transmission Rights Krimmer contracted for, the greater the potential payoff, or the greater the hit to his bottom line if the weather never got weird and remained calm and barbecue-friendly. "You decide how much you want to bet, chief."

"How much we want to *invest*," Krimmer corrected him. "How confident are you, Sam, that it's likely to develop into an EF5?"

Samantha's face fell. "I've already called my grandma and told her to stock up on groceries. Nothing perishable," she added as she anxiously ran her hand through her hair.

Krimmer frowned and nodded sympathetically. "I'm sure everything will work out OK," he said. "What about Norman? What do they have to say?" Norman wasn't a person, but rather a place: Norman, Oklahoma, the headquarters of NOAA's Storm Prediction Center, bastard child of the National Oceanic and Atmospheric Administration. They were the same bunch of clowns who were always nattering about climate change, although they usually had the decency and political awareness to hedge their claims about how much was natural variation and how much was man-made.

"They haven't issued an official watch," Samantha told him. "You know how the secretary came down on them last month about crying wolf. They don't want to cause unnecessary panic, so they'll underplay it until they're sure the atmospheric disturbance is that big. Especially since, historically, peak tornado season in those parts is March to August."

That was just about the funniest thing Krimmer had heard all day. "Peak tornado season's March to August?" he yelped. "Hah! Since when?"

CHAPTER 3

SAMANTHA LINGERED IN KRIMMER'S OFFICE AS ROBERT WENT OFF TO rerun the numbers. After her gloomy greeting and her anxiety about her grandmother, Krimmer had no idea what to expect next.

"How are you feeling about everything, Jake?" she asked, causing his antennae to begin to vibrate. Unless it was a personal matter, Samantha always called him *Krims* at work. *Jake* was for afterward.

"I'm feeling great, Sam," he replied cautiously. "You've done it again. That prospective EF5 looks like a really big opportunity."

"That's not what I'm asking," she said, her face an expressionless mask.

Krimmer tensed, then exhaled. "I'm sorry, I shouldn't have kidded about drinks," he said, as he looked around his desk for something to do with his hands. "It must have been a touch of spring fever." When she didn't immediately smile, he made it bigger and brighter. "Can you beat that, Sam? Spring fever in October!"

Samantha was not amused. "Sometimes people can't say what they mean unless they joke about it."

"No, I think it's better if we stick with our arrangement," he said automatically, sounding surer than he truly was. He started fidgeting with his pen. "I think it's right for both of us."

When his former meteorologist quit, Krimmer's headhunter had sent him half a dozen candidates, but none clicked until Samantha Richards showed up to interview for the job. Her education, experience, and salary history were ideal, and the confident and brainy way she handled Krimmer's barrage of questions reassured him that she wouldn't wilt in the pressure cooker of a small office with big-money decisions on the line.

That Sam's looks and personality also checked off all his boxes did give him momentary pause. The last thing he needed was to throw sand in the gears of a smoothly functioning business with an office romance; but in the end, he decided she was "safe." It wasn't a problem that she appeared to be past the cusp of thirty—with maturity came more realistic expectations. But like many women her age, she had emotional complications. In her case, it wasn't the ticking of a biological clock, but a difficult personal situation—a divorced, single mom riding herd on a six-year-old boy. Instant buzzkill for your basic bachelor, even before he had experienced the aforementioned boy firsthand.

So Krimmer was more surprised than anyone when the professional admiration forged in the close quarters of the office, together with the increasingly frequent celebratory drinks after work, led to something more. Those moony, dream-fueled sessions revealed some embarrassing, mutual retro passions, like sappy Puccini operas, anything by Fitzgerald or early Hemingway, and a pair of classic films—*Casablanca* was a slam dunk, but for a half-court buzzer beater, you couldn't match the sci-fi cult movie *Galaxy Quest*. Throw in a devotion for the local sports teams—the Nationals, the Wizards, the Commanders, and Georgetown basketball—add two adventurous appetites for anything from bison burgers to Vietnamese *bánh mì* sandwiches to haute cuisine, and chase it with some great sex, and before he knew it the relationship was in grave danger of getting serious. Well, serious for Samantha anyway. And truth be told, serious for Krimmer as well— very serious, even though he was never willing to admit to himself she might be *the one*, much less come right out and tell her so.

Krimmer's unanticipated state of bliss presented a dilemma. He was self-aware enough to know that his track record was less than sterling. Despite his best efforts and intentions, his girlfriends tended to become *ex* sooner rather than later. His relationship with Samantha was rapidly approaching a point where sitting tight would no longer be an option; he would be expected to declare himself one way or the other. What's more, the longer he ignored the unstable status quo, the more acrimonious any breakup was likely to be, and Sam was too valuable an employee to lose. The firm's revenue had almost doubled in the nine months they'd worked together.

After much soul-searching and uncharacteristic waffling—*What am I really afraid of?*—he broached the idea of a "structured separation" in the most flattering and financially lucrative terms. To both his surprise and relief, after an initial, vituperative outburst and two days of frosty silence—Krimmer had expected no less—Samantha came around to the idea of a personal *entente cordiale*, where she would continue being the weird-weather guru in the outfit in return for a strict hands-off policy. A sizable raise and generous cut of the profits sealed the deal.

Samantha stared him down until he stopped fiddling with the pen. "Oh, I guess you're right, it's working," she finally said, seeming to capitulate. "It's just . . . it's just that . . ."

"It's just what, Sam?" Krimmer asked. Something was bugging her badly, and he certainly didn't want to aggravate the situation by appearing uncaring.

"I'm sick at heart about my grandma out there in Tornado Alley," she said, running her fingers nervously through her hair again, jeopardizing her customary look of perfection. "My ninety-one-year-old grandma."

"You called her, you've warned her," he said. "What else can you do?"

"I don't know," Samantha said, shaking her head. "I guess what I'm saying—it's not just her. Do you know what it's like when a big twister touches down?"

"The Great Plains is one part of the country I've never had the pleasure of visiting," he said, shaking his own head with great solemnity, as though even if he didn't know firsthand, he surely understood.

"But you've seen the devastation afterward."

"Of course, I've seen the videos on the *Journal*'s website. And on the Weather Channel. It can be horrible."

The worry lines between Samantha's eyebrows deepened. "So you know, even if people do take precautions, sometimes it doesn't matter," she said. "All this extreme weather has a way of sticking it to a lot of innocent folks, even if they know it's coming."

He had sense enough to keep quiet as she crossed her arms, fingering the cameo brooch like a rosary bead, her eyes filling and her cheeks puffing out as though she was getting ready to burst. "I'm afraid all my anxiety is starting to affect Timmy. He woke up in the middle of the night, screaming about monsters in his bedroom."

Finally. That was probably what was on her mind right from the beginning.

"Oh, children always have scary dreams. He'll be all right," Krimmer replied, going out of his way to be supportive.

"And he's acting out at school," Samantha said, still struggling to hold it all in. "Why do you think I had a conference this morning?"

"What happened?"

"I don't want to talk about it," she said irritably.

"Oh, c'mon Sam, cheer up. I'm sure whatever he did, it wasn't all that bad." *Certainly not as bad as the time we took him to that god-awful mouse movie.* When all Timmy wanted to do was drib-ble popcorn down the collar of the little girl in the row in front of them, until finally her mother turned around and yelled at him— Krimmer!—as if he were the one responsible, and not just for some harmless teasing but for molesting her daughter. At least that finally got Sam to wake up. She apologized profusely to the mother, and then to him for not paying attention, so much and so loudly that half the theatre started shushing her because they couldn't hear what the goddamned rodent on the screen was squeaking to his buddy the cat.

"Besides, I know you're worried, but we need those EF5s," Krimmer said, smiling in encouragement. "They pay the rent and then some."

Samantha stared at him uncomprehendingly, as if he were from another planet—one of the eight-armed Thermians in *Galaxy Quest* perhaps, except their holographic simulators could make them cud-dly and sympathetic, and he clearly wasn't. "You don't have a clue about what I'm getting at, do you, Jake?" she said, the sadness in her voice draining it of any energy. "You try to raise a rambunctious six-year-old by yourself and see what it's like."

"I do understand," he protested.

Samantha's stare had devolved into a stony silence.

"I really do know what it's like." *Trust me, how could I forget?*

"Have you called Jared back yet?" she asked, snapping out of her funk. "He was very anxious to speak with you."

"What, is something wrong?"

"You obviously haven't called him," Samantha said. "I'll let Jared tell you about it."

Before he could say anything in his own defense, Krimmer's smartphone erupted with Mortenson's personal ringtone: two long woofs and a short yip. The barking reflected not only his dual status as both loyal friend and faithful canine, but also his desperate need for attention, Morse code for *me.* In the same spirit, the hello-photo couldn't have been more different than his big-dog lawyerly portrait on his office line. Jared's blue-eyed, silver-hair-cropped-short, rugged-Viking look was complemented by a South Beach tan and a tight-lipped, clown-sized, crescent-shaped smile that looked like it was about to burst into a shit-eating grin.

"Speak of the devil," Krimmer said.

Samantha gave him a quick, anxious glance, then turned and stormed out of his cubicle. "Some other time, I guess."

Krimmer decided she was just on edge about Timmy—what else was new? But as he let his smartphone ring a second time, it echoed a little alarm bell that was ringing deep in his brain, just like it had earlier when he noticed Samantha was dressed to the nines. *What was that all about, her jumpy look and peevish reaction when Jared called?* Given his pal's proclivities with the ladies, Krimmer knew suspicions were never unwarranted, although it wasn't clear to him why he might care. *A deal's a deal, isn't it?* Even if from time to time he thought about backing out?

When he tapped the photo on his new toy's big screen, it almost felt like he and Mortenson were about to have a face-to-face conversation—that's how real it seemed. Unfortunately, it was the lawyer's Beltway face, not his good-time Charlie mug, that was sitting across the desk from Krimmer, ready to pounce. "Didn't you get my message, boyo?" he asked. "Why haven't I heard from you?"

"I wasn't in the mood for bad news."

"So I have to trick you into answering?"

"You don't have to cancel golf tomorrow, do you?"

Mortenson scowled at the frivolous question. "Did you bother to read the article yet?"

"What article?"

"What's the matter with you, Jake? I emailed you the link."

"Stop trying to make me feel guilty, Jared. I was involved," Krimmer said. His inflection left no doubt that his involvement was with a person of the female persuasion. That was the only excuse

Mortenson would accept, and besides, there was no harm in wishful thinking about Rita. *Why not, since both Sam and Connie are out of the picture?*

The lawyer snorted unsympathetically. "So who's the lady? Anybody I might know?"

"She's not RFPT," Krimmer said, not untruthfully no matter who *she* was. He and Mortenson had a cutesy private code when talking about women. RFPT was Ready for Prime Time. If a lady wasn't RFPT, the jury was still out on her prospects or her longevity, so she wasn't ready to be discussed.

"Well, I guess I'll have to wait to hear. In the meantime, you need to concentrate on an important issue that could seriously impact your livelihood. Get your mind off your sex life for a minute, like me."

"Hah! Since when?"

"Since I saw the article in question," Mortenson said with sobering seriousness.

Krimmer pulled up the link on his computer. It was from the *Miami Herald*, which unlike so many other daily newspapers around the country, was managing to hang in there, thanks to the digitally impaired reading habits of the retired snowbirds from up north. Five elderly women in an assisted living facility in Ft. Lauderdale were being treated in the local hospital for heat prostration, all because Sunshine Energy was rationing electricity and the establishment's backup generator had failed. A sixth—a ninety-four-year-old widow on a stationary high-flow oxygen concentrator—had died, and her daughter, no spring chicken herself at seventy-three, was talking lawsuit.

"That's a horrible story," Krimmer said, "but what's it got to do with me?"

"What's it got to do with you?" The attorney shrank back in disbelief. "You supplied the power to Sunshine Energy. Or, in this case, maybe you didn't. At least not in a timely fashion."

"I didn't actually supply it, Jared, you know that. I exercised a Financial Transmission Right. The utilities up north supplied the power." He blinked. "I assume they did, anyway."

Mortenson tut-tutted at his client's innocence. "You were part of the daisy chain, Jakester."

"C'mon, Jared. They can't blame anyone for the thunderstorms. It was an act of God."

"Don't be so naïve, Jake. A tort's a tort, and the Almighty is beyond the reach of the legal system. So why wouldn't the daughter sue you? What has she got to lose? The risk is all the trial lawyer's, and you know how they start to salivate when they smell deep pockets."

"Like a dog," Krimmer agreed, mentally conflating Mortenson's face with one of Pavlov's mutts.

"You got it, Jake. As a financial wheeler-dealer, you might as well have a target painted on your back."

"Tell me again, Jared. How could I possibly be held responsible?"

"If your Financial Transmission Right contributed to an artificially inflated cost for the electricity, and that inflated cost caused the utility to delay delivering the power for some reason, let's say because the Southeast Power Combine had done a lousy job hedging, and that delay, in turn, resulted in a temporary brownout that was the proximate cause of the elderly widow's demise, then you could be held partially liable."

"That's bullshit, Jared, and you know it. The cost would have been higher no matter what."

"*Crede quia absurdum est.*"

"What does that mean in English?"

"Loosely translated, it means you better believe it precisely because it is bullshit. What jury is going to understand your business, anyway?"

"Well, what do we do? Should I send flowers?"

"Good God, no. That would practically be an admission of culpability."

"I was just kidding."

"We do nothing for the moment. We let them figure it out first."

"How long will that take?"

"A couple of months if they decide to file. I mean, how much could the old lady's life be worth, considering her advanced age?"

"Is that what they base the lawsuit on? How much time they've got left?"

"Yeah, if they can establish an amount of lost income for the deceased. But with an old bird like this one, where they get the hammer out is for emotional pain and suffering. That's where the daughter comes into play." Mortenson's voice brightened as he thought about the sticky situation some more. "But we can always tie it up in discovery for years. With a little luck, the daughter will be dead by then, and maybe she doesn't have any kids of her own."

Krimmer couldn't believe it. "Holy Christmas, Jared, do you know what you just said?"

"What?"

"That it would be a good thing if the daughter died."

"Well, from the perspective of the defense, it would be. If she doesn't have any heirs, a trial lawyer would have to be desperate to pursue the case for the estate. Although . . ." Mortenson scratched the stubble on his chin with the back of his hand, a sure sign he was thinking more about the problem.

"Can you knock it off," Krimmer snapped, still irritated by the lawyer's callousness. "Or get a shave."

"Hey, you know I don't shave after Wednesday, Jakester. A little beard helps me look younger for the weekend."

"I don't want to think about Florida anymore. How about a game of squash tonight?"

"Isn't it too late to book a court?"

"It's the Friday of a holiday weekend." The Athenaeum's squash courts usually went begging after work on normal Fridays. Most of the members were too tired to play after a long week—their average age was pushing seventy—or they had decamped to their home districts.

Another furtive flurry of scratches and then, "No can do, buddy. I think I've got a date."

"You think?" Krimmer asked.

"Well, we haven't finalized the particulars."

Mortenson's post-divorce afterlife was one long blur of compensation, but his standards were minimal. "Do I know her?"

"Sorry, she's like your honey, Jakester. She's not RFPT either." A little puff of air escaped the side of the attorney's mouth, a whistling hem and haw. "She's more like an experiment."

"Isn't every woman an experiment as far as you're concerned?" Krimmer joked, even as he idly wondered again about Sam.

Mortenson made a face. "Don't be late tomorrow. Our tee time is 10 a.m."

"Don't be late yourself. Don't fuck up your experiment."

Mortenson acknowledged Krimmer's admonition with his customary dazzling, if oily, smile. "Just what do you think experiments are for, old buddy?"

CHAPTER 4

SOMETIMES IT WORRIED KRIMMER, HANGING AROUND WITH JARED AS much as he did, about who was rubbing off on whom. Mortenson was top-notch as a lawyer, but he could be a little slippery, as he had just proven. For sure, he was fun to be around, except when he fell back into his slippery, lawyerly ways, which he tended to do at the most inopportune times. Still, Krimmer valued Mortenson and what he could learn from him. He was well aware he occasionally needed a measure of slipperiness himself to compete. After all, in this high-stakes FTR game, he was a lone wolf up against the big boys.

After graduating high school in Chevy Chase, just outside of Washington, Krimmer followed in his father's footsteps to Columbia. That elite, Ivy League college on Manhattan's Morningside Heights instilled in him a high regard for a broad liberal arts education structured around a core curriculum of foundational works of literature, history, music, and art, along with the unspoken knowledge about the economic futility of same. So after four years of broadening his mind and honing his long-into-the-night debating skills, off he went to Harvard Business School, where English majors and other free spirits in need of a career go to die.

Although the B-school provided a first-rate education in high finance, it was as blissfully ignorant as the average American about the arcane and complex racket of Financial Transmission Rights. Krimmer didn't discover his true calling until he joined the herd of his fellow high-achieving scholar-capitalists and descended on Wall Street to make his fortune. A near-top class ranking was enough to bring him to the door of the exalted, old-line firm of Gould & Baggett, but not enough to enter the inner sanctum of institutional client services. He served his professional apprenticeship in a Wall Street sideshow, learning the ins and outs of what was then the financial world's latest line of legal larceny, the under-the-radar FTR trading scheme. This sketchy new business was facilitated by the quants at the big banks and hedge funds, who had developed sophisticated statistical models based on historical weather patterns, demand curves, and a utility's maintenance record and outage rate. These algorithms, or "algos," as they were called, could forecast with acceptable accuracy which utilities would need to supplement their power output and when, and how much any congestion revenue was likely to be worth.

Krimmer was no dope. Despite the endless hundred-hour workweeks, the writing, career-wise, was on the wall. FTR trading would never be the fast track to partnership at Gould. Although profits were steady, the short-term nature of the contracts increased the risk to the firm. They couldn't be bundled and securitized and sold to gullible investors, affectionately referred to as "muppets." And the Wall Street quants with their algos were thriving like an out-of-control, silicon-based life form, sucking the air out of deals with high-frequency trading, using computers to move in and out of huge positions in fractions of a second. They dominated every market, making competition increasingly cutthroat, slashing margins, and transforming FTRs into a business of slow pennies rather than fast dollars. Besides, the allure of a trader's life in New York was wearing thin. If Krimmer never had another hundred-buck cigar or two-thousand-dollar bottle of vodka at a "gentleman's club," it would be all right with him. He never lacked for female company.

An opportunity is just a problem turned upside down. Although trading FTRs might be pocket change for the Gould & Baggetts of the world, Krimmer saw how they could provide a big payday for an independent operator. His time served in those hallowed halls of finance had inculcated a fierce belief that there was a market to be made in anything, even bear gallbladders, so why not other people's troubles? To net lottery-sized payoffs in Financial Transmission Rights trading, it was only necessary to find the potentially catastrophic disruptions to the grid, the ones that could make headlines, the ones where millions in property and even lives were at stake, the ones that struck so swiftly and seemingly capriciously that the historical-data-modeling quants had little chance of predicting their appearance with their precious algorithms. Bingo—weird weather.

And lest he forget, a crack meteorologist to forecast when and where weird weather would strike.

Unfortunately, his crack meteorologist now seemed to be setting off on a guilt trip about the latest catastrophic disruptions to the grid, past tense in Florida, future in her home state of Oklahoma. Krimmer was about to call Samantha back to see what he could do to buck her up, when he was waylaid by yet another call. A glance at the computer dashed his hopes that it might be that indigo-eyed, cocktail-party newbie-cum-imaginary waiter, the lovely Rita hunting him down.

A picture of two smiling faces, both capped with full heads of snow-white hair, had popped up on the screen: his parents. It was a call he felt obligated to take, as a good and loving son always would. And he did truly love them, despite still having to push back against the burden of being an only child, together with an intermittent guilt trip of his own for so handily eclipsing his father's career, at least monetarily.

His mom and dad were a picture of relaxation and contentment, sitting shoulder to shoulder on the dark green, forest-friendly deck in front of their bungalow on the Chesapeake Bay side of Maryland's Eastern Shore. The deck was Jake Sr.'s latest do-it-yourself project, constructed with plastic lumber made from recycled milk cartons. Although the temperature was springlike, even summery, the water was still agitated from the same line of storms that had devastated Florida. In the background, angry whitecaps rose and battered the bright blue sky, as though they were trying to crash their way into heaven.

"How you doing, son?" Krimmer's father asked, as enthusiastic as a slap on the back. He never was a big man physically, but he always had the energy of a big man and that deep, sonorous big-man's voice.

As usual, his mother was more restrained, a circumspect bird to her husband's exuberant bull. "How are you, Jake?"

"Fine, fine," Krimmer said.

"Are you having any fun?" his mother asked, "or are you still married to your business?"

His dad was more direct. "Yes, anyone new in your life we should know about?"

Since the two of them had despaired of ever becoming grand-parents, they had lost any sense of shame about making his love life, or lack thereof, an appropriate topic for indelicate inquiry. Krimmer sometimes wondered if their strategy was to constantly embarrass him in the hope of driving him into a legal state of permanent bliss. In all the years he'd been back in Washington, he had only introduced them to one girlfriend, one time, and that turned out to be a disaster. They loved Samantha. So much so that they never spoke her name again after he broke the news to them about their new arrangement, or never asked how it was working out, their silence and lack of curiosity being the ultimate reproof for his selfishness.

"Yeah, I met *the one* at a cocktail party, but I struck out when I told her how beautiful her eyes were. She wanted to know what was wrong with the rest of her."

"Oh, Jake," his mother sighed, as though she believed him.

"How're you guys doing?" Krimmer asked.

"We're fine, too, son. Now the sun is back out."

"Just fine," his mom trilled, although her smile didn't make it past her lips. "Just fine."

"Everything's going great, really great," his father reiterated as if he was trapped in a loop.

"Really great," his mother echoed, glancing over her shoulder at the turbulent Chesapeake.

Krimmer had to marvel at his parents' tenacious hold on happiness. Born at the tail end of the Baby Boom, Jake Sr. and Susan Krimmer were poster children for the fate of their generation, or at least those lucky ones who rode the pig in the python to success and riches as though it were a galloping thoroughbred. Too bad their gallant steed had to go and stumble before it reached the finish line.

The only child of a well-off but by no means wealthy Chicago family, Jake Sr. had navigated smoothly eastward, the first Krimmer to attend Columbia, then onto Harvard Law rather than the B-school, and finally to the epicenter of power in Washington where he jump-started his career as a clerk to the chief judge of the federal appeals court for the DC Circuit. That ennobling experience led to a succession of increasingly influential positions, in government and out, culminating in a senior partnership in the capital's most prestigious and wired-in law firm. With that booming voice and a keen sense of what worked in the courtroom, he was a superb litigator. Over the ten-year stretch before his retirement, he'd argued some twenty-odd cases before the Supreme Court, more than any other attorney in the country, winning all but two.

While the dominance of her husband's oral arguments was being compared to SEC football and the old Yankee dynasties, Susan Krimmer turned her passion for art appreciation, honed at Wellesley, into a thriving business. The Krimmer Gallery, conveniently located not far from K Street, rapidly became the go-to destination for any of the capital's elite who needed to fill an empty wall with something impressive but not outrageously expensive or potentially off-putting, the artistic equivalent of a respectable cloth coat rather than a showy mink. Patriotism was a big draw, so the gallery prominently featured American primitives and any oil paintings with the Stars and Stripes or scenes from the Old West, preferably with cowboys and horses but no Native Americans, and lots of sky-blue colors.

That was then. Krimmer's parents had found it prudent to relocate to what had been their weekend house in the glory days. Taxes were a pittance compared to Chevy Chase. And they didn't need all that room to rattle around in, they said, since it was just the two of them and the dog. Shopping and golf were a half-hour drive, and the hospital was only adequate, but if the problem was serious enough, they could always hop over to Washington to see a world-class specialist. Health care, as it turned out, was the least of their problems.

Seventy-five was the new fifty-five, so even though they were edging up in years, there was enough gas in their tank and tread on their tires to keep them chugging down the road. They faced the same problem as so many other successful baby boomers victimized by the hype of the Wall Street–Bubblevision sell-side talking heads—"this time it's different." How many market meltdowns could an IRA withstand? Seniors staring retirement in the face had to grit their teeth and accept infinitesimal interest returns on their nest eggs or buy into a bubblicious stock market that made the speculative frenzy of the Dutch-tulip mania seem like sensible investing.

Sure, his parents were more fortunate than most of their contemporaries—over-seventy was one of the fastest-growing age cohorts in the labor market. Nonetheless, they were grateful for Krimmer's help to supplement their savings and an underfunded Social Security system that was under constant attack from the deficit scolds. Outliving their money was a big concern.

"Hey, son, I wanted to tell you the transfer hit our account."

"Yes, we wanted to thank you, Jake," his mother echoed. "Your little contribution helps with the extras." She bit her lip. "You know I didn't mean to imply that what you send us is not enough," she added quickly.

"C'mon, Susie, let's not have any worries. We've got nothing to worry about, do we, son?"

"Not as long as I'm around," Krimmer agreed, although their gratitude for his monthly largesse was one of those things that always made him feel uneasy. The role reversal from childhood was like a warning shot of impending mortality—his as well as theirs.

"How's Ben doing?" Krimmer asked. Ben was their shag-rug of a rescue dog, black and hairy as a Newfie but only the size of a Lab. Shades of Mortenson, the miserable-looking puppy had showed up one rainy day at Krimmer's townhouse, skinny and wet, and made himself at home. When no one claimed him, he and Samantha had talked about adopting him permanently—Timmy was crazy about dogs. When that plan fell through, collateral damage from the demise of a more ambitious daydream, Krimmer's parents had volunteered to take Ben in. "You're still feeding him that fresh, organic dog food, aren't you? The stuff that gets delivered? They say it's human-grade."

"You bet," his father boomed, seeming relieved to change the subject. "Ben's eating like a horse."

"Your father takes him for a long walk every day."

"Assuming the weather is OK."

"Oh, my God, the weather," his mother said, rolling her eyes. "Did your father tell you about the last storm? We had water up to the roses."

"Up to the roses, really?" Krimmer asked. "Your garden's got to be fifteen, twenty feet above sea level."

"You get an ordinary nor'easter, son, and all hell breaks loose with the storm surge."

"I'm worried about my roses, with all that salty water."

"It's not that salty, Mom, it's just brackish."

"Show him, Jake," she said, giving her son a dirty look.

His father stood up quickly, and just as quickly made a grab for his right hip.

"What's the matter, Dad?"

"Nothing, just a twinge," Jake Sr. said, as he picked up the phone that had been sitting on the table and pointed it over the railing so the camera could capture his mother's beloved roses, the glorious, densely matted hedge of *Rosa rugosas*, some forty feet long and six feet high, that served as the rear border of her flower garden. With the warmer weather, it should have been speckled with pink blooms, even now, early in fall. Instead, brown, both stalks and blossoms, was the predominant color.

"I think you should prune them back and see what happens next year," Krimmer said, trying to be helpful.

That innocent suggestion seemed to irritate his mother out of all proportion. "What do you think is going to happen, Jake? There are going to be more storms, and bigger storms, like there are every year." She promptly redirected her ire at her husband. "Show him the flags."

His father dutifully pointed the phone at the thirty-foot nautical flagpole bolted to the deck. Old Glory was blowing in the brisk breeze, and a red square flag with a black square in the middle was flapping from a six-foot crossbar, the yardarm.

"He hardly ever takes that storm warning flag down anymore."

Jake Sr. made the mistake of weighing in. "That's true, but I guess you shouldn't mind the storms so much, son. That's how you make your money."

"Killing roses?" his mother asked, redirecting her glare to the camera.

"You're such a kidder, Susie Q."

"Well, you're the one who brought it up."

"I mean, you know Jake works in finance."

"My understanding is Jake makes his living off of other people's misery," his mother said tartly.

"Hah, since when, Mom? I make my living being smart about the weird weather, that's all."

"That's what I meant," Jake Sr. agreed, thereby compounding his error.

What followed was a short awkward silence, during which his mother's eyes flicked back and forth between her husband and her son, as though she was debating which one she should take on first.

"Hey, guys," Krimmer said, stepping in like a referee. "Let's call it a draw, OK?"

"Well, he makes me so angry sometimes."

"You learn to put up with it, son."

Krimmer quickly improvised. "Look, I've got to hang up. Got another call coming through. Love you both."

What the hell was that all about? He had tried to be genuinely sympathetic about the roses. Of course, the old man didn't help any with that fatuous comment about his making his money from storms. While that was factually correct, at least in part, it was a gross misrepresentation of how he did make his money. He liked to believe he anticipated the way the damage caused by storms and other natural, weird weather–related phenomena could be rectified and minimized by rapid response and more efficient management of the electric grid. Viewed that way, he was not profiting from other people's misery; he was profiting from helping alleviate it.

So when the *phone* icon on his computer flashed again, he was already rehearsing his belated rebuttal before he noticed that no picture had popped up on the screen. Instead of a callback from Mom and Dad, it simply read *Private Caller*. Still, with two big deals in the bank, or nearly so, he didn't hesitate to click. *Good things come in threes.*

CHAPTER 5

"JAKE KRIMMER, PLEASE." THE WOMAN SOUNDED VAGUELY FOREIGN, the way she pronounced his last name, landing hard on the *k*'s and extending the *m*'s into a throaty, musical hum.

"Speaking."

"This is Rita, Jake. Rita Ten Grieve."

Well, whaddaya know? Ms. Indigo-Eyes has come around. "Nice to hear your voice," he said, not skipping a beat as he leaned back in his chair and swung his feet up on the desk.

"I wanted to get back to you."

"I'm glad you did." He reached over and switched on the white noise machine, just in case the conversation got interesting.

"I wanted to follow up on what we spoke about."

"You mean you're ready to have dinner?" he suggested.

"Dinner? With you?"

Rita Ten Grieve sounded more than puzzled, positively baffled, as though it were an alien concept. So maybe she didn't remember. Maybe she had been a little tipsy, too.

"I'm talking about our conversation about climate change," she informed him.

It was Krimmer's turn to be positively baffled, so much so that he didn't automatically say, "You mean weird weather." Instead, he fudged his comeback, "We talked about *that*, you and me?"

"You mean you don't remember, Jake? Perhaps you had a little too much to drink?"

"I remember you," Krimmer declared. "Very clearly."

"You're sure?" Rita asked.

"I'd be surer if you turned your camera on," he said, suddenly anxious to have a look at her. The screen within a screen on his computer was still blank.

Her reply was quick and crisp. "I can see you fine, Jake. That's all that's necessary."

His mind raced, settling on something he hoped was light but pointed. "That's not very friendly."

"This is a business call."

"Oh, I see." Krimmer hadn't thought of the cocktail-party newbie in terms of business. "You know, I've been trying to reach you, too."

"I'm aware of that. There's a record of every Internet search on the Nimbus."

"The what?"

"The Nimbus. It lives above the Cloud in the datasphere. I couldn't get anything done without it."

"Oh sure, of course, the Nimbus." *Whatever the hell that was. There was always something new.*

"I'm disappointed you couldn't remember my name, Jake," she said matter-of-factly. "We're not off to a great start."

"I remembered it as soon as you said it, Rita. Besides," Krimmer added, going for a little warmth, "I remember the color of your eyes."

That didn't get him very far, either. "You're not the first, and you won't be the last."

"That's still not very friendly."

"Did I mention this is a business call?"

Krimmer made one last attempt to flirt. "Well, if we're going to do business, it would be nice to actually see you. How do I know that you're not just another chatbot?" In fact, that's what she was sounding like, so cool and detached and self-assured.

"Did I look like a chatbot at the cocktail party?"

"You know what I mean. I've gotta know who I'm doing business with—gotta look 'em in the eye, I always say." Indigo, as it were.

"Oh, all right," she said, "if you insist." The screen-within-a-screen flickered to life, puncturing Krimmer's ballooning anticipation. Instead of Rita's face, it was an aerial view of his mother's roses in full bloom, no brown in sight.

"What the . . ." Krimmer started to stay. *Where did that come from, a drone flyby earlier in the summer? How did she get a hold of it?*

"Does that help?" Rita asked.

Krimmer slipped his feet off his desk, back to solid earth. "What's going on, if I may ask?"

"Touch the roses, Jake."

"Why?"

"You said you wanted to get to know me better, didn't you? Sweep your finger across the screen. See what happens."

Krimmer hesitated until curiosity won out. He ran his finger across the image. The vibrant swath of pink and green withered instantly, as if his touch was toxic. The hedge was as brown as it was in real life.

"Don't worry, you don't have to grieve for them this time. Do it again and you'll see."

He swiped the screen, and the pink roses were back in bloom. "Hah, magic! How'd you manage that?"

"Didn't I already tell you? I couldn't do my job properly without the Nimbus."

He wasn't going to give her the satisfaction of asking what the hell she was talking about. Instead, he fell back on a tried-and-true negotiating tactic: the abrupt change in direction. "So what's the deal, Rita?" he asked, hunching forward in his chair and putting on his poker face. "What do you want from me?"

His caller responded in kind. "I have a proposition for you," she said.

It didn't sound like the kind of proposition he would have welcomed. "A business proposition, I assume?"

"Yes, but not entirely. What are you doing this weekend?"

"That depends on the nature of your proposition."

"I want you to play a little game with me."

"With you personally?"

"In the flesh."

That piqued his interest again. "What kind of game?" he asked, going along.

"You'll see. But it will be fun, I promise."

"You mean more parlor tricks, like with the roses?"

"Even more spectacular," Rita said.

"That would be something," he acknowledged. "But can it wait until next week? This is beautiful weather for golf."

There was a long pause, as if the connection had been lost. "No, it can't wait," she said, clicking back on. "There are other considerations that I'm not at liberty to disclose."

Something was starting to smell fishy. "So what's the objective of this little game?" he asked. "I'm beginning to think you might have some ulterior motive."

"I thought I made that clear right up front. I want to continue our conversation about climate change."

Krimmer didn't hesitate to correct her this time. "You mean weird weather."

"I know that's what you like to call it, Jake. But the weather's not just weird, it's destructive and vicious and getting worse every day. It's bringing misery to the entire planet."

He finally saw her for what she was, and it wasn't the hot cocktail-party newbie he'd been remembering. "Holy Christmas, you're a Green. I should have known. All you want to do is rag on me about how the whole world's going to hell and what an awful person I am not to care."

"It would be better if you just thought of me as Rita, Jake," she replied, as calm as he was keyed up. "Rita Ten Grieve. Someone who wants to help you see the truth about what you do for a living."

"How about helping me find the best Gouda cheese, instead?" he said, excessively pleased with himself for correctly pronouncing it *How-duh*, and underscoring the *H* with a rolling, guttural *G*, a deliberate exaggeration of her faint accent.

Much to Krimmer's disappointment, Rita didn't seem offended. "Oh, my name, you mean? It's just an alias. Kind of a *nom de guerre*. It's an old custom. You take the name of the place where you come from."

"And it's not from Holland."

"No, not Holland."

All this verbal sparring was becoming tiresome, now that it wasn't likely to go anywhere. "Look, Rita Ten Grieve, or whoever you really are. Get to the point."

"I thought you were interested in getting to know me, Jake."

"I am . . . I was. Until you started with this save-the-planet bullshit."

"Is that any way to talk to an attractive lady?" she asked with a little lilt in her voice, sounding almost human for a change.

"How many times have you told me this was a business call?"

"I can be flexible."

"You mean dinner?" he asked, although the question was purely *pro forma*. The attraction was fading rapidly.

Her tone grew throatier and low, a canny reminder of how she came on to him at the cocktail party. "We'll have to see. It depends on how our little game goes."

Krimmer always was a sucker for a sexy voice. He stirred in his chair, conflicted. Part of him simply wanted to click off then and there. He'd run into her kind before: Greenpeace babies, NOAA nymphets, smug, self-righteous, sanctimonious prophets of doom. Hearing them talk, we'd all be better off forswearing beef, taking cold showers, and driving around in battery-powered go-karts. He'd rather be subjected to an Al Gore–Hillary Clinton porno movie, and he didn't mean that ancient chestnut, *An Inconvenient Truth.*

The other part of him couldn't forget the cocktail-party newbie's considerable charms, which perversely now seemed all the more enticing. No question, it was a delicious challenge she presented— the transgressive thrill of sleeping with the enemy. Besides, he wasn't afraid of naughty bedtime games, if that's what she had in mind. He'd let a woman blindfold him once and have her way with him. As long as it doesn't involve dress-up role-playing, which hadn't gone so well. More to the point, since it had ended with Sam, he hadn't clicked with anyone. Impostors all, they seemed so boring, so conventional, and not just in the sack. Besides, what else did he have to look forward to this weekend, now that Connie was a no-show?

"So what's this game all about?" he asked gruffly to hide his glimmer of interest.

"It's simple," Rita said, any sexiness draining away, replaced by the officious voice of a determined bureaucrat. "I get ten chances to share with you why I grieve for our future if we don't do something to change it. Ten chances to make you grieve, too."

What was I thinking? It's never going to work. "Oh, now I get it," Krimmer said, giving his cheek a melodramatic slap. "Rita Ten Grieve. Can one of the grieves be for the taxes on my townhouse? They're killing me."

She was just like his mom, the way she slapped him right back with a few choice words to keep him in line. "When did you start to be a clown, Jake, or were you born that way?"

What he hadn't learned at Columbia or Harvard B-school, he'd picked up from Confucius. *What did the old boy have to say? Best defense is a kick-ass offense.* "Now that I've heard your pitch, Rita, I don't think I want to play your little game."

Something was very odd about Rita Ten Grieve's response. Either that or something was suddenly very wrong with Krimmer's hearing. Rita's words didn't sound like they were coming from his top-of-the-line Apple. If the computer speaker had been the source of her words, they would have sounded tinny compared to the way they sounded now, far richer and more sonorous than any chatbot and oh-so-measured, as though they were drifting to Earth from high above. There was no denying the chill he felt as he heard her say, "I don't know why you're so reluctant to become a better person, Jake: more in touch with your true self, more caring about those you love."

"Some people think I'm very caring already," he said.

"You mean because you send a little money every month to your mom and dad? I did notice how they thanked you for it a few minutes ago."

Krimmer was flabbergasted. Out of respect for his parents' feelings, he never mentioned his lending a helping hand to anybody. "What the . . . did the Nimbus strike again?"

"Look, Jake," Rita said, once more his mom, paying him no mind. "Assisting your parents is good as far as it goes. The fact that you're generous to them tells me that you're not completely irredeemable. That's one of the reasons I agreed to take your case, even though I knew it would be a challenge."

"My case? Don't tell me you're a lawyer or something. I had you figured for PR or a political aide." And he was sure he had her figured right, the way she was so relentless about staying on message.

"So what do you say, Jake? Anyone as intelligent and educated as you can't be totally ignorant of the facts. You're aware of the danger we're heading for, but you're not only a denier—you're also milking climate change for all it's worth, profiteering every time there's another weather disaster."

"Profiteering?" How had an innocent, bantering conversation descended so quickly into such a contentious exchange?

"Yes, profiteering, because deep down you have doubts about all your climate change denial. Deep down you sometimes feel dirty about the way you make your money, don't you?"

"Hah, since when?" he said with as much bravado as he could muster. The answer wasn't any farther than lunch at the Athenaeum.

To his relief, Rita didn't start harping on dead oysters. "Maybe this will help your memory." His mother's roses disappeared, replaced by a photo of the front page of the *Washington Post*, the old-fashioned print edition, with its banner headline trumpeting the news: SUPREME COURT UPHOLDS AMERICAN CLEAN ENERGY ACT, 5-4.

Words failed him as he stared at the screen.

"So you do remember," she said.

"Of course I do," Krimmer snapped, stunned that a cocktail-party newbie, even one with the Nimbus in a holster on her hip, could so easily discover where the bodies were buried in his family. "Who can forget the ACEA?"

The most momentous and far-reaching federal statute since the passage of Obamacare was a rare, heroic act of Congress. The American Clean Energy Act was the first piece of legislation—as opposed to questionable executive orders—that attempted to put limits on the amount of greenhouse gases spewing into the atmosphere. The act was further notable for enshrining the term *climate change* in the bill's particulars, although the legal language waffled about whether it was *man-made* or a *natural variation*.

The ACEA lurched into law after the pols could no longer ignore the public outcry about the dramatic increase in über-violent thunderstorms, Cuisinart tornadoes, coast-devouring hurricanes, raging atmospheric rivers, ark-worthy rains, dust-bowl droughts, scorched-earth heat waves, bone-freezing cold spells, crippling ice storms, baseball-sized hail, bomb-cyclone blizzards, serial nor'beasters, roof-high snowmageddons, and so-called hundred-year floods. Not to forget the knock-on effects like Vesuvial mudslides, Hades-style firenadoes, Atlantis-like inundations, and the general sense that the world was coming to an end.

The increasingly numerous and vocal Greens had led the charge. They found an unlikely ally in the hidebound US Chamber of Commerce, which had begun to make gurgling noises about how all the weather-related damage was choking off their member companies' bottom lines. The nation's elected representatives were further goaded into action by fear of losing face internationally. The Chicoms-in-name-only weren't satisfied with being crowned the world's largest economy. The go-to producer for cheap shoddy goods and crappy knockoffs was boldly reinventing itself as the cuddly Great Panda, promising to lead the global response to climate change.

Despite their many good qualities and policies, the Republicans were moral invertebrates, masters of obfuscation and inaction. Their primary objective was to hold on to as much power as possible while the America they thought they knew was slip-sliding away. But with the world lining up against them, and the base increasingly anxious, they felicitously discovered that the vestigial bone in their backs was a spine. In the most miraculous conversion since Saul became Paul on the road to Damascus, the GOP wise men decided it no longer mattered that they weren't scientists. They were now capable of joining with the Democrats and Greens, and having an informed opinion about the overwhelming evidence that man-made emissions of greenhouse gases—carbon dioxide and methane—were, at the very least, contributing to all the weird weather.

Popular opinion was divided as to whether the prescribed corrective measures went too far or not far enough. But in the Krimmer household, the opinion was unanimous. The American Clean Energy

Act was a sore subject. Jake Sr.'s argument before the Supreme Court to quash the law resulted in the second and final legal defeat of his career. His partners immediately grew concerned that he was losing his mojo, and perhaps he did, too. In any event, his retirement soon followed.

Rita brought Krimmer back to the present with a gentle gibe. "Didn't see that one coming, did you, Jake?"

"Everyone makes mistakes," Krimmer said in a subdued monotone. "Even my old man, as smart and as experienced as he was."

"C'mon, Jake," Rita coaxed. "Do you really think your father *lost* that case?"

CHAPTER 6

THE AMERICAN CLEAN ENERGY ACT WAS A THREAT TO KRIMMER'S career, as well. Congress went for the jugular, targeting the power plants that burned coal and natural gas to generate electricity, producing a quarter of all US greenhouse gas emissions.

A market-based cap-and-trade system was quickly deemed a nonstarter; Republicans had spent too many years demonizing it as a Democrat-inspired job killer. Taxing the carbon content of fuels drew even less support. Both parties deemed that any new tax, no matter how well intentioned, was both semantically repulsive and politically suicidal. Geoengineering the problem away by fertilizing the oceans with iron to absorb more carbon, or injecting particles into the atmosphere to reflect sunlight into space, was also ruled out. Evangelicals strongly objected to the government attempting to "play God." And pouring more money into the development of much-ballyhooed nuclear fusion wasn't going to help. It wasn't funding that was the roadblock, but rather the seemingly intractable engineering challenge of scaling laboratory results into a near-term commercial enterprise.

Other than kicking the can down the road yet again, that left only one alternative: the oxymoronic siren song of Clean Coal and its kid brother, Green Gas, which packed less of a wallop of CO_2, but more methane. Now, anyone who ever saw a power plant belching plumes of pure pollution into a clear blue sky, or observed the conga line of begrimed miners escaping a shift change at the pit, or witnessed exotic flames shooting from the kitchen faucet thanks to the fracking wellhead next door, or felt the earth tremble after all that bothersome wastewater was injected back into the ground to get it out of sight and out of mind, might scratch their head in wonder at these artfully arranged confluences of contradictory words. But if an act of Congress could somehow legitimize those compelling euphemisms, the lawmakers could be seen as doing the right thing by the electorate while sparing irreparable harm to the Political Action Committees that funded their careers.

Thus, as finally passed into law, the American Clean Energy Act required power companies to embrace carbon-capture-and-storage technology, or CCS. Every existing plant would have to be retrofitted to trap greenhouse gases right at the smokestack before they could enter the atmosphere, and no new plant would be permitted to go online without it. Sure, the technology was currently expensive, but the price would fall with increased demand and improvements driven by good old American know-how. Sure, there was some debate about the net amount of CO_2 reduction, once a CCS-equipped plant's need for a greater quantity of fuel to produce a comparable output of electricity was factored in. And sure, there was that nagging problem of sequestration—what to do with all that CO_2 extracted from the combustion process—but some bright geek would come up with an app for that.

Thankfully, of all the possible solutions, CCS presented the least immediate threat to Krimmer's livelihood. It wasn't at all clear that this legislative brainstorm would survive the inevitable legal challenges. If a power company did not purchase the required equipment, or if their emissions were not reduced to the prescribed level within the prescribed time frame, consequences would ensue. It was the nature of the consequences that proved troublesome. Congress had predictably eschewed any mention of a tax in the bill. Instead, the revenue to be paid to the federal government for failure to comply with the CCS regulations was termed a *carbon shared responsibility payment*—or in simpler parlance, a corporate mandate. Whatever it was called, it was treated as a penalty, not a tax—a lexicological workaround that inevitably propelled the law into the meandering court system.

Twenty-six utilities joined together to file a lawsuit, contending that the ACEA's reliance on the capacious umbrella of the Commerce Clause, which had long been interpreted to give Congress the power to regulate just about any aspect of business that involved crossing state lines, was unconstitutional. They maintained that by mandating the purchase of CCS equipment and threatening financial penalties, the government was interfering with the basic business model of the corporation. It would be like making an individual citizen purchase a product that, however socially useful and personally beneficial, that citizen did not desire. After several contradictory decisions at the federal appeals level, the case was fast-tracked to the Supreme Court.

Enter Jake Sr., the Babe Ruth–Nick Saban of the legal world, sure to put to rest any of Jake Jr.'s worries. As eloquent and persuasive as ever, he successfully argued on behalf of the National Association of Energy Providers that upholding the penalty would "open a new and potentially vast domain to congressional authority." The Commerce Clause rationale for the act was duly struck down, 6–3. But cleverly, the government also put forth several other backup arguments in support of imposing the corporate mandate. Unexpectedly, the reigning Supremo, a staunch conservative himself, but deeply concerned about the legitimacy of the court, twisted the arm of his would-be successor to side with the court's three-member liberal wing. Semantics aside, the penalty was nothing but a tax, they reasoned, which, *ipso facto*, Congress had the constitutional authority to levy. With their deciding votes and complementary victorious visages—a trademark smirk and a frat-boy grin—the ACEA became the law of the land.

"It's funny what you think about when something like that happens," Krimmer told Rita as he tore himself away at last from the grim headline on the screen. "At first, I was angry with my father. I thought his mistake was going to kill my business. But all the new regulations just screwed up the power grid even more."

"The ACEA still isn't fully implemented, and there are lingering technical problems," she admitted, "but, all in all, it's a good thing for the country and the planet. It's helping postpone Armageddon for a few more years."

"It wasn't a good thing for my old man. He never anticipated that the court might buy the tax argument. *Tax* was a dirty word to the presidents who appointed those justices. It was a political decision, not a ruling based on law."

"A rookie mistake for such a successful litigator, wouldn't you say?"

Krimmer shrugged off her insinuation. "You've got my father mixed up with somebody else. He knows and I know that there's no proof that weird weather isn't just a natural variation in the climate that's been going on since God was a boy. Why, we were still in an ice age ten or twelve thousand years ago."

"And starting fires with flint and keeping warm with animal skins. Our knowledge has progressed since then."

"Phony knowledge from the science nazis. They'll manipulate data and tell any lie to get grants or tenure. Remember Climategate? The suppressed emails?"

"Eight different scientific and political committees investigated the allegations. And none of them found any evidence of fraud or misconduct. Face it, Jake, nine of the ten hottest years since record keeping began in 1880 have occurred in the last decade, and it looks like this year is going to be the hottest yet."

His lonely-looking calendar was a lingering temptation, but after that heated back-and-forth, Krimmer was ready to throw in the towel. "Look, Rita, I don't need any lectures about weird weather. Let's end this conversation right now. I've got a busy afternoon ahead of me."

"But what about the weekend, Jake?" The bureaucrat receded into the background as the little burr in her voice once again sounded more like a purr. "Are you already booked solid, or would you like some company?"

So she's a mind reader, too? "Hey, I don't even remember what you look like anymore."

"I thought you remembered the color of my eyes," Rita teased.

Krimmer did remember, of course, and her streaky blonde hair and slender, curvy body, as well. It was just enough to prevent him from being rash. "OK, sure, I'd like to spend some time with you, but can we take a break from all the talking points?"

"Is that all you think they are? Maybe we should let your father weigh in?" Without waiting for an answer, the two snow-capped heads suddenly popped back up on the computer screen.

As surprised as he was, Krimmer's first instinct was to give them a friendly wave. "Hi Mom. Hi Dad," he said.

"They can't hear you, Jake. When you hung up, I had the Nimbus keep the connection live and record their conversation."

"You what?" Her little magic act was getting out of hand. "Who said I wanted to play your stupid game?"

"You automatically gave me admin rights to your computer when you swiped the roses on the screen."

Krimmer was so astonished that it took him a moment to register that her behavior wasn't just audacious; it was positively creepy.

"I never said I wouldn't cheat," she told him.

He knew it was a fight-or-flight moment. But either option would likely mean that the only company he'd have for the next few days was Mortenson, so he settled for a gentleman's withdrawal. "All right,

I surrender, Rita. Why don't you tell me what it is that you're so anxious for me to hear."

Although he couldn't see her smile, it came through plain as day. "How about the truth for a change?"

The phone was where his father had left it on the picnic table, the lens still pointed at the two of them sitting on the bench, although now there was enough space between his parents to see a distant sailboat bobbing up and down in the rough waters of the Chesapeake. Instead of all smiles, their faces were by and large expressionless, with just the hint of frowns. Jake Sr. was staring straight ahead. His mother was turned slightly toward her husband, her eyes focused somewhere off-camera. Krimmer was unnerved by their sudden resemblance to a computer-animated version of the farm couple in Grant Wood's *American Gothic*, their lips flapping mechanically as they spoke sideways to one another.

"Why did you have to go and upset him, Susan?" His father's voice was uncharacteristically flat and unemotional.

"Why did *I* have to upset him?" his mother asked, mirroring her husband's tone. "It was you who upset him, Jake."

"You were the one who brought up the dead roses."

"Who said he didn't mind all the storms?"

"Why would that upset him?" his father protested.

"I can't imagine," his mother said, inching farther away.

"Look, Susan, I was simply trying to pretend I was fine with what he does for a living. I didn't want to make a ruckus."

"Why not just tell him the truth?" his mother asked.

Krimmer braced himself for a big revelation, but what she had to say was barely a blip. She had leaned Green for years.

"Weird weather, weird weather," his mother mocked, as she sat up taller and squared her shoulders with a hint of pride, looking directly at the camera, as if she knew Krimmer was watching. "I'm so sick and tired of euphemisms. As far as I'm concerned, from now on it's anthropogenic climate change," she said, the emphasis on the accusatory adjective. "Man-made."

"That's going to be a big help, Susan," his father said. "Whatever you call it, his income depends on it."

"And our little extras, too. I know that's what you're thinking. But we're putting self-interest ahead of truth," his mother scolded. "The money is not all that important. If we had to, we could live just fine without it."

"You're right, but don't you get the feeling it's important to him?" Jake Sr. asked, glancing at his wife.

She seemed to think it over forever. Her next judgment, when it finally came, did catch Krimmer off guard. "You know, I believe you're right. It's one of the few ways our son knows how to show his love."

After that less-than-chummy exchange, the two of them sat, silent and morose, each in their own world, to the point where Krimmer assumed the conversation was over, and he was left wondering why Rita had made it out to be such a big deal. Sure, there were a few surprises, but nothing earth-shattering, nothing that was going to make him feel fundamentally different about his parents, or frankly, about himself—not even his mother's unflattering observation about the work-around for his emotional reticence. That's when she finally spoke up again, her voice warmer and more philosophical. "Sometimes I think Jake is just like you," she said seemingly out of nowhere. She nodded in vigorous agreement with herself as she echoed Rita with her hurtful verdict. "Deep down, he's ashamed of selling out."

From his reaction, Krimmer got the feeling his old man didn't like what his mother had said any more than he did. "My God, Sue. 'Selling out.' I haven't heard that term since college," his father said, springing up from the bench and raising his arms in frustration.

"Well, I wasn't exactly jumping for joy all those years when you were the mouthpiece for your rich friends."

"I never heard you complain about our lifestyle," he said, wincing as he grabbed his hip again. "Chevy Chase, the bungalow, the fancy clothes and cars, the vacations in Europe."

"Oh, sit down, Jake, before you hurt yourself."

His father obeyed, giving in to his arthritis if not to his wife. "Anyway, it all worked out in the end. I wouldn't have been in a position to do what I did if I hadn't been such a successful mouthpiece." He added with a wink, "What could have possibly gotten into me, letting that case get away."

"Doing the right thing, perhaps?"

"It took me long enough," his father said with a wry smile.

"Almost as long as it took you to agree to use recycled plastic to build our deck."

Jake Jr. started fidgeting in his chair as his father's smile went from wry to sly and his voice began to regain that storied courtroom traction. "Once I came around to your point of view, Sue, that climate change wasn't a hoax, the rest was easy," he admitted. "I knew the chief justice would be looking for a way out. He was in the same pickle with the ACEA as he was with Obamacare. He didn't want the court to lose even more credibility with another contentious, politically driven decision."

"Did you really have to think twice about it?" his mother asked as she resettled herself on the bench, moving closer.

"Don't forget, it cost me my job," his father said, moving closer as well. "As soon as my partners saw the transcript, it was over. They knew I had given the tax argument short shrift, as if it was a nonstarter. If it were a tax, I argued, why wouldn't Congress simply say so?"

Krimmer wanted to shout "No!" It wasn't possible that his father would have deliberately thrown the case.

No problem for his mother; she was all for it. "You may have lost your career, but on the way out, you kept your integrity."

"At the price of my reputation."

When two gears mesh, if one rotates, the other must rotate in the opposite direction—just as his parents did, turning inward creakily but reliably, their glances flicking this way and that until finally there was no other alternative but to settle on each other. "There's nothing wrong with your reputation with me," his mother said, girlishly batting her eyelids.

"You don't blame me for all those years of denial?"

Krimmer could only surmise what was going through his mother's mind, as she inched her face higher, and said with a forgiving sigh, "Nobody's perfect, Jake Krimmer."

At that point, their lips were perilously close and everything went dark, both on the screen and in his brain. As shocked as he was by his father's confession, Krimmer kept up the façade. "Nice job, Rita—cutting it right there, just when we were about to see the money shot."

When Ms. Indigo-Eyes didn't say anything, he was quick to bluster, "But I don't know if I believe any of it. I mean, now that I'm beginning to understand what kind of dirty game you're playing, how do I know it was on the up-and-up?"

Krimmer turned toward the window, as if he could see her as clearly as she could see him, and he was trying to avoid looking at her. "That could have just been some kind of video mash-up you cooked up with your beloved Nimbus."

When she still didn't answer, he asked, "Did you hear me, Rita? How do I know any of what I was seeing and hearing was real?"

No response again. Krimmer swiveled around, ready to repeat his accusation face to no face. That's when he saw the sign-off message on the screen. *Have to go, another client appointment. See you tomorrow. PS—Sorry about the oysters.*

CHAPTER 7

WHAT THE HELL WAS GOING ON? SO HE HADN'T BEEN SEEING THINGS at the Athenaeum after all. Krimmer's head was spinning as he hunkered down in his cubicle, which suddenly didn't seem so over-sized. He was determined to sort out the issues one by one before the walls closed in.

Who was this Rita Ten Grieve? Greenpeace operative? Point person for some mysterious, deep-state conspiracy or NOAA-led, wild-eyed crusade? Ghostly emissary from the datasphere, wherever that might be? Or just a crazy stalker, a crackpot on a mission?

How did she pull off that gender-bending impersonation? Most of the members of the Athenaeum were big-name politicians or other assorted Washington muckety-mucks. Tight security was a given.

What was she really after? Or what were *they* really after—who-ever it was who had assigned her to his *case*.

What kind of "grieves" did she have in mind? Should he be ner-vous about them, even a little afraid? Whatever the Nimbus was, it was certainly nothing to mess with. Look how it had spied on his old man, exposing his deepest, darkest secret. What might it do to him?

See you tomorrow? What nerve! Did he miss the memo that he had agreed to play her little game?

Google was no help with answers. Rita Ten Grieve produced only 516,000 results, a pittance by search engine standards, and none of them had anything to do with the mysterious, wraithlike person in question. Unless the first hit, a book titled *After Long Grief and Pain*, a nineteenth-century Victorian tearjerker by an author identified only as "Rita," was some kind of omen.

Frustrated, Krimmer turned back to the window, watching the crowd of tourists enjoying the unusual warmth and sunshine on the National Mall. He wondered if any of them were giving this day's variety of weird weather a second thought. *That's where Rita ought to be if she truly wanted to get her message across, down there herself, handing out flyers and engaging as many people as she could round up, explaining why they should not be quite so pleased and complacent about enjoying June in October.* Instead, she was picking on him, just a poor guy trying to make a decent living. What's with this coy, now-you-see-it, now-you-don't, act of hers? Sure, she's attractive enough, but so was the spider to the fly.

"Lost in thought, Krims?"

Krimmer spun around, caught unawares. Samantha was standing there in all her elegant glory, a rolled-up sheet of paper in one hand, a crumpled tissue in the other.

"How long have you been standing there, Sam?" he asked as he switched off the white noise machine.

"I assume you want to have a look at the numbers again," she said, ignoring his question. The look on her face was decidedly serious, reminding him of her parting words as she stormed out of his office a half hour ago. "Some other time" was apparently going to be now.

"Oh, the numbers," he said, wondering about his little twinge of disappointment. "Whaddaya got?"

"Robert ran the Oklahoma spreadsheet one more time," she told him, unrolling the printout and handing it over.

"And?"

"Take a look. The financials are still pretty good," she said, betraying a little upswing in her enthusiasm. "There's been very little trading in the Central States Power Pool FTRs over the past day or two, so it looks like the field isn't crowded. It's our ball if we choose to run with it."

Like any trade, the trick with Financial Transmission Rights was to get ahead of the crowd. Once the competition detected any sign of momentum, either buying or selling, they were quick to jump in and front-run the deal. "So it's an empty net?" he asked, deliberately picking up on her lacrosse jargon.

Samantha's smile was barely detectable, but it was there. "Maybe not altogether empty. Robert thinks there might be a midfielder or defender waiting for us down by the goal."

Krimmer nodded and quickly scanned the changes in the asking price of FTRs. "Don't you think we should have Robert in here?" he asked.

"I told him I'd cover it with you," she said.

Krimmer let that backhanded admission that this was indeed that "other time" hang in the air between them for a moment, then, with great ceremony, laid the sheet of figures on his desk. "OK, Sam, why don't you sit down. I wasn't sure, either, that we'd finished our earlier conversation."

"I wasn't sure we had an earlier conversation," she said, emotionally flatlining again as she settled herself primly on the couch.

"Will you please let me in on the secret?" he pleaded. "What's really on your mind?"

"I thought you spoke with Jared."

What was on her mind, as always, was Timmy, and the story in the *Miami Herald.* Somehow she had conflated her son's latest episode of antisocial behavior with the old lady's death in Ft. Lauderdale, resulting in a clear and present danger from tornadoes to her grandma's knitting circle halfway across the country in rural Oklahoma. At least that was the sense of what Krimmer was getting.

"Please tell me, Sam," he pleaded again. "Exactly what did he do in kindergarten?" Timmy was a year behind his age group; Samantha had redshirted him to give him the advantage of being older than his classmates.

"You know how they play musical chairs, right?" she replied. "He left a pile of poop on his chair, and when the music stopped, the little girl was so anxious to sit down, she didn't notice."

"Was the poop . . . you know, spontaneous, or did he plan it out in advance? Like hiding it in a piece of toilet paper?"

"For God's sake, Jake, what does it matter?"

What did it matter? Unlike Rita Ten Grieve, this real, flesh and blood woman was looking so lost and forlorn. He had an overwhelming urge to get his day back on track. *What did Confucius have to say? Sometimes you gotta break the rules.*

"Hey, I've got an idea," Krimmer said, almost before he knew he had it.

"What's that?" Samantha asked, kneading away at her tissue.

Or maybe even my life, it was occurring to him for the third or fourth time today, as he heard himself asking, "What are you doing tonight? You have any plans?"

Sam looked up quizzically. The tip of her tongue peeked out between wary lips. "I have a date. Why?"

"Cancel it. We can talk more over dinner."

"Dinner? You know we agreed . . ." She didn't need to finish.

Krimmer nodded understandingly. "We did."

Samantha's squint was pure suspicion. "What, you think I've got an on-off switch or something, like your noise machine?"

"You're obviously a little down in the dumps, that's all," he said. "As your employer, it's my responsibility to keep you happy, cheer you up."

"I don't know, Jake—"

"Jake," she called me. "What don't you know?"

"What's behind this sudden desire to lavish money and attention on me?" Samantha asked, still suspicious.

What was behind it? "Hey, what better way to start the long weekend? Help celebrate Columbus Day."

"Indigenous Peoples' Day, Jake," she corrected him.

"Oh, right—Indigenous Peoples' Day, sorry. You know, old dog, new tricks."

Samantha took her time deciding. "Well, nothing's set in stone," she said. "We're supposed to talk to firm things up."

The little alarm bell went off again. *Nothing set in stone* reminded Krimmer of Mortenson's not finalizing the particulars with his "experiment."

"Hey, don't tell me Jared is your date."

His crack meteorologist just laughed. "Why would you *ever* think that?"

The *ever* got him thinking that maybe she really was Jared's experiment. That made him all the more insistent. "C'mon, Sam. It's getting late, and I've got to put in these bids."

"Well, I do have a babysitter . . ."

He pressed the advantage. "How about Tout Va Bien at seven thirty. Give you a chance to go home and freshen up and say good night to Timmy."

Was he right or what? Women were as changeable as weird weather. "How about the Palm instead," she said, perking up all at once. "I haven't had a big, juicy steak in ages."

"I was thinking of someplace more . . ."

"More convenient to your fancy townhouse?" she asked, giving him an exaggerated evil eye.

"Someplace quieter where we can have a serious talk."

"Oh, I thought you wanted to cheer me up, and now you want to get serious, too. Don't tell me my job's in jeopardy again," she said, as light and airy as a wink.

Krimmer didn't miss her not-so-veiled reference to the danger of office liaisons. "It might be if you're wrong about that EF5 in Oklahoma," he called out as she stood and turned to leave.

Samantha stopped and peered back over her broad and magnificent shoulder; her look managed to be both beguiling and triumphant. "It might be, too, if the dinner goes too well."

Krimmer was barely able to suppress a guilty smile of anticipation. Could she be thinking along the same lines he was? Then again, how could she possibly be, when he wasn't sure himself what he was thinking. *Time to make those trades and go home and take a shower.*

Buying and selling Financial Transmission Rights had come a long way since Krimmer's early days in the business. Initially, almost all the action was in a monthly auction. As the various players grew more sophisticated and honed their algorithms, and the weather became ever weirder, and the disruptions to the grid less predictable, it was apparent that the substantial and frequent fluctuations in the price of FTRs would be better served by a more flexible and timely mechanism for initiating and closing trades. As a result, day-ahead and real-time markets were established, where the availability and associated costs of delivering electricity could be determined with more precision, and final positions could be confirmed or modified, even at the last minute.

For traders like Krimmer, these innovations introduced a new and destabilizing element to their quest for larger and more profitable transactions. Simply put, transparency was not a speculator's friend. If everyone knew what you were up to, it was difficult to get an edge. Combine that with the 20/10 vision of the quants with their trusty algos and their high-frequency trading strategies, and you had a classic prescription for diminishing returns. The obvious solution for the Financial Transmission Rights market was the same as it had been historically for equities—dark pools, the private exchanges where bilateral trades between could be made under a cloak of secrecy, without fear of tipping a hand.

The dark pool that Krimmer tapped into on his computer was G&B, an outfit so discreet that they never even revealed what the initials stood for. The jokey rumor had them pegged as Goldberg & Bagwell, an off-the-books, accessory business of Krimmer's former employer, Gould & Baggett—kind of like a useful crevice tool for the so-called "giant, sucking vacuum cleaner of Wall Street." *No matter.* G&B paired him with a willing counterparty, processed the trade swiftly and accurately, collected his winnings or paid off his loss, and credited and debited his account with unerring precision.

As Krimmer entered Robert's recommended bids, it was easy to forget that the numbers dancing across the screen represented more than just a well-thought-out strategy wrapped in a game of chance— not all that much different from liar's poker or backgammon. The notion that underlying all his high-stakes derring-do, lives were at risk or misery was being commoditized or the demise of the planet was being facilitated—that wasn't something that normally would have entered into Krimmer's thinking. But today was not a normal day. Today was the day the women had decided to gang up on him. His mother, Rita, even Sam, in her own outwardly stoic but nonetheless persuasive way. As he checked his bids one more time and clicked the *submit* button, Krimmer had to wonder if his life had actually worked out as well as he liked to think it had. For whatever reason, at that precise moment he felt profoundly and inescapably alone.

CHAPTER 8

TOUT VA BIEN WAS ONE OF KRIMMER'S FAVORITES, AND NOT JUST because its name was so aspirationally apropos. *Everything is fine, all goes well.* Tucked away on a side street in Georgetown, not far from the university, it was the kind of retro French bistro defined by a wall of red-leather banquettes, travel posters from Normandy to Nice, and Piaf's haunting *chansons* on the sound system. Krimmer savored the opportunity to mingle with an academic crowd rather than the usual Washington politico posse—it hearkened back to "Lit Hum," Literature Humanities, an essential part of the core curriculum at Columbia. He would have broken out a tweed jacket instead of a blue blazer, were it not for the weird weather.

Getting into the Gallic spirit, Krimmer passed on the customary single malt and ordered an aperitif, a Ricard, making sure to pronounce it with a raspy *R*, as though clearing his throat. He didn't want Samantha to think that he needed to gulp his drink while he was waiting, so he nursed it carefully, adding a bit of water from the pitcher after every sip. Each drop made the amber pastis from Marseille turn cloudier. By the time she walked in the door, he was dealing with a full glass of milky liquid.

"Wow, Sam." Off with the Victorian look, on with the sparkling diamond studs and a slinky, V-neck, emerald-green dress, the beltline and the narrow straps trimmed with glittering sequins to accentuate her athletic waistline and bare, broad shoulders. "This joint ain't the Ritz, you know," he said as his hand went to his open collar. "I'm feeling underdressed."

"Hey, can't blame a girl for trying," Samantha said as she checked her options, then slid to Krimmer's left on the curved, corner banquette.

So far, so good, Krimmer thought, until she added archly, "Besides, I had it all laid out for my date tonight. You remember, the one you made me cancel?"

"Let's not go there," he said. His eyes gravitated to the faint, three-inch scar embossed on her right shoulder, a souvenir from a chronic lacrosse injury she'd once told him about in passing, as though it were hardly worth mentioning. Still, she never tried to hide the scar, as some women would. In fact, she seemed to go out of her way to show it off.

Samantha must have thought he was still ogling her other charms, the way she used her index finger to reorient his chin, and with it his admiring gaze. "Let's not go there, either," she said. Then, noticing his glass, "No Scotch?"

"Just an aperitif."

"I guess you weren't kidding," she said, pretending to go wide-eyed. "This really is going to be serious, huh?"

Just how serious, he couldn't be sure. The day had started off the same as any other, until without any warning the smooth ride had turned into a rough trip, buffeted by doubt and confusion and unexpected anxiety. The good news was that all the clear-air turbulence had a way of concentrating his attention on the choices he had made, or hadn't. And maybe the mistakes, as well.

Krimmer knew he risked raising expectations tonight, both his own and Samantha's, beyond what was best for either of them. *Was it just because I have no other weekend plans? Or that the cocktail-newbie turned out to be a nutcase*? Or was it another, more hazardous, question that was beginning to make its presence known? Perhaps even felt? How much of this flare-up of desire was his slow-burning recognition that Samantha might be *the one*, after all?

"So what'll you have, Sam?" he asked, signaling the lone, frazzled waiter.

"I'll have what you're having," she said without cracking a smile.

They didn't spend much time looking at the menu. Samantha was always quick to decide. "So what's on your agenda for tonight?" she asked as they waited their turn to order.

Thankfully, his cotton khakis had a firm grip on the leather upholstery, keeping him from squirming. "There's no agenda, Sam. I just thought a little relaxation would be good for both of us."

"Yes, you did seem busier than usual, on the phone all afternoon."

Krimmer thought that was as good a place to start as any. "How much did you overhear?" he asked.

"Who can overhear anything? Your noise machine does a good job."

"Not that good a job. Things were getting pretty heated there for a while."

Sam sought refuge in the tableware, rearranging her knife and fork. "I did hear a woman's voice, that's all."

"My mother?"

Sam shook her head. "Younger." She took a sip of Ricard and grimaced. "Too bitter," she said.

"Take another sip. It will taste more like licorice."

She stared down at the milky liquid. "Anyway, you sounded so animated, I thought she might be a new girlfriend."

Krimmer wondered if Mortenson had planted that seed. *Better not to ask.* "Oh, you mean *her*," he said. He paused to choose the least inflammatory description. "She's a bit of a stalker."

Samantha's head jerked up. "You're a rock star now?" she asked brightly before appropriating his favorite trope. "Hah, since when?"

"OK, OK," he said. "So I met her at a cocktail party a couple weeks ago, and I guess I made an impression." He was already regretting he didn't just let the new girlfriend comment drop. "She called me to do some networking."

"You sure she's not smitten with your good looks and bank account?"

"You can hold the sarcasm, Sam."

"Not a chance," she replied with a grin.

Krimmer pushed the basket of bread aside, making more room for his tightly clasped hands. "What about my parents. Did you catch what was going on with them?" He glanced at her out of the corner of his eye, trying to monitor her reaction. "My conversation with them kind of got me thinking about things," he said, trying to make it sound like they were things that might be of interest to her, as well.

But Samantha seemed to be off in her own little world. "I was focused on your lady friend," she admitted, shaking her head so imperceptibly it might have been nothing but a nervous tremor.

They successfully avoided any more awkward questions or confessions or recriminations until the kitchen did its usual job of turning out a splendid dinner, which had a welcome calming effect on both of them. Over soft-shell crabs for him—the warmer water in the Chesapeake had extended the season into October—and hanger steak for her, plus two glasses of wine apiece, Sancerre and Côtes de Rhône AOCs respectively—Krimmer knew his *appellations d'origine controlees* like his ABCs—he told Samantha a carefully edited version of what had transpired, making it seem like one extended conversation rather than two, with his parents confessing all rather than him spying on them through Rita's electronic keyhole.

He started with their bickering about the roses and the way he made his money, segued to his mother mocking weird weather as a euphemism for climate change, and ended with his father's admission of deliberately botching the attempt to kill the ACEA in the

Supreme Court. To make up for the self-serving omission about Rita in either of her guises—Washington cocktail-party newbie, Nimbus secret agent—he went into ponderous detail, explaining everything from the ins and outs of the Commerce Clause to how to keep *Rosa rugosas* blooming, while preventing them from invading any neighboring sand dunes. The more he talked, the more comfortable he felt, sharing his thoughts and hopes and doubts about the ups and downs of the day, just like old times. Not so Samantha, who was looking less fascinated than bored.

"Well, that's quite a lot to digest in one sitting," she said as the waiter took the plates away. Krimmer had finished up with one final twist, his mother's unnerving observation that his little monthly gift was one of the few ways he knew how to show his love. Of course, he first had to reluctantly admit that there was such a thing as a little monthly gift.

Sam reached over and patted his hand. "At least she recognizes you have a good side, too, Jake."

"You mean as opposed to my bad side, profiteering from weird weather?"

"Your mom actually accused you of profiteering?" she asked, leaving her hand in place, over his.

"No, that's my word," he said guiltily, remembering whose word it actually was. "But that's what my mom meant, I'm sure."

Samantha paused before asking, "So is *weird weather*, isn't it? Your word?"

"Yes," he acknowledged after a pause of his own.

Krimmer knew Samantha was waiting for him to elaborate, but he couldn't figure out how to go there without involving Rita and her unsettling magic show. It didn't seem credible that he was beginning to have doubts just because his parents had made clear their point of view, however emphatic they had been.

"Are you starting to think it might be something else?" Sam asked. "Is that it?"

"Is *what* it?" he asked, taken aback by how easily she had zeroed in on the source of his discomfort.

"Is it really just weird weather? Is that what you wanted to talk about?"

"No, I was more interested in the profiteering part," he said, attempting to backtrack, to move the conversation in another direction, less all-encompassing, more intimate. "Is that what you think we do, Sam?"

"Profiteer?" she asked, withdrawing her hand. "Well, it's true, there's certainly something exploitative in the way you make your money."

"The way *we* make our money."

"Are you lumping us together?" she asked, looking everywhere but at Krimmer.

"From a business perspective, yes. We do have a deal, you know," he said, dragging out the words, hoping that she would get the idea, and that everything would just flow naturally, from business to personal. "If that's how you really feel about what we do, if you think it's exploitative, why are you still here?"

Samantha took her time responding, and even then, her answer slipped out at an oblique angle. "I don't know, Jake. I guess I'm an imperfect human being."

How guilty could a man be made to feel? "Who told you to say that?" Krimmer snapped.

Samantha's head spun around, matching his intensity. "Say *what*?"

"Nothing, nothing," he mumbled, just as quickly retreating. "It just reminded me of something . . . something my mother said."

Samantha appeared to take pity on him. "Well, I guess I've been doing a lot of thinking lately, too," she told him, finishing her wine.

"About how you feel about work?" he asked.

"About that," she agreed, "and . . ."

Krimmer looked up. It was a long way back to Alexander Pope and eighteenth-century Brit Lit, but hope always does spring eternal. "And maybe about our arrangement?"

"Yes, and about our arrangement," Samantha said, leaning away as far as she could without falling off the edge of the banquette. "Did it ever occur to you that the two might be connected?"

"It has crossed my mind," he said without fanfare, relieved that however painful it might prove to be, the subject was at last out in the open. He swirled his empty glass in the air and glanced around for the waiter, the real *garçon*, not an imaginary one.

"Well, let me assure you, it crosses my mind every day." There was nothing in Samantha's tone to suggest that she was happy it did so. "If you really want to know, Jake, the only time I feel fine about the connection is when I go online and check my bank account."

Samantha raised her empty wine glass an inch or two and nodded. That was all it took for the busy waiter to come right over. "For you as well, sir?" he asked.

She waited until they were alone again to explain. "Timmy's private school is expensive, you know."

"Oh, I didn't know you had decided to send him to private school."

"Yes, I'm able to afford it because of our arrangement."

"Well, I'm glad it's working out," Krimmer said.

"I think the expense is worth it. Timmy gets a lot of individual attention. I can see the change in just a month. He's growing up."

"So the poop on the chair was just an aberration?" he asked, trying to be supportive, but also trying to keep it light.

Apparently that's not how Sam heard it. "Timmy really bothers you, doesn't he?"

Krimmer strenuously objected. "I didn't mean anything by it. I swear."

Samantha's eyes narrowed into slits, like loopholes in a medieval battlement, the better to defend her son. "You never mean anything, Jake. You never do."

"Look, I'm sorry," Krimmer said. To make amends he asked, "Tell me about the changes you've seen." When Sam didn't immediately relent, he said, "Please, I mean it—tell me."

"Well . . ." She drew it out as if she was evaluating how interested he truly was. "For one thing, Timmy no longer wants to be a fireman."

"That's a good thing, huh?" One look told him that wasn't enough. "So what does he want to be when he grows up?"

Samantha hesitated, as though she was in no hurry to reveal too much, too quickly. "They've been teaching astronomy and space," Samantha said. "Would you believe, Timmy now wants to be an astronaut?"

"An astronaut, huh? Good decision," Krimmer said, ratcheting up his enthusiasm. In retrospect, he should have left it at that, but he felt the need to expand on his approval, although not so much as to get the conversation any further off track. "I bet he'd like *Galaxy Quest*, or do you think it's a little old for him?"

"Why are you so dubious?" she snapped.

"I'm not dubious. I'm really not."

By now it was clear there was nothing he could say that would make Samantha happy, except maybe confessing that he, too, once wanted to be an astronaut, so he applauded Timmy's ambitions. *Although with the mood she's in, it could just as easily lead her to question my sincerity, so maybe it's better to just try to get us back to why we're here.*

"Look, Sam . . ." he began, even as he noticed how his hands resting on the table were not resting anymore. They had taken on a life of their own, the fingers rubbing and pressing and kneading together as if they were trying to get a firm grasp on something, and not just his whisked-away wine glass.

"Look, Sam," he began again. "I'm sorry for involving you in my problems when it's clear you've got enough of your own to deal with. I just wanted . . . I just needed . . ."

Samantha had noticed his hands, too. She didn't let him finish. "A shoulder to lean on?" she asked with another touch of sarcasm. Although perhaps she had already forgiven him, the way she crossed her left arm over her chest to touch her own ample shoulder, bare and real, not metaphorical, as if she were telling him it was OK anyway to rest his head on it, physical and emotional scars be damned.

It was all he could do to finish his thought. "I guess I was disturbed by my father hiding the truth."

"Well, at least he thinks enough of you to confide in you at last," she said, a little warmth creeping back into her voice.

Krimmer was afraid that his crooked, phony smile would give him away. "What happened to our wine?" he asked.

Samantha's tinkling laugh sounded forced as well. "Maybe the waiter feels we've had enough."

"Well, it's getting late. You want coffee?"

Samantha waved him off. "It'll only keep me up. I've done enough thinking for one day."

By now, it was clear to Krimmer that nothing about their future was going to get resolved tonight. "I'll get the check then," her said. "I've got a golf game in the morning. What about you?"

"You know I don't have time for golf, Jake."

"I mean what are you going to do tomorrow? You have plans? Maybe we could pick up where we left off." When he saw the startled look on her face, he quickly clarified. "Pick up the discussion, I mean. Where we left off tonight."

"Timmy and I have some shopping to do." She seemed to think about it before she added, "And the only way I could cancel my date tonight was to promise to reschedule for tomorrow."

Timmy again, always Timmy. He made sure not to show his disappointment. "How about Sunday, then? How about brunch?"

Samantha's initial look of astonishment had settled into something more pensive, part question, part doubt. "Why don't we see how tomorrow goes," she said. "I'll let you know."

While all this frantic calendar negotiation was going on, Samantha was still maintaining the separation up top, but their knees were close enough to brush; perhaps to even touch more purposefully, Krimmer couldn't be sure. He kept thinking they both wanted to say something more, but neither wanted to say it first, and before he could get up his nerve the moment had passed.

When he finally did speak, the best he could manage was, "Sure, let's see how tomorrow goes."

Samantha stared at him sympathetically, her lower lip protruding and curled, protecting her dignity. "Oh, Jake, what can I say? Speaking as your crack meteorologist, I can confidently forecast that the sun will rise tomorrow on what's sure to be another lovely day."

Krimmer nodded his assent, but in his mind he was echoing that other Jake, Hemingway's, who never cleared the high bar for Lit Hum but who knew all about how love stories ended. Or sometimes never did. *"Isn't it pretty to think so."*

CHAPTER 9

THE SUN DID RISE, JUST AS SAM PREDICTED, STREAMING THROUGH THE double-height windows and sliding glass door and nudging Krimmer's eyelids open. Curtains were for losers, people who didn't have a good reason to get out of bed in the morning. Besides, during the gut renovation of his Federal-era Georgetown townhouse, he'd had the contractor wall in the back garden to protect himself from spying eyes, indigo or otherwise.

Krimmer's freshly ground and brewed coffee was waiting for him, as programmed. He added a splash of milk, cinched the belt of his robe, and checked his computer and phone. No email, but Samantha had sent him a text, an adjective-free, one line thank-you. Just as well, he told himself as he headed out to the flagstone patio. Any further thoughts about what happened at dinner last night and what didn't, what was said and what wasn't, any regrets as well, he banished from his mind. So too, any further dwelling on his high-tech stalker, attractive as she might be. "See you tomorrow?" *Hah! Since when?* Even his uneasiness about his parents' disapproval of his line of work evaporated in the unusual warmth of mid-October—definitely even more like summer now, not even a hint of frost or a leaf on the ground. The greens would be true and the fairways immaculate, a great morning for golf. "Tomorrow" was indeed a lovely day.

Krimmer scrolled through the *Wall Street Journal Weekend* as he sat at the smoky-glass-and-stainless-steel table and sipped his coffee. The news from Florida wasn't all bad. The ban on daytime air conditioners had only been lifted from noon to four. That meant Sunshine Energy was still running below capacity, and that congestion pricing along with his FTRs were still in effect. Just as happily, there was no update on the nursing-home debacle, so maybe the newshounds were chasing bigger game.

One article that did catch his eye was how wind and solar now accounted for more than forty percent of Australia's residential electricity supply, more than doubling in the past ten years. With all the devastating effects of weird weather they had to deal with—the scorching heat, the year-round bushfire season, the parched outback, the flash floods—the Aussies had gone all-in, building football-field-sized arrays of Tesla lithium-ion batteries to store alternative energy. The technology was far from cost-efficient—it was underwritten by government subsidies—but it was effective, supplying electricity when the sky was cloudy or the air was still, or when weird weather came calling. *Well, good for them, because if there's anything they have too much of Down Under, it's sun and wind.* Of course, if the US ever followed Australia's lead, it could put a severe crimp in his business model. But that was a problem that he didn't expect he would have to deal with, given his twenty-years-at-most career horizon and the foresight-free track record of the big thinkers in Washington—the ACEA excepted.

Krimmer gulped the rest of his coffee, raced through his shower and banana, and skipped down the stairs to the underground garage. Along with the naturally cooled wine cellar, the garage was the finishing touch of his gut reno. Cleverly constructed beneath the adjacent alley, it housed his lovingly maintained, Sebring Orange, premature midlife crisis: an antique 2019 Corvette ZR-1 convertible, the last model year before General Motors decided bigger was no longer better. Krimmer sat up straight in the low seat at a street-friendly Formula One angle, his legs and one arm fully extended to reach the pedals and the wheel, his free hand fondling the gearshift of the seven-speed manual transmission. As soon as he turned on the ignition, the prehistoric 755-horsepower, supercharged 6.2-liter V-8 engine would respond with a full-throated roar, not the sissified silence that greeted the drivers of electrics and hybrids. Too bad there wasn't a stretch on the twenty-minute drive up to the country club where he could take his baby from zero to sixty in 2.85 seconds without becoming instant bear bait.

When he finished fantasizing, the massive engine responded with a rapid series of puny clickety-clacks. The solenoid was working overtime, futilely attempting to overcome a case of Down-Under revenge: a dead battery. Krimmer turned off the ignition, counted to ten and tried again. Same result. Another rewind; same result one more time. Not wishing to test the limits of the definition of insanity commonly attributed to Professor Einstein, he reached for his smartphone. Maybe this "tomorrow" wasn't so lovely after all.

No Uber or autonomous Yellow Cab for Jake Krimmer. He liked to ride in style. "You're in luck," the dispatcher at the limo company told him. "We have a car in the area."

It wasn't even two minutes before a jet-black, all-electric stretch Caddy squeezed through the gauntlet of parked cars lining the narrow Georgetown street and glided to a stop in front of his townhouse. The automatic door slid open, and Krimmer threw himself into the back seat, grunting a thank-you as the limo silently accelerated, heading down P Street towards Wisconsin Avenue. The glass panel between the front and rear seats was shut, so the driver asked over the intercom, "Liberty Country Club, Bethesda, is that right, sir? No golf bag?"

"It's at the club," Krimmer answered without looking up. "Text Mortenson," he said into his smartphone. "Tell him my battery died and I may be ten minutes late."

"That's a surprise, given the advances in battery technology," the driver said.

"Personally, I think the Aussies are smoking something," he grumbled as he verified the readout on the screen. The phone genie had thoughtfully added, *Sorry.* "They'll never make any money."

"Anyway, we're really lucky with this weird weather, don't you think, Mr. Krimmer? June in October?"

"Yes, we are lucky," he said, tapping the *send* icon, still not thinking twice about the driver's choice of words.

"Good thing it isn't really June. Why, with the higher levels of CO_2 in the air these days, all the trees and plants would be having one heckuva pollen party. I don't know if my allergies could handle it."

Krimmer's head jerked up. It wasn't just the *weird weather* and the cheap-shot follow-up about elevated levels of carbon dioxide— something else wasn't kosher. Washington limo drivers tended to be Bangladeshi or Pakistani men who were refugees from the parts of their countries that were now more or less permanently under water. This driver looked not only distinctly American—no humanitarian visa required—but also unquestionably female, her light brown hair verging on flaxen, pulled back into a short ponytail and glistening with artfully contrived streaks of blond. He couldn't tell if it was the microphone that made her sound kind of throaty, but she definitely was no wilting soprano.

"Excuse me?"

"I said I didn't know if my allergies could handle it," the woman said good-naturedly. "It's a weird thing, I mean—the way the pollen count gets higher every year as it gets warmer because of all the CO_2."

"Would you mind opening the partition," Krimmer asked, searching for FaceFinder on his phone. "I can't hear you very well."

"No problem, sir." As the glass divider slid open noiselessly, the driver glanced at Krimmer in the rearview mirror, making it unnecessary to activate the facial recognition app, even if it had worked this time. The eyes that greeted him under the shiny visor were that familiar, deep, distressing shade of violet-tinted blue that had been haunting him, for better or for worse, ever since his aborted lunch at the Athenaeum.

"Rita," he acknowledged, barely audibly.

"I assume you got my message."

"'See you tomorrow'?" he asked, perplexed, as if it hadn't occurred to him that tomorrow was today.

"The planet doesn't have a lot of time to waste."

"Neither do I," Krimmer said, but that wasn't what was bugging him at the moment. "You screwed around with my Corvette, didn't you? You understand you're responsible for any repairs. What did you do, get into the onboard electronics?"

"Through OnStar," Rita admitted.

"I canceled OnStar years ago."

"All the circuits are still installed," she said breezily. "They can be accessed through your GPS."

"Holy Christmas, Rita," he said, unsure whether he should be frightened or flattered that she'd go to such lengths. "What's going on here? Just who are you, and who do you work for? The goddamned Nimbus?"

"Nobody works for the Nimbus. The Nimbus works for us."

"Who's us?"

"Honestly, Jake," she said, laughing off his question. "I thought you were smart enough to have figured it out by now. I'm Rita Ten Grieve, and I work for you."

Krimmer was too frustrated to argue. He might regret it later, considering that his dinner with Sam at Tout Va Bien hadn't completely erased the alluring image of the cocktail-party newbie—and who knew how the impasse with Sam would be resolved, or even how he wanted it to be. But at this point, after Rita had ambushed him by messing around with his pride and joy, he was ready to take his chances. "Well, then, Rita Ten Grieve. If you work for me, drive me to the club and then get out of my life."

"I can do that if you're sure that's what you want," she said, not bothering to play coy with the rearview mirror again. Instead, she took her hands off the steering wheel and turned her head around to direct those haunting eyes right at him—freezing him indigo-ly. "If you really think it would make Samantha happier not to have me around anymore," she added without blinking.

Krimmer wasn't overly concerned that the driverless dreadnought wouldn't make it down the insanely narrow street without leaving mayhem and destruction in its wake—he assumed Autodrive was on the case. What was commanding his attention, what immediately sent his adrenaline level soaring, was the introduction of this new variable into the equation. How did Rita know that his sexy seer was the ultimate X factor? If his earlier questions had peaked at two standard deviations above normal volume, this one was off the charts. "Samantha? What do you know about Sam?"

Rita was unflappable. "Just the basics. She works for you. You were once in a relationship. Now you're not. A few other things that she had to say in her email to you last night."

"You mean her text," Krimmer said, not pausing to consider how outlandish it was that Rita could have access to anything Samantha had sent him. "'Thank you for dinner'?"

"No, her email," Rita insisted blithely, taking a quick look out the windshield to make sure the cameras and radars and Lidar light sensors were doing their job. "What Samantha had to say to you was much too long for a text. Much too complicated."

Krimmer finally began to get the picture. "Wait a second. Are you trying to tell me that your Nimbus friend has been spying on my valued employee?" he asked, trying to imply it was only confidential trade secrets that concerned him.

"Yes, and that she wrote you an email as soon as she got home from Tout Va Bien."

"I didn't see it in my mailbox," he snapped.

"I guess Samantha decided not to send it."

The full import of Rita's offhand disclosure finally sank in, along with a shiver of uneasiness. *This is one crazy broad.* But he had no reason to disbelieve her, not after that monkey business with the roses and her instant replay of his parents' little tiff. Besides, it would be just like Samantha to go home and do an emotional data dump, get out everything that she'd been holding in that evening, everything that for whatever reason she didn't want to say when they were together. So Rita was now aware of where Sam stood in regard to the two of them, how she felt about him, and where she saw their relationship going. Or didn't.

Krimmer's first instinct was to explode in fury, embarrassed and even afraid of what Sam might have revealed. But initial instincts were often the bane of a shrewd trader. He wouldn't get anything out of Rita with threats or anger. "Please don't tell me I gave the Nimbus admin rights to Sam's computer, too," he said with preternatural calmness.

"No, you don't have to feel guilty, Jake. I cheated again." She turned her head back to the road and placed her hands on the wheel as the limo approached the corner where P Street took a jog as it crossed Wisconsin Avenue. "I decided to take a gamble. I set up an open line into all of Samantha's electronic communications."

Krimmer was aghast that Rita could do such a thing, but he immediately saw the upside. *Talk about a golden opportunity. She might as well have set up an open line into Samantha's psyche.* Though his next thought surprised him. *Was that OK?*

"You really think that was wise, Rita? Cheating, I mean?"

"'All's fair in love and war,'" she replied, as cheerful as could be. "Isn't that what the Bard said?"

"As a matter of fact, no. That isn't Shakespeare." *It wasn't war either, so to make it fair, make it right, it would have to be love. Or a close approximation.*

"Well, whatever. I only cheat when the end justifies the means."

Krimmer stared out the limo window as they headed north on Wisconsin, trying to get more comfortable with the idea—several ideas, actually. The spacious, sloping grounds of the Naval Observatory were hidden behind historic Georgetown's minimally invasive commercial strip, making him wonder if Rita had learned all the clichés back on Thermia, when they were perfecting the English-language synthesizer.

"Did Samantha delete the email or just not send it?" he asked, hoping it was a little harmless feeler.

Rita sounded as though she was swallowing a chuckle. "Is that your way of asking me if I'm aware of what Samantha had to say about the two of you?"

Before Krimmer could come up with a plausible denial, she said, "Seriously, Jake. I have to protect everybody's privacy."

That was as funny as peak tornado season from March to August. "Hah! Since when? You spied on Samantha, didn't you? You call that protecting her privacy? And what about my privacy? Whatever Sam wrote has as much to do with me as it has with her."

"You have to trust me, Jake. This is one of those times when the end does justify the means. Remember, I work for you, and I want to see you happy."

"I thought you wanted to convince me to accept climate change for what it is and change my ways," Krimmer retorted.

The mirror flashed indigo again. "Did you ever consider that the one might be related to the other?"

Where have I heard that before? "Oh, puh-leeze," he said, although he couldn't help thinking about what Sam had said at dinner, her ambivalence about the connection between their work and their relationship.

"Climate change is a contentious subject, Jake. It can bring people together, or it can pull them apart. You saw that with your parents. Didn't that have any impact?"

"It had an impact all right," Krimmer conceded under his breath.

"Yes, Samantha thought so, too. She hoped it would help you be more forgiving."

"Forgiving of what?"

"C'mon, Jake, I've said too much already."

"Look, Rita, if you really want to help me like you say you do, just give me a hint of what Sam's thinking. We're both going through a very mixed-up period, and it would be much better if we could work it out one way or the other and move on with our lives."

"You mean together?"

"Or maybe not together. I don't know. It's all so confusing right now. Between the business and the personal stuff, who can tell?"

Rita seemed to sympathize. "Well, there is one way I could see my way clear to giving you a little more insight. Open the kimono a bit."

"What's that?" Krimmer asked hopefully.

"Have I mentioned I'd like to play a little game with you?"

Hope died.

They were stopped at one of DC's notoriously long traffic lights, where ninety seconds seemed like five minutes. Rita had plenty of time to turn around again and go into full sales mode. "Ten grieves, Jake, that's all I'm asking for," she said, sounding as preachy as a Sunday-morning TV evangelist. "Ten chances to help you realize the harm you're doing to yourself, and the planet, and the people you care about."

"My parents, you mean," he said, sitting up straight and rigid, willing himself to look away from the messianic face framed by the partition.

"Samantha, too. I know you're thinking I'm some kind of weirdo nut job, and this is the last place you want to be right now, but I also know you do care about her. Isn't that why you're still listening?"

When he didn't immediately answer, she added, "And don't you want to know if she still cares about you?"

Cares about sounded an awful lot like *a close approximation*, aggravating Krimmer's qualms. *What am I afraid of? What I might find out?* "OK, how long does this game take?" he asked after a protracted pause.

"If I don't succeed in convincing you by midnight on Indigenous Peoples' Day, I won't bother you anymore. You can go back to your destructive way of making a living and being your old, self-centered self."

"Three days, that's all you need?"

"Scrooge was converted overnight," Rita said, laughing. "I thought you might take a little longer."

"What's the rush?" he asked sarcastically.

"Did you forget? There are other considerations."

"Oh, right," Krimmer scoffed; it was one more example of Rita's insistence on being mysterious and obscure. "That you're not at liberty to disclose, of course."

"What I can tell you is that I've got a long list. You're not the only jerk who's trying to destroy the planet."

"Yeah, but how many are as good-looking as I am?" he joked, just as the light changed.

Krimmer didn't know Autodrive could accelerate that fast, sending him reeling backward.

"Listen, Romeo," Rita growled as she made a quick check on the health and well-being of her passenger. "If I can't convince you in three days, you'll never be convinced."

"What you're describing doesn't sound very much like a game to me," he said as he sat up straight again, and they glided silently up the street.

"Well, I intend to keep score. And I have all the powers of the Nimbus at my disposal to make it interesting."

He reminded himself that, as spooky and audacious as it was, "all the powers of the Nimbus" could go a long way to helping him figure out where both he and Sam stood. "I still don't get it," Krimmer said, although he knew he had already rationalized the decision to go forward. "How exactly does one win this game?"

"Well, I win if I convince you, obviously," Rita said.

"But how do *I* win? This is my livelihood you're talking about."

Her piercing eyes flashed in the rearview mirror again. "This is also your planet that we're talking about, Jake, and your children's planet, and your children's children," she said with great solemnity.

"Ten chances, huh," he said, not sure what to make of Rita's oracular pronouncement, considering that children were the farthest thing from his mind right now. Was she intimating that Sam had brought up the M-word in that email? Or Timmy?

"Ten grieves to lift you out of the ignorance and complacency and cupidity that you deal with every day."

He had to admit that despite the sermonizing, she had one thing right. The stench in Washington was something Krimmer had no problem relating to. Not that he was overly bothered that the whole political establishment was the moral equivalent of an overripe durian. It stank like a slimy, putrid, decomposing body, but once you cracked it open, it was a land of milk and money. Frankly, if anyone in government had any common sense or overarching vision, they would have shut down his symbiotic racket long ago—parasitic might have been a better description. And reregulated the power grid while they were at it, fixing the parts that were broken.

"See, Jake," she said, "we do agree on something." The blinker clicked to make the turn onto Massachusetts Avenue.

"Holy Christmas, does my mind get beamed up to the Nimbus, too?"

"Not yet," she said, laughing again, "but we're working on it."

"I suppose that piece of theatre with my parents was one of your ten . . . ten . . ."

"One of my ten grieves. Yes, it was."

"So all I have to do is survive nine more?" he asked.

"Seven, actually—assuming I need all ten. Digital access to Sam cost me one grieve, and let's not forget the oysters. You don't want to know what tricks I had to play to get past security at your fancy club."

"How could I possibly forget the oysters," he asked theatrically, placing his hand over his heart.

She laughed him off for the umpteenth time. "The Athenaeum was kind of like a test; my way of judging if you were a good candidate for conversion. I wanted to evaluate how uncomfortable I could make you."

"I gather I passed," he mumbled.

"So what do you say, Jake? Are you going to let me be your personal guide and teacher?"

"I don't know, Rita," he said, glancing at his watch. Krimmer realized how successfully this arguably psychopathic stalker from God-knows-where had perverted his sense of reality. Sam or no Sam, why else was he even contemplating playing her little game? "You never did tell me how I win," he said, in a last-ditch attempt to forestall the inevitable.

"C'mon, Jake, do you ever listen? You win if at the end you're a happier person."

Flummoxed by yet another maddening platitude, Krimmer noticed they were traveling south on Massachusetts Avenue, not north, cruising right through the heart of Embassy Row. "If you're heading for the club, you're going in the wrong direction," he warned her.

"Oh, am I?" Rita said gaily, as if it was of no more significance than if they were sightseers, out for a relaxing Sunday drive. "I was thinking you might enjoy the scenic route."

CHAPTER 10

THE TOURISTS WERE STILL EATING BREAKFAST, SO THE SATURDAY morning traffic was virtually nonexistent by Washington standards. The limo cruised down Massachusetts Avenue and merged onto Rock Creek Parkway, and in another minute or two they were passing the Watergate Complex and the Kennedy Center. The wide, gray Potomac lay hidden off to their right, out of sight behind the massive, ten-foot-tall earthwork berms topped with concrete floodwalls that had replaced the former bike and walking trail.

Krimmer's implicit capitulation seemed to have put Rita in a chipper mood. "Thank God for the Army Corps of Engineers, right Jake? If they hadn't built the levees, we'd need a boat to get down this highway after that last storm."

"But we did build them," Krimmer reminded her. "We adapted."

"We built them because we were getting tired of hundred-year floods every twelve months."

After that smart-alecky exchange, Krimmer decided silence was the prudent option as they sailed alongside the unseen river. He was beginning to worry about exactly what he had been suckered into.

Since he hadn't filed a formal protest, or chained himself to the two-foot-high wrought-iron fence that protected the strip of boxwoods in front of his townhouse, it was clear he was now officially playing Rita's little game. As much as he hoped it would only prove to be a harmless amusement rather than something more sinister and consequential, his confidence level wasn't high. Rita's behavior was bizarre at best—even eerie, the way it bordered on the supernatural. And if he stopped to think about it, despite how useful it might be in working things out with Samantha, the reach of this thing she called "the Nimbus" was certifiably terrifying.

Krimmer was still dealing with his assorted anxieties as Rita picked up Ohio Drive and circled the back of the Lincoln Memorial, then made a quick zigzag up to Independence Avenue. They sped on until the Tidal Basin, a placid inlet of the Potomac about a half-mile in diameter, was shimmering on their right, the Jefferson Memorial gracing the far shore.

Rita executed a deft but highly illegal maneuver, jumping the curb into the row of parking spaces that paralleled the edge of the water. "Sorry about the bump, but I know you're in a hurry," Rita said.

"You're the one who's in a rush," Krimmer loftily observed. "It shouldn't take long, anyway. I've been coming here since I was a kid."

"Why do you think I chose it for your next grieve?" she asked. "According to our records, you were six years old on your first visit—the same age as Samantha's son."

He was beyond questioning whose records they were or why his age was so important. Still, he sat there for a moment, body and mind untethered, before he realized the rear door had slid open and she was standing there, smiling patiently, waiting for him to slip out into the sunlight and appreciate the beautiful view. Two beautiful views, in fact.

The cocktail-party newbie had been all indigo eyes and streaky blond hair, the latter grazing the former until she coyly smoothed it back in place to lure him further in, transforming the would-be pred-ator into prey. All that flirty kinesis, combined with a few quick belts on an empty stomach, had left Krimmer with only an impressionistic image—attractive for sure, but hazy. And what he could see from the back seat, even when she turned toward him, had been constrained by the partition and his own uneasiness. Now, as he stepped out of the limo, it was as though he was seeing Rita Ten Grieve for the first time.

The baggy, unflattering, chauffeur's uniform did a good job of camouflaging Rita's figure, but Krimmer was struck by her clean-cut, all-American face, framed by a broad, unruffled forehead and a gently tapered but determined jaw. A straight, assertive nose, more pendant than button, softened her cheekbones and deepened the hollows of her eyes. When she smiled, her ample lips stretched wide and opened generously, revealing the tiniest of flaws, an adorable little gap between her upper two front teeth. If it weren't for her unnerving trademark, the withering, indigo stare, she could have been the girl next door, albeit one with something more than the boy next door on her mind.

Too bad that ship has sailed, he acknowledged to himself, now that he had weightier matters on his mind. The cocktail-newbie certainly had her charms.

Rita gestured toward the serene expanse of the Tidal Basin and the stately, alabaster Jefferson Memorial across the water. "It will be interesting to see what you remember," she said pointedly. "So let's have a quick look."

Curiosity vied with suspicion as Krimmer followed Rita down the concrete path that circled the Basin. What "interesting" things did she expect him to dredge up from his childhood visits that might make him a believer about climate change? What repressed memories did she hope would give him a good smack upside the head? What Krimmer did recall was boringly benign: how every year during the Cherry Blossom Festival his family would make a day of it, touring the

Memorial, picnicking in the little grassy park, and renting a pedal boat to paddle around the calm water, surrounded by a living wall of gnarly trees and fragrant, candy-colored blossoms.

As if on cue, just before the two of them reached the point where the walkway bulged out into the Basin, they had to duck an over-hanging branch of one of those famed Japanese cherry trees: a gift from the people of Tokyo in the early twentieth century. From that spot, the view of the shrine to America's third president was an iconic photo-op for tourists. In early April—or more often now in March—when the cherry trees were a blaze of pink, the panorama became picture-postcard stunning.

The sprawling steps and columned portico of the neoclassical, white-marble edifice seemed to rise directly from the unruffled pond. Behind the portico, a colonnaded rotunda topped by a shallow dome, inspired by Monticello, Jefferson's beloved home, gleamed in the morning sun. Krimmer could just make out the silhouette of the majestic bronze statue in the center, open to the elements except for the protection of the dome and the columns and—he did remember something else, after all—a selection of Jefferson's timeless words chiseled into four marble panels inset at equidistant points around the rotunda, highlighted by the opening lines of the Declaration of Independence.

"Here, try these on. They might wipe the smile off your face." Rita handed him a pair of glasses, the large, oval lenses set in a solid-looking, black plastic frame. Krimmer noticed the temple arms were thicker and more substantial than normal, half the height of the lenses at the hinges and tapering only slightly towards the earpiece in a kind of wraparound design. Still, other than the chunkier sil-houette, there was nothing to indicate that the glasses were anything special—just a little dorky. "Are these supposed to make me see things differently, Rita?"

"Why don't you put them on and find out for yourself?"

Krimmer wasn't accustomed to wearing eyeglasses, but this pair was surprisingly light and comfortable. They didn't change or distort what he was seeing in any way. It was like looking through a spotlessly clean window.

"Let's ease into it, considering you're a rookie and I don't want to get you too alarmed," Rita said. "I'm going to use a grieve to show you what it was like the first time you were here. It will help you get accustomed to VOCS—Visual Output Computer Simulation. It's virtual reality like you've never seen it before: instant head-tracking and a 360-degree field of vision."

Before Krimmer could remind Rita that his nerves were made of steel, the lenses fogged over for an instant, then cleared all at once, like condensation on a windshield suddenly swiped away. The stately Memorial and the Tidal Basin were gone, and he was inside the rotunda, looking up at the monumental, nineteen-foot-high statue of Jefferson, heroic in his calm dignity, shoulders squared, arms and hands hanging peacefully at his side, confident gaze directed north towards the Washington Monument and beyond to the White House.

From his perch on a step, halfway up the statue's four-foot granite pedestal, everything looked just like Rita said it would, just as he remembered it, although Krimmer was surprised that his parents were nowhere in sight. He searched for them in vain in the crowd of chattering, picture-taking tourists who were circling the statue behind a purple velvet rope. He wondered if they were hidden behind all the people, reading one of the quotes on the marble panels. Staring up like a little kid at Jefferson's feet, Krimmer had an idea. If he could just get his own foot up on the base of the pedestal, he could grab the great man's leg and pull himself up to get a better look around. Which was exactly what he was preparing to do, then and now, when a panicky voice that could belong to no one but his mother, sliced through the background noise of this mash-up of memory and reality like the affectionate cuff of a momma bear determined to get the attention of her cub.

"Jake Krimmer, don't you even think about climbing on that statue," she scolded. "You know you're not supposed to be inside the ropes."

"How the hell—" It was as though he had literally been there, not just observing it. Krimmer the boy felt frustrated, thinking he had done nothing wrong. Krimmer the man felt astonished and exposed.

"The frames are connected by Bluetooth to the Nimbus, which is converting the accessible data and generating the image."

"You know what I'm asking, Rita."

"Unlike your mother, your father thought you were just a spunky little kid, so he was videotaping. I don't know if you're aware, but your parents had all their photos and tapes digitized. The Nimbus accessed them from their computer."

"It felt like it was real," Krimmer said, unsure whether to be more amazed or frightened.

"It ought to feel real. A low-powered laser shines the image onto a holographic reflector in the lens, which shoots it into your eyeball, directly onto your retina."

Krimmer whipped off the glasses.

"You don't have to worry, Jake," Rita reassured him. "The laser is too weak to do any damage. Barely class one. Doesn't even need a permit."

Embarrassed, Krimmer glanced at his watch. Dazzling technology aside, if the flashback tour of the Memorial was one of Rita's coveted ten chances to convert him, one of her ten grieves, he was thinking it could use a little more pizzazz. "Well, thanks for the trip down memory lane," he said, "but let's not forget I have a tee time at ten."

Channeling an inner momma bear of her own, Rita cocked her head and granted him an indulgent, frowny smile. "I hope that doesn't mean you're bored, Jake. I'll add the audio with my next grieve."

As Krimmer slipped on the VOCS glasses, he had a premonition that it was the wrong time to forget Confucius. *Be careful what you wish for.* At first he thought he was under water, as if he had somehow fallen into the Tidal Basin. He could barely see for the waves splashing into his eyes. It took him a moment to realize where he was and that he still had the perspective of a six-year-old. He thrashed around until he figured out how to move his head so he was clear of the surface, and that's when Rita's next grieve delivered more pizzazz than he had bargained for.

"Welcome to the future, Jake," was the last thing he heard her say.

All those summers on the Chesapeake, Krimmer had learned to love the soothing regularity of the waves, from the roar of the big, barrel rollers crashing on the rocks, to the little lapping noises as the tide was turning. The size of the waves he was seeing now, hungrily nipping at Jefferson's feet and snapping at his timeless words on the wall, fell somewhere between those extremes. Not so their memory-shattering sound. Neither regular nor soothing, the audio assault was amplified as the troubled water sloshed randomly in the confined space, and intensified as it bounced off the hard marble surfaces, and magnified as it echoed around the concave interior of the dome. At once shrill and harsh and out of phase, the cacophony of wavelengths was unbearably painful, like twelve-tone music played by a sixth-grade orchestra, boomed out over the sound system of the Commanders' football stadium. Krimmer covered his ears with his hands, but it did no good. Just as the troubling images were being beamed directly onto his retina, the horrifying noise was being funneled straight into his eardrums, and from there, directly into his conscience.

"Holy Christmas, what the hell is going on?"

"It's so cute how you always say that. Did your parents teach you not to swear?"

Krimmer groaned in frustration. "Jesus Christ, Rita, what do you want from me?"

"What do you think, Jake?"

"I'm going to take these goddamned things off right now."

"Don't, Jake. You'll want to see what's next."

"What are you going for this time? Smell or touch?"

"I was thinking more along the lines of enlightenment."

With that, everything became eerily quiet, and they were standing back where they began. The Jefferson Memorial still rose in the distance, and the sun still streamed down brightly on the dome, but the resemblance to the earlier reality ended there. The water level had risen to engulf the Memorial's sweeping marble steps and inundate the majestic rotunda, flooding the surrounding shoreline until the Tidal Basin was half again its former size. Instinctively, Krimmer took a step back, as if afraid it was about to soak his shoes.

"This is why it was so noisy in there," Rita said.

Krimmer hid behind a quip. "It looks like an island green."

His personal guide and teacher sighed. "You don't have to worry. I'll get you to the golf course on time."

"Well, what do you want me to say? It's not sexy enough for YouTube?"

"It's not a video, Jake, it's the future. Real data is fed into the program and the Nimbus creates the appropriate images and displays the results."

Krimmer slipped the glasses down his nose and looked back across the Tidal Basin, prediction and reality side by side. "So what am I seeing, one of those hundred-year floods?"

"No, just a supercharged nor'easter, like the one that killed your mother's roses. This is what happens when the storm surge is fifteen feet above the high tide level."

Krimmer pushed the glasses back. Something else wasn't right. Where were the lush plantings that surrounded the Memorial, and the famed cherry trees that crowded the banks of the Basin? As he swiveled his head, all he saw was a gruesome palisade of dead sticks, poking above the surface of the water.

"They're gone."

He didn't have to explain to Rita what he meant. "After too many storm surges, their roots simply drowned," she said.

On the heels of his memory of long-ago picnics, Krimmer suddenly felt the little boy he used to be had been violated. "But we'll adapt, won't we?" he asked, almost sounding like that little boy. "Look how they're farming oysters now in the Chesapeake."

"That's a different order of magnitude, Jake. What would you suggest? Build a levee along the entire East Coast and make God pay for it?"

Krimmer had no more to say as he continued to scan the denuded landscape, embarrassed that his sentimentality might be hanging out like a sloppy shirttail.

"I hate to tell you, Jake, but this is really nothing. If we don't stop the rise in global average temperature soon, Earth won't just become unpleasant, it will become unbearable, maybe even uninhabitable."

Embarrassment begets nastiness. "Oh, you mean that measly one-point-five degree limit they keep talking about."

"One-point-five degrees *Celsius* compared to pre-industrial levels. Two-point-seven Fahrenheit. And if we don't slash greenhouse gases now, we're going to blow through that level in the next few years."

"Like you said, the ACEA will take care of that."

"Do you ever listen? I said the ACEA was a baby step, like putting a Band-Aid on a rupturing aorta. Neither you nor most of our elected representatives seem to have a clue about the enormity of the problem."

"All is lost, is that what you're trying to say?"

"No, but it won't be any fun. For every tenth of a degree above one-point-five, you can count on more deadly heat waves, more flooding, more cataclysmic storms."

"So it will be good for business."

Rita exploded. "You can't really mean that, Jake. If we ever reach two degrees centigrade, Earth will be unrecognizable. No more Arctic sea ice, low-lying coastal cities under water, deserts where there used to be productive farmland."

Well, maybe not so good. No Arctic sea ice, no EF5s? "We'll figure out a way to deal with it. We always have."

"There's only one way to deal with it," she insisted. "We have to face the damage we're doing to the planet. We have to change our thinking and our reckless disregard for the consequences of burning fossil fuels." Rita turned her eyes away to contemplate the calming presence of the Memorial. After she caught her breath, her impatience was gone, replaced by an almost forlorn note of distress. "When you were inside, didn't you see what the great man wrote?"

Krimmer, too, was tired of arguing. "What are you talking about?" he asked wearily.

"The words right there inside the rotunda, Jake, Jefferson's words carved into the marble on the southeast portico."

"All right, let's have it. What did our founding father have to say about weird weather? 'We hold these truths to be self-evident'?"

"That's true too, but it's his words about your favorite solution—adaptation—that you need to take to heart. It's worth another grieve to send you back so you can have a look yourself."

"I don't think so."

"I'll tone down the audio. The sooner you do it, the sooner you get to play golf," Rita said, perking up to once again play the part of his mother.

It can't be any more depressing than the drowned cherry trees, and it's one less grieve I have to deal with. As he took a tentative step forward, Rita did lower the sound, but the Nimbus ramped up the force of the storm surge to compensate, immersing him completely in the chaotic scene. He was a little boy again, and the turbulent water had climbed above the statue's knees, threatening to submerge Jefferson's words beneath the rapidly rising level of the Tidal Basin. Krimmer had to breast the huge, incoming swells as he struggled toward the inscribed slab of marble. By the time he half waded, half swam, close enough to read, the last sentence was beginning to sink beneath the whitecaps, and he was barely able to make it out before it disappeared entirely. Jefferson was speaking about governments, and his eighteenth-century language was stilted, but his impassioned call for open-mindedness and change—and Rita's message about adapting to the new realities—was clear.

> . . . *as new discoveries are made, new truths discovered and manners and opinions change, with the change of circumstances, institutions must advance also to keep pace with the times. We might as well require a man to wear still the coat which fitted him when a boy, as civilized society to remain ever under the regimen of their barbarous ancestors.*

As the waves leapt higher, Krimmer frantically searched for the exit. He couldn't escape the sensation that the water level was rising above his head. Or was he simply being pulled under?

CHAPTER 11

KRIMMER COULDN'T MAKE A PUTT TO SAVE HIS LIFE. THE BALL KISSED the inside right edge of the cup, spun around the back, then ejected as impudently as Timmy sticking out his tongue, coming to rest about six inches away and eliciting from Mortenson an off-color remark that passed for sympathy on the golf course. "Prick tease."

Mortenson drew a little circle around his own magnificent 7 on the scorecard to indicate he'd won the fourteenth hole, a long par 5. "That's gonna cost ya, boyo."

"I wouldn't be bragging about a double bogey, Jared," Krimmer retorted as he tapped the ball into the cup with the back of his putter for a triple, an 8.

Although the uneventful trip up to the Liberty Country Club had done nothing for Krimmer's game, it was a welcome respite after Rita's haunting grieves. Once they left the Jefferson Memorial, they had crossed the Potomac and headed north on the George Washington Parkway to avoid the tourists, who were beginning to overrun the streets. Rita had kept her opinions and arguments to herself, as if she wanted to give Krimmer all the time he needed to process what he'd just seen. The closest she came to alluding to weird weather or climate change was when they were briefly stopped where a towering tree had come down along the side of the road, roots and all. The human dung beetles in their yellow hardhats and orange reflective vests who were chewing up the remains had halted traffic to haul away a truckload of chips.

"That big oak blew down last week," Rita informed him. "The heavy rains made the ground spongy, and it was finished off by the high winds."

"Nature's way of making room for the next generation."

"You're a fine one to talk, Jake," was her cryptic response.

Despite the additional delay, Krimmer was only twenty minutes late when they pulled up to the clubhouse. Mortenson was standing next to their cart, waiting. He was giving Rita the once over even before she opened her window, until she settled him down with a disarming gap-toothed smile.

"Do you want me to pick you up after your game, Mr. Krimmer?" she asked politely.

Mortenson butted in. "Nah, I'll give the lamebrain a ride back," he said to her. "I mean, you're a professional. How difficult is it to keep a battery charged, I ask you?"

"Just bad luck, I imagine," Rita replied.

Krimmer rolled his eyes for both their benefit. "I'll be sure to let you know if I need you," he told her.

She smiled at him as though she expected he would.

"How'd you do it, Jakester—rate a looker for a limo driver?" Mortenson asked as the stretch Caddy disappeared down the driveway, the crunch of gravel the only sound.

Thankfully, Jared didn't demand any further explanation. Although it would have been relatively easy to concoct a story, compared to what he would have to deal with if he ever found out the truth about Rita, whatever the truth might be. *Sex object* and *savior of the planet* would give Mortenson a lot of ammunition. He would have a field day with the former, the latter being largely irrelevant to his circumscribed worldview. At least Jared had never said otherwise, never contradicted Jake's assertions that weird weather was simply a natural phenomenon.

"Where are the other guys, Jared?" Krimmer asked. He had been looking forward to the match. Most of the time it was close. Most of the time he and Mortenson came out winners.

"They went on ahead as a twosome."

"What, they couldn't wait a few more minutes?"

"I told them to go," Mortenson said. "I saw on Immer how you were stuck on the parkway." Immer, meaning *always*—borrowed from the German, like Uber—was the phone app that allowed them to keep track of each other, mapping their location wherever they went. As a sign of their solidarity and devotion to their kindred pursuits and business interests, they were always a green spot on the grid, except when one of them was involved with a lady in prime time. "I'm surprised you got here as fast as you did."

"I had a good driver."

Mortenson agreed wholeheartedly. "I'll say, boyo, and for the sake of your wallet, I hope you still do."

"No pun intended, I'm sure," Krimmer shot back, even as it was sinking in what the day was going to be like. Mortenson wasn't his partner. He was his opponent.

As they approached the fifteenth tee, his pal announced with an obnoxious burst of enthusiasm, "You're four down with four holes to go. You're dormie."

Krimmer winced. He had to win all four of the remaining holes to tie the match.

"I'll press," he muttered, making a bet that he would win more of the remaining four holes than his alleged buddy. What was another fifty bucks when you were looking at losing four ways—the front nine, the back nine, and double for the match—two hundred dollars, already?

"Isn't that what you've been doing since the first hole, pressing?" Mortenson asked. The shadow cast by the bill of his baseball cap accentuated his deep tan, making his teeth glow whiter than pearly as he punctuated his little jab with a grin. "It wouldn't be that your new girlfriend, the one who's not ready for prime time, is giving you a little agita, would it?"

"She sure as hell is not giving me anything else."

"I don't know what she looks like, Jakester, but I'd be thinking it's time to dump her. You're going to be lucky to break 100 today."

"You're going to be lucky if I don't bean you with the ball first."

"Haven't you noticed that for once I'm observing the niceties? I'm making sure to stand behind you every shot."

That was the thing about weekend golf. You were supposed to go out and have a good time with your friends and colleagues. Instead, you ended up not only trying to screw them for a few lousy bucks, but also messing with their psyche.

What made his inept performance especially frustrating was that the course was in perfect shape. All summer it had been like playing in Dubai, with enormous splotches of dormant grass marring the closely mown fairways, turning them so brown in places that it made the sand traps look like patches of virgin snow. But now that the beautiful, weird, fall weather had kicked in, and the club had pumped enough water through the sprinklers to sink Atlantis, Krimmer could only admire the luminous, short-green grass from a distance, as his balls persistently nestled down in the thick and unforgiving rough.

"How're you going to play this, Jakester? You got yourself a plan?" Mortenson asked, not so much grinning this time as hungrily baring those fluorescent choppers. A hundred-and-thirty yards away, the fifteenth hole, a postage-stamp par-3 green surrounded by bunkers, was beckoning.

"I think I'll try to knock it on the dance floor," Krimmer said, deadpan.

Thanks to winning the last hole, Mortenson had the honors, so he was first off the tee. He struck the ball cleanly, but it sliced to the right, just catching the edge of the fringe of taller grass that surrounded the green. Still, it was only twelve feet from the pin.

Most days, Krimmer would have pulled the 8 Iron club out of his bag. Today, he chose a longer club for extra distance—the 7 Iron.

"Going with the artillery, I see."

"Shut up, Jared."

"You know what they say, aim for the angel. That way God will save you if you slice." The top of the tallest spire of the Mormon Temple was visible in the distance, the eighteen-foot-high gold-leaf statue of the Angel Moroni blowing his horn over the left edge of the green.

"God didn't help you all that much."

"We're not on the best of terms lately."

"Maybe you shouldn't have wished the old lady's daughter dead?"

"Hey," Mortenson said, parrying with his favorite subject. "Your new girlfriend ever give you such a come-hither look as this hole, Jakester?"

As Krimmer took his stance, he tried to clear his mind of the psychological debris that had been piling up all day, blocking him at every turn. No Rita Ten Grieve admonitions or arguments, no Samantha unsent emails, no VOCS horror shows, no mechanical Tin Man moves to the ball. He concentrated on feeling the head of the club as he brought it back and up in a smooth arc, then down and through. His sole aim was to get inside Mortenson, inside his ball and inside his head.

Every sport that involves striking a ball has its sound of success. For an iron shot in golf, that sound is just a faint click, barely audible to the player. The reason is simple. The objective is not to hit the ball but to swing through it, in effect to smite air, and sometimes the turf afterward, scalping the grass to create a divot.

Krimmer's hopes were not to be denied. The little white ball rose gracefully and high, paused for the briefest blink against the pure blue sky, then plummeted earthward, bounced once, and settled on the green less than three feet from the flag. Even Mortenson was impressed, rewarding Jake with a boisterous high five.

Krimmer let Jared drive the cart. He wanted the satisfaction of walking up to his ball, watching it grow larger and closer to the hole with every step. For the first time since his morning cup of coffee, he was feeling as if he had regained a measure of control. Until he bent over to repair his ball mark, as cute as a dimple on the flawlessly smooth, manicured grass, and heard Mortenson say, "Sorry, pal, it appears to be just outside of gimme range."

"I wouldn't want you to concede a birdie putt anyway, Jared," Krimmer said, taking a long look himself as he placed a shiny dime behind the ball, marking its spot before picking it up to clean it.

"Hey, a rule is a rule," Mortenson maintained, as he laid his putter on the ground on the line between Krimmer's marker and the pin. "I'd say your ball is two inches outside the leather."

Among the twenty-four major rules of golf, along with the hundreds of sub-rules and official, learned interpretations, there was nothing about conceding a putt when the distance from the hole to the ball was less than the distance from the blade of the putter to the bottom edge of the grip. In other words, it wasn't a rule at all, just a rough approximation of what, in a friendly match, good sportsmanship would usually allow.

"You're away, Jared," Krimmer noted. "Last time I checked, twelve feet was farther from the hole than three."

Tiny, par-3 greens are generally not only tiny. Golf course architects like to trick them up with slopes and level changes. Mortenson's putt from the fringe looked like a double breaker and fast, starting left down the hill and then swerving right at the end. Krimmer figured he'd be lucky to get within two feet. The ball came to rest inside ten inches.

"That's good," Krimmer said, conceding Mortenson's putt as he lined up his own, as straight as it came on this green, just outside the hole.

As Krimmer stood over the ball, Mortenson called out, "Hey, that's good, too."

"I already told you, Jared. You can't concede a birdie. A rule is a rule, even when it isn't."

Krimmer stroked the putt straight and true, but not quite hard enough. The ball quivered on the front edge of the cup, then just sat there, still as a spooked mouse.

"Buck up, boyo. A lotta guys lose their nerve when it comes time to put it in."

The two pars ended their bet on the match. Krimmer was four holes down with three to go, but the press was still in play. They tied the sixteenth and seventeenth par 4s, both shooting bogey 5s. Krimmer extended his string of bogeys to the eighteenth with another 5, but Mortenson parred with a 4 and took the press as well, one stroke and one hole better.

"Here you go, Jared, two hundred and fifty bucks," Krimmer said, as he counted out the bills on the varnished oak table in the air-conditioned taproom. They had decided it was too hot to sit out on the patio in the sun.

"Much obliged, Jakester." Jared pushed the cup of dice to the side. "Forget rolling for the drinks. I'll buy. I can't stand the thought of seeing a grown man cry." He motioned for the waitress, a pretty girl with long blonde hair, and they ordered two drafts, a Bud Light for Mortenson and a Newcastle Brown for Krimmer. "Nice moves," the lawyer said, following the waitress's progress as she swung her way around the tables, heading toward the bar.

Maybe it was just the humiliation of such a sound defeat, or perhaps Mortenson was getting under his skin with his ceaseless roving eye, but in either case, Krimmer was curious. "Can I ask a personal question, Jared?"

"Fire away."

"How old are you, anyway?"

"Forty-nine," Mortenson said proudly. "I bet you never guessed."

"You win that bet, too."

"It's the porcelain veneers, Jakester. Right after my divorce, I had just enough left to make my dentist a rich man. They make old guys like us look ten years younger, don't they?"

"Twenty years, I'd say."

"Now you're talkin'," Mortenson said, as he glanced over at the waitress standing by the tap. "Speaking of moves, what's going on in your world that's making you so jumpy?" he asked. "The way you were swinging the clubs, it looked like you had a bad case of Mature Golfer Movement Disorder, otherwise known as the yips. And here I thought it was only supposed to be a problem with the putter."

"It was just one of those days," Krimmer said, although that did prompt him to ask, "Say Jared, did you ever hear of something called the Nimbus?"

Mortenson clasped his fingers around the bridge of his nose and shut his eyes. "I see hair. Does this Nimbus have anything to do with hair?"

"No, it's a computer thing."

"Never heard of it, boyo. Why're you asking me?"

"I just thought you might be up on that stuff."

"What stuff?"

"Just computer stuff."

That seemed to remind Mortenson of the link he'd sent yesterday. "Hey, I hope I didn't get you riled up with that article in the *Miami Herald*. Old ladies die in nursing homes all the time, so I don't think it will come to a lawsuit. And if they do file, I'll be on the case."

Krimmer had to bite his tongue.

Mortenson's blonde-haired object of desire returned with their beers, setting them down hard, a virtual slam, as if she knew all about tall, dark, and handsome older guys with that casually horny look on their face.

"Anything else, gentlemen?" she asked, holding her pad and pencil over her breasts for protection.

"No gentlemen at this table, miss," Mortenson said with his gleaming, dentally-enhanced smile. To prove it, he gave the waitress one of his patented, over-the-top, big-dog winks. She returned the favor by flouncing off defiantly.

"You know, Jared, there are other things in life besides getting laid," Krimmer said, suddenly wondering if that's how he came across all the time, too. If so, no surprise the dinner with Samantha had ended with a thud.

"You're a fine one to talk, Jakester," he said. "Speaking of which, any new developments with the amazing Okie Amazon?"

"We had a pretty good week," Krimmer replied, assuming the lawyer was switching to business. "Sam's unbelievable," Krimmer said, as he initiated several maneuvers to help him maintain his equanimity, sliding his mug toward Mortenson's for the obligatory clink and easing the conversation back to FTRs. "The reason we've been so successful is that she can see how things are developing before anyone else does."

When Krimmer finished filling Mortenson in about the continuing congestion in Florida and the brewing EF5 in Oklahoma, going into great detail about the record low level of sea ice in the Arctic, and the likely disastrous outcome when the polar vortex collided with the warm, moist air from the Gulf of Mexico, all the lawyer said was, "I'm thinking you still have a hard-on for her."

Krimmer was growing increasingly uncomfortable, hearing Jared talk that way, especially about Samantha. He scraped the chair back from the table to give himself more room.

"I gotta hand it to you about your arrangement," Mortenson went on, the expression on his face the same as when he was ogling the waitress. "Sam's a tough one to lay off."

Krimmer began to wonder if his buddy was clueless or just rude, but he pretended to be unfazed, even as he recalled Samantha's uneasy laugh and theatrical *ever* in response to his spur-of-the-moment query if she was Jared's Friday-night experiment. "The prospect of killing the golden goose concentrates the mind wonderfully, or something like that," he said, reaching back to Brit Lit at Columbia instead of Confucius, paraphrasing Boswell's Dr. Johnson.

Mortenson was watching him intently as he attempted to pry one more time. "Golden, sure. But not silly, I'd bet."

"No, not silly," Krimmer agreed, his wariness not just intact but soaring. "Not silly, for sure."

"Well, if it's not biz or a terminal case of remorse about your ex-honey, what is it?" Mortenson asked. "You looked like a spaz out there on the golf course."

"Anybody can have a bad day."

Or maybe not. "I figure it must be your new girlfriend," Mortenson said with a sly, one-eyed look.

"New girlfriend?" Krimmer said with a hoot of derision. "What new girlfriend?" He was sure now that Sam and Jared had been comparing notes. Why else would they both be harping about a new girlfriend?

"C'mon, Jakester. Stop holding back."

"I'm sorry to disappoint you, Jared, but there is no *new girlfriend*," Krimmer said, taking a big gulp of beer in the hopes that would dampen his smoldering suspicions. There was something telling about his pal's insistence that he must have a *new* girlfriend, ergo he had no interest in an *old* girlfriend, like Samantha. Of course, that would suggest that Mortenson had some modest capacity for guilt, or was truly concerned about screwing up a friendship, qualities that heretofore had gone largely unobserved.

The lawyer pressed his case. "You didn't deny it when I brought the subject up on fifteen."

"I was just playing along with your mind games," Krimmer said. "There was no need to deny it."

"But you admit you were talking to a lady just before I finally got through to you yesterday?"

"And I told you she was not RFPT. Does that sound like a new girlfriend?"

"Well, at least you confirmed *she* exists."

Krimmer's attempt at a smile was pensive at best. "I wouldn't be so sure about that."

"OK, OK, I know when to back off. I'm getting the impression this is serious."

Just as well that Mortenson was congenitally oblivious to sarcasm. "Oh, it's serious, all right."

"So I guess I'll have to wait to hear more."

"Hey listen, drink your beer, it's getting late," Krimmer said. "Are you going to give me a lift back to town, or what?"

"What's the rush, you got something going tonight?"

"Maybe I'll take in a movie."

"That sounds exciting."

"All right, how about squash? Double or nothing?"

"No can do, sorry," Mortenson said, as he peered down into his mug, as though it were suddenly important to determine how much beer remained. "Gotta deal with my experiment."

"Sorry, myself," Krimmer said, unable to refrain from scratching that nagging itch. "Two nights in a row, huh?" he asked, innocent to a fault.

"Nah, just a rain check. She canceled on me yesterday at the last minute."

What chutzpah! The dots that had been threatening to connect since yesterday had snapped into a straight line; they led to nowhere Krimmer wanted to go.

"Hey, let's move it," Mortenson said, standing up and draining his Bud Light. "You're the one in a hurry."

"You know what, Jared," Krimmer replied, flashing the sandbagging snake a smile that may not have been as fluorescent white as his, but was certainly more sincere and convincing. "There's no need to rush after all. I'm going to hang around and practice my putting or something. See if I can salvage what's left of my game."

CHAPTER 12

WHAT COULD HE BE THINKING? *SAMANTHA WOULD NEVER STOOP THAT low.* That optimistic mantra got Krimmer through the next twenty minutes as he waited for Mortenson to slither away from the premises. First, by eschewing putting practice and taking out his frustration on a bucket of balls, smashing them in all directions on the driving range, then taking his time toweling off in the locker room, and finally sneaking unobserved into the pro shop to punch his yip-filled 104 into the computer, where it would surely do wonders for his golf handicap.

When Krimmer eventually emerged from the front door of the clubhouse, it was almost three o'clock. He'd had a premonition that he wouldn't need to order a car. Nonetheless, he had mixed feelings when he saw the jet-black, EV, stretch Caddy waiting for him under the canopy. He wasn't looking forward to more preaching, but the matter of Samantha's unsent email had become more urgent.

"Well, look who's here," he said to Rita as the passenger door slid open. "Why do I feel another grieve or two coming on?"

"Gotta make hay while the sun shines," she said with her most radiant gap-toothed smile. "Remember, I'm working on deadline."

"So fire away. I'm too broke to make any other plans."

"I know," she said sympathetically. "I checked Mr. Mortenson's score earlier."

"I suppose you checked mine, too."

"I didn't bother. I figured you wouldn't be in any shape to beat it."

As they started down the gravel driveway, Krimmer noticed that Rita had left the partition open. He prepared himself for an inspirational, post-game harangue about climate change, or at least a bracing lecture, but none came. In fact, the only thing she said was that she was going to take the Cabin John Parkway south to the Barton because they were still doing tree work on the G.W.

"So what did you do with the rest of your morning?" he asked. "Gas up and polish the Nimbus?"

"C'mon, Jake," she chided. "So do you and Mr. Mortenson play a match every weekend?"

"Is it possible you don't already know?"

"I was just making small talk."

"So was I."

"I do know that you spend a lot of time with Mr. Mortenson."

"So you're aware that customarily we're partners."

"Oh, yes," she said, drawing out her acknowledgment so thoughtfully that it occurred to Krimmer that he'd reminded her of something else concerning Mr. Mortenson.

He decided not to beat around the bush. "I think Jared's making a play for Samantha. You haven't heard anything about that, have you?"

"Honestly, Jake. If I had, I couldn't say. You understand the need for privacy."

"You're a fine one to talk about privacy," Krimmer scoffed. "I thought you were willing to open the kimono."

"Only when I see some signs of progress," Rita said with an impertinent glance in the mirror.

Sam wouldn't stoop that low, he told himself again, preferring to think of it as reasonable hope rather than self-deception. *Then again, Jared would.*

As they sped down the parkway, Krimmer pulled out his phone and checked Immer. So far, so good. The pulsing green dot that marked the location of Mortenson's self-proclaimed chick magnet, a secondhand, baby-blue Miata convertible that was junkyard-ready under the hood, was circling behind the Pentagon on Washington Boulevard. That meant Jared had bypassed the Roosevelt Bridge, a straight shot to the newly gentrified neighborhood of Columbia Heights, and Samantha's row-house apartment. It looked like he was headed home, at least for now, to his Alexandria high-rise with the sweeping view of the Potomac and a ready supply of potential conquests, thanks to a communal swimming pool and in-house gym, where, conveniently, most of the members were single, female, and twentysomething. For women who were subsisting on a government salary, crammed in with two or three roommates, Jared's one bedroom must have seemed like a penthouse. Equally conveniently, any random divorced females, not yet of a certain age, were likely to be on the prowl as well. With those kinds of easy pickings, why did Mortenson feel the need to chase after Samantha?

Maybe in his desire to emulate his good pal Jake, Jared failed to understand that just because it sometimes seemed that Krimmer went through girlfriends faster than a box of tissues, he didn't necessarily regard them as disposable. In the time that he was with a particular lady, long or short, Krimmer honestly cherished every moment, or so he told himself. For sure, as soon as it was clear they were never going to be *the one*—or it got complicated as it had with Samantha—it was over. But more than once, not just with Sam, sadness had been the dominant theme of the breakup—sadness for yet another missed opportunity. He kept in touch with several of his exes, emailing birthday greetings when prompted by Facebook or LinkedIn and forwarding off-color jokes, that sort of thing. He'd even attended two weddings: Beth's and Stacey's.

More charitably, perhaps Mortenson was just trying to test the limits of their relationship, their sibling-like rivalry. Wasn't that what he was doing when he was trash-talking on the golf course, and bragging afterward about how much younger he looked, implying Jake needed to invest in a set of porcelain veneers? The only thing to do was to put Jared's mind games aside for the moment. Krimmer told himself again that Sam was a grown-up, even if Jared wasn't. She could handle whatever came along. It might even be a positive thing if Samantha were merely testing the limits, too. But limits of what? How far he was willing to go to alter their arrangement? What might he say or do to convince her to permanently change its nature?

Consumed by all this thorny speculation, Krimmer had lost track of time. When he looked out the window, he saw that they were already back in DC, lurching along in the Saturday afternoon traffic on Constitution Avenue, heading east just past the Vietnam War Memorial.

"Are we there yet?" he asked.

"Such an impatient little boy," Rita said.

"It looks like we're going to my office." If they continued straight for another half mile, his building would be one block north, to the left, toward Pennsylvania Avenue.

"Doesn't all that green space behind the trees give you a clue?"

"The Mall?" Constitution Avenue ran alongside its entire length.

"The *National* Mall, Jake," she reminded him. "We'll just make a quick stop."

"I see it from my office window every day. Great view."

"I know. So I don't have to waste another grieve reminding you what it's like," Rita said, trying to coax a smile. "I really botched things this morning, having to use three at the Tidal Basin."

"Three?" he exclaimed, quickly doing the arithmetic. "You mean each grieve is a one-off? Even though it was the same place and the same guy?"

"Every time I go back to the Nimbus with a different request, my account is charged."

"Whatever," Krimmer said, secretly delighted that she had only four withdrawals left.

As they edged past the Washington Monument, Krimmer was gloating that cars were parked bumper to bumper on both sides of the avenue. "You're never going to find a parking space," he was about to say, only to have a Winnebago RV pull out just ahead of them, leaving a space more than large enough for the stretch Caddy.

"Shall we have a look, Jake?" Rita asked with a self-satisfied smile.

The great public space of the National Mall was nothing less than the capital's town square, a broad green, well irrigated swath of parkland that stretched for almost two miles in the very heart of the city. They took the short walk up a gentle incline to the base of the Washington Monument, affording them an unobstructed view in both directions. The grassy lawn to the east was flanked by light-brown gravel paths, rows of trees still in full leaf, and a dozen museums dedicated to American arts and science and history, including the original Smithsonian Castle. In the distance, presiding over the far end of the Mall, was the soaring, tiered dome of the United States Capitol. Dotted with memorials to the dead of major wars, the sweeping lawn continued to the west, surrounding the Reflecting Pool and ending at the brooding presence of the Lincoln Memorial.

Krimmer didn't hesitate when Rita silently handed him the VOCS glasses. On a pure entertainment level, he'd gotten a kick out of the special effects at the Jefferson Memorial. In fact, if the technology ever went commercial, he'd be the first in line to buy stock. What harm was another sound-and-light show if he could learn more about the Samantha situation?

When he slipped the glasses on, the wide-open space was suddenly claustrophobic. The expanse of grass was inundated by a sea of boxy, flat-roofed FEMA trailers, white shipping containers with a door and a couple of tiny windows. Thousands of them were lined up end to end in precise, straight rows as far as the eye could see, from the steps of the Capitol in one direction to Lincoln's imposing statue in the other. Even the Reflecting Pool had been boarded over to accommodate the flimsy-looking dwellings.

"What do you think of the view now, Jake?" Rita asked. "Worth the exorbitant rent every month?"

Krimmer tried to bluff his way through. "I always did think of the Mall as the heart of a dysfunctional nation."

"Welcome to Hooverville, the new, improved, twenty-first-century version. Government-issued quarters instead of cardboard shanties make for better PR."

Krimmer took a couple steps forward and suddenly he was in the middle of the crowded settlement. The trailers were packed in so tightly that there was no room to drive a car between them. The little grass that had survived was brown and flattened, leaving a network of dirt sidewalks to connect one neighbor with the next. Every trailer had an AC vent and a fan—and a good thing, too, the way the air shimmered as it rose from the roofs baking in the sun.

"People actually live here?" Krimmer asked, his voice as bleak as the scenery.

"They have no place else to go. About half are permanent residents, displaced by one weather calamity or another. The rest are seeking shelter temporarily, until the floodwaters recede or the forest fire is contained or whatever else is going wrong at home gets back to normal. If it ever does," Rita added.

Krimmer wasn't sure why he was taking it so hard, the sight of a refugee camp at the very center of the nation's capital. Maybe it was because Washington was his hometown. Or more likely, it was a carryover from being dragged back to his boyhood at the Jefferson Memorial. He was imagining how he would have felt if his beloved tree house in the Chevy Chase backyard had been seized for a homeless shelter through eminent domain.

Rita must have been thinking along the same lines. "How would it be for children to grow up in a place like this, Jake? What would it be like if Samantha had to raise Timmy in this environment?"

"No fun," he conceded, even as he noted that although this wasn't the first time Rita mentioned Samantha's son, it was the first time she'd mentioned him by name. He wouldn't be the least bit surprised if Rita knew how conflicted he was about Timmy. *Hell, she knows about everything.*

"I don't see any kids," Krimmer said. "The place looks deserted."

"They're not here yet. The Nimbus hasn't populated the encampment because there's still a slim chance that if we act quickly, we can prevent this tragedy," Rita replied, her voice aching with a hollow, sepulchral sadness. "But if we don't, scientists now hypothesize that if the rise in average global temperature exceeds two degrees Celsius, which is beginning to look likely, we're going to quickly accelerate to three or close to it, because of the inertia baked into the climate by all the carbon dioxide that's been absorbed by the oceans. And three degrees higher is when *uninhabitable* starts to come into play, unless you're a dinosaur. Three degrees higher was the average temperature in the Jurassic."

"Scientists hypothesize," Krimmer groaned as he shed the glasses and handed them back. "What that means is nobody has all the facts. Nobody knows for sure."

"If we wait until we have all the facts, Jake, it's likely to be too late to do anything about them."

He knew he'd get further ahead, Samantha-wise, if he gave Rita a little encouragement, but after the kind of day he'd had, and the sudden injection of a second X factor, Timmy, into the equation, he was in no mood for her insistent moralizing.

"That doesn't mean the rising temperature is caused by human activity," he shot back.

"It's basic physics, Jake. Burning fossil fuels produces CO_2, and the higher the concentration in a gas like the atmosphere, the more heat the gas can trap. Scientists have known that since the nineteenth century, before anybody ever thought about climate change. Ask the Google about John Tyndall, eminent Victorian."

"You've heard about photosynthesis, haven't you? CO_2 is necessary for plants to produce oxygen. How did it get rebranded as dangerous?"

"Too much of anything can kill you," said Rita, unable to suppress a suggestive little giggle. "Even you-know-what."

You know you're losing when you're on the wrong end of a risqué tit for tat. No pun intended.

"I don't care what you say, it's all still hypothetical," Krimmer said, determined to finish what he'd started. "Where's the evidence that the CO_2 is doing any damage? And don't tell me about the cute little polar bears stranded on ice cube–size ice floes, that's old news. Where's the waterfront property in Las Vegas? The Gulf Stream petering out into a trickle?"

"The Colorado River is practically dry," she pointed out.

"OK, so how about the retreat of the glaciers on Mount Kilimanjaro?"

Rita shook her head in disbelief. "You do know it's actually the glaciers on Everest that will go first, Jake."

Why haven't I learned by now? Debating Rita was like one of those late-night bull sessions at college, the kind where the other guys in the room always seemed to have had one less beer, the way they could counter every argument with an overlooked and persuasive fact. "So lives will be saved," he muttered. "The world's tallest mountain will be easier to climb."

From the sympathetic look on her face, Rita was a compassionate victor, ready to put him out of his misery. "Your real problem, Jake, isn't that you're unaware of the science. Your real problem is that you're threatened by it. What you perceive as self-interest is making you stupid."

Here come the oysters, Krimmer predicted, but instead, she finished up with something even closer to home.

"I don't have to tell you about the most compelling evidence of all, what the greenhouse gasses are doing to the climate." Rita skipped a beat, giving him time to anticipate the *coup de grâce*. "It's how you make your money every day—the damage and destruction caused by your beloved weird weather."

Krimmer bowed his head. He knew he had pushed back too hard, causing her to veer off the factual, as theoretical as it might be, into dangerous personal territory. *Not dead yet*, he stubbornly reminded himself. "Didn't you forget the scariest stuff?" he asked with what must have been a phony grin. "You know, when civilization collapses and the only thing that survives the heat are the zombies—or is it the homicidal motorcycle gangs? I forget."

Rita rewarded him with a tight-lipped smile, but her eyes betrayed her seriousness, indigo becoming somber blue. "If you need apocalyptic visions before you're convinced, go to the movies, switch on the TV, read trashy cli-fi novels," she told him. "The reason they're all so popular is that they're so far removed from reality that they can be enjoyed without any fear that they might actually happen. It's *schadenfreude* on a cosmic scale, risk without consequences. As thrills go, they're somewhere between the haunted house ride at the amusement park and bungee jumping from a helicopter over the Grand Canyon."

"I didn't mean—"

"Look, Jake. The problem is that all those prepackaged dystopias get in the way of dealing with the real issues. Who would believe that FEMA trailers on the National Mall were a problem after seeing that crap? The only thing they all get right is that unless we do something, civilization as we know it will assuredly, unquestionably end."

She stopped to take a breath. When she continued, her tone had softened. "If you haven't figured it out yet, what I'm trying to do is show you stuff that you will see in your own lifetime with your own two eyes."

She paused again, but only briefly. When she finished up, it was not with a flourish but with a muffled wail. "The terror of the ordinary, Jake. My job is to show you the terror of the ordinary."

That sounds like Timmy, all right. But he didn't need Rita to tell him the joke wasn't funny.

CHAPTER 13

As he climbed back into the limo, Krimmer had nothing more to say. Rita was playing him like a fiddle, that was for sure. First, leading him on with her considerable charms, then taking advantage of his escalating anxiety about his relationship with Samantha, such as it was. Not to mention how she was starting to get under his skin with the kid business. Like he couldn't possibly care what happened to the country, to the world, unless he had a genetic stake in the future? She should worry about having children herself, the way she jumped to conclusions about a guy.

"Home, Jeeves," Krimmer directed when he finished buckling himself in.

"Yes, sir," Rita replied, but much more pleasantly, as she executed a death-defying U-turn on Constitution Avenue. Krimmer was about to tell her that it might be the most direct route back to Georgetown, but given the Saturday afternoon traffic, it wasn't going to be the fastest. That's when she revealed the full extent of her guile.

"What would you say to a quick stop at the White House, Jake? We'll pass right by."

"C'mon, Rita. Haven't we had enough for one day?"

"You know we're supposed to finish our little game this weekend, and I'm booked wall-to-wall tomorrow with another case."

"Two-timing me, huh?"

"No, just allowing the terror of the ordinary to marinate."

Despite his outward coolness, even low-grade hostility, Krimmer couldn't help but be a little troubled. The stark images at the Memorial and the Mall may have been generated by a computer, but they had pricked at his disbelief in a way that was sharper and deeper than all the dire statistical projections of the doomsayers. "So how many grieves is it, so far?" he asked.

"Seven down, only three to go."

No wonder he was having a few qualms. *Nothing serious, though.*

As always, Rita acted as though silence meant agreement, as she made a hard right at the tarped-over Haupt Fountains. What was technically an extension of Sixteenth Street was cordoned off by a steel-plated barrier-arm gate, and according to the sign, entrance was reserved for Executive Office Building staff parking. After a few words with the heavily armed Secret Service guards, they were waved through and onto the road that ran around the Ellipse, the fifty-plus-acre oval field just south of the White House.

"Don't tell me that's where you work, the EOB?" Krimmer asked. "What are you, Office of the President? National Security Council? Spook Central?"

Rita laughed him off, as usual. "None of the above. I just have friends in high places."

Literally or figuratively? Krimmer stared out the window at the broad, flat expanse of brown grass that was the Ellipse. Weird weather in Washington meant scorching, dry summer days, broken up by periodic vicious storms. The unrelenting heat baked the soil so hard that when the rain came down in buckets, instead of soaking into the ground, the water simply ran off. The irrigated National Mall

was still a showpiece, but the dried-out Ellipse, along with the rest of
the President's Park and the South Lawn of the White House, were
collateral damage of the permanently drought-stricken southwest.
After three years of a politically correct no-watering policy, they had
become scruffy-looking, vacant-lot embarrassments in the president's backyard.

At least there's plenty of room for more FEMA trailers.

Rita pulled into another extremely convenient parking space a
few steps from the wall of waist-high concrete blocks that blocked
the path of any photo-intent ordinary citizens walking in from Seventeenth Street, keeping them away from the fourteen-foot-high
wrought-iron fence that guarded the rear of the White House. She
had another few words with the security personnel, and a moment
later she and Jake were ushered through a narrow opening between
the blocks, right up to the black iron bars.

"With your clout, shouldn't we be using the front door?"

"Insiders know where the real action is," she said as she handed
Krimmer the VOCS glasses.

He paused for a long moment, looking around at the formerly
elegant grounds, the glasses loose in his hand. Beyond the sad-look-
ing fountain on the brown South Lawn, drained dry in solidarity with
those water-challenged states formerly dependent on the Colorado
River, the less-familiar side of the White House glowed in the distance, a couple hundred yards away. The few specimen shade trees
that had survived were already losing their leaves, so they did little to
obscure the imposing façade of the Executive Residence, dominated
by the semicircular columned portico, with its second-floor balcony
built during the Truman administration. To the left, a one-story
colonnaded structure framed the famous Rose Garden, now equally
brown, and connected the main building to the West Wing, the president's place of business. To the right, the mirror image led to the first
lady's domain in the East Wing. Soaring high above the very center

of the building, a single, vivid spot of color—a giant American flag—completed the dignified, if bedraggled, tableau.

"What are you waiting for, Jake? Are you worried about what you'll see? Put the glasses on."

Goddamnit, I am worried. As much as he disliked and distrusted politicians, the presidency was different. It was OK that the House and Senate were hotbeds of self-interest and duplicity; that's how business got done in Washington. All the more reason the country needed a president to rise above the soulless scrum to be the moral voice of the nation and a bold leader. The fact that few, if any, presidents within memory—Jimmy Carter was before his time—had lived up to that ideal was distressing to Krimmer, even though it was personally beneficial. It was the entrenched mediocrity and shortsighted vision in government that allowed him to perpetuate his lucrative weird-weather FTR scheme. But in the final analysis, he could not completely escape his upbringing. He had been raised in the political epicenter of the country by patriotic and civic-minded parents, who had taught him to have a reverence for the office, if not the man. And the serene and stately structure in the distance, the symbol of that office, was about to be sullied by another grieve in a way that he suspected would make their hearts break—and quite possibly his.

"Put them on, Jake."

Reluctantly, he complied. The lenses fogged for an instant, then cleared to reveal the White House from the vantage point of the South Lawn, midway between the fountain and the columned portico. Despite the closeup view, the building looked blurry, as if it were moving almost imperceptibly, as if the signal from the Nimbus wasn't strong enough to anchor it in one position. The more Krimmer strained his eyes to focus, the more the illusion of movement grew, until he realized it wasn't an illusion at all. The entire building was beginning to shake as a tiny, dark smudge appeared in the midst of all the brown in the sorry-looking Rose Garden, and quickly spread into a circular depression, accompanied by a low, sustained rumble, like the muffled booms of distant cannons. As the rumble grew louder, the shaking became more violent, until the vibration of the structure seemed to resonate with the oscillation of the sound, but with a higher pitch, more like the horrifying shriek of a victim tortured on the rack, stretched beyond the breaking point. Instinctively, Krimmer took a step back as the ground quickly fell away and the dark depression became a landlocked whirlpool, expanding centrifugally in all directions until it reached the columned portico on one side and the West Wing on the other. He watched in horror as the building let out one last discordant cry and the corner of the West Wing collapsed into a giant, yawning cavity that looked straight out of Sinkhole Alley in west-central Florida.

"That would be the Oval Office," was Rita's only comment as silence at last prevailed.

Krimmer slowly removed the VOCS glasses. He must have been screaming without realizing it, either that or the sickening noise had been loud enough for everyone to hear, the way all the tourists were snapping his picture, as if they thought he was either responsible for the commotion or had gone bonkers. "You call that the terror of the ordinary, Rita? Hah! Since when?"

"Do you always have to use that expression, Jake?" she asked coolly. "Does it make you feel superior or something?"

Krimmer hadn't thought about it that way, but it was true. It was more than his cocksure way to register disagreement. It was meant to ridicule.

"C'mon," he said, still exasperated. "This is nothing but a myth. Washington wasn't built on a swamp. It's just a convenient metaphor for all the political dysfunction."

"Maybe not a swamp, Jake," she replied with otherworldly calm, "but the city was built on tidal marshes. And the ground is silt and sand and clay. Not exactly the most stable soil when sea levels are rising and acidic water is infiltrating the sedimentary bedrock, turning it into lace. Did you forget about that big sinkhole that opened up between Constitution and Pennsylvania Avenues, near your office? Or the one up in the Petworth neighborhood that swallowed a school bus?"

"But the Nimbus had to go and have the sinkhole open up under the President's home?"

"It's not the first. There was a baby sinkhole on the North Lawn when Trump was in the White House."

Krimmer did remember all the jokes on social media.

"It seems to bother you, Jake."

"You bet it bothers me. I'm still an American."

"Then as an American, consider yourself responsible for your fate," Rita said, her irritation beginning to show. "It's a nonpartisan effort, making sure that pesky international agreements don't interfere with the American way of life, number one in everything— including per-capita emissions."

The way she was reacting, she must have been sitting next to him in Brit Lit. "Patriotism is the last refuge of the scoundrel," Dr. Johnson had famously pronounced.

"Who deserves the blame more than our leaders?" Rita asked rhetorically. "Bush gutted the Kyoto Protocol that almost two hundred countries had signed to limit greenhouse gasses. He stood right there in the Rose Garden, right where the sinkhole opened up, with Cheney by his side, piously proclaiming he believed in man-made climate change, but sucks-to-be-you, America, he just wasn't going to do anything to help stop it."

"Are you saying Obama was any better?"

Party loyalty didn't seem to matter to her; she was an equal-opportunity derider. "Obama did to the Copenhagen Accord what Bush did to Kyoto. He flies off to a meeting of more than one hundred world leaders, all of whom are trying to grapple with the threat to the future of the planet, and what does he do? The thing he does best—make a speech. He claims that time is running out and America will meet its responsibility. Only he doesn't make any new commitments, and the commitments he does put on the table are far less than any other advanced nation. That's not audacity; that's hypocrisy."

Krimmer certainly was no knee-jerk flag-waver, or no Obama fan for that matter, but he was uncomfortable with Rita's diatribe, especially standing right there in the beating heart of Washington. It was like hearing someone swear inside a church. He could only shuffle his feet and look away as she launched into the conclusion of her rant.

"And you don't want me to even get started on Trump pulling out of the Paris Accord and the termites in his administration who ate away at the few sane rules and regulations we had to keep emissions in check," he heard Rita say. "Or the current occupant of 1600 Pennsylvania Avenue, whose one positive contribution was to sign the ACEA, and who seems to think that not watering the White House lawn is enough of a sacrifice to ask of the voters."

"You skipped over Biden," Krimmer felt compelled to note. There had to be some president who wasn't totally in the tank when it came to thinking long term.

"You're right, he did what he could, given how the opposition was so dug in. Half the Republicans maintained climate change was a hoax, the other half were all convinced that doing anything about it would kill the economy. So he had to pretend we were fighting inflation, not climate change. At least you can thank Scranton Joe that the next Corvette you buy is going to be more powerful than that dinosaur you drive now, precisely because it's all-electric."

That'll be the day, he wanted to say, but he held his tongue and took another look at the real White House, not the Nimbus-generated image. He could have sworn the entire structure was listing sharply—the ship of state run aground. "How you can be so negative about America?" he asked, although it came out less like a question than a plea. "After all, it's your country, too."

Her expression suggested it might not be. In fact, at that moment he was back to thinking it might not even be her home planet. After spouting off like that, most human beings would be beet-red, but not Rita. Her face was still a pale, spectral white, unmarked by any sign of emotion other than the resignation in those indigo eyes, larger and sadder than ever before, as deep-set as footprints in newly fallen snow.

"OK, how do I know any of this is real?" Krimmer asked. "I've seen all the tricks you can play with computers. So what if your fancy VOCS program spits out not-so-pretty pictures instead of numbers. Garbage in, garbage out. The data on which everything's based come directly from the usual bunch of Chicken Littles, doesn't it?"

"You're right, Jake. It's like your line of work. It's all probabilities, where that twister will touch down. That doesn't stop you from buying FTRs and making barrels of money, does it?"

Krimmer made one last try, out of frustration or perhaps the early stages of fear, he wasn't sure. "Even if I give you that there's a problem, I'm sure it would take a thousand years to produce that kind of damage you showed me today."

"Don't you ever listen? All it would take would be an increase of three degrees Celsius, or five-point-four degrees Fahrenheit, according to the projections of the Nimbus."

"But how many years?"

"The latest report from the United Nations says if we don't get to net zero emissions quickly, say by 2050, we're on course for tyrannosaurus time by the end of the century."

OK, maybe not the last try. "So what if all this did happen? So what if we turn the National Mall into a trailer park, or need to take a boat to get to the Jefferson Memorial. It's all just optics anyway."

"You're too smart to believe that."

"I could have sworn that just a few minutes ago you were calling me stupid."

Rita just stared at him with those grieving, indigo eyes. She suddenly seemed less spunky than distressed. "Isn't any of this getting through?"

Krimmer let down his guard, although he was quick to explain it to himself as a need to demonstrate a little progress, plus offer up a little timely chivalry. After all, she was trying so hard. "If you want to know the truth, Rita, it's starting to get to me, emotionally, I mean. Especially that trick with my parents."

Exposed by the resulting beam of satisfaction, all he could do was glance at his watch and mumble, "Don't you think it's time we get out of here?"

Rita eyed him up and down like a kennel show judge checking for conformation. "I'll spare you any more sermons, Jake. Something tells me you've already got plenty to think about."

It wasn't clear to Krimmer if it was an excess of chivalry or an unruly stab of self-doubt that made him say with a nervous laugh, "Well, at least you didn't bring up the kid business again."

In either case, it was a good thing it slipped out the way it did. Rita kept her part of the bargain and opened the kimono a little more, just enough to confirm his nagging suspicion. "What makes you think I'm the one who keeps bringing up Timmy?"

CHAPTER 14

KRIMMER CALLED SAMANTHA FIRST THING SUNDAY MORNING. ACTUally, he called her at precisely nine o'clock, which was as close to "first thing" as he dared. The way he figured it, she would have been up since seven thirty. He knew from experience that was about as late as Timmy would ever let her sleep, even if she had been out late, even if her "friend" was forced to spend the night "on the couch" because his car had broken down, or some other lame excuse that would pass muster with a six-year-old when he discovered a man making coffee in the kitchen. Krimmer also knew from experience that there was no sense in trying to have a serious conversation with Sam until she had fed Timmy breakfast and ingested the requisite quantity of caffeine, an amount that could fluctuate wildly, depending on whether or not she did indeed have an overnight visitor.

The possibility of catastrophic engine failure in Mortenson's baby-blue Miata had kept Krimmer up late last night. As soon as the limo had pulled away from the White House, he began checking Immer obsessively, making sure that Jared's pulsing green dot was still happily ensconced in Arlington, which it was until it wasn't.

By six-fifteen, when Krimmer texted his dinner order to China Joy, Mortenson was already crossing the Roosevelt Bridge, a straight shot to Columbia Heights and Samantha's apartment. Twenty minutes later, after Krimmer had answered the bell, paid and handsomely tipped the delivery guy for his fried dumplings and moo shu pork with pancakes, and cracked a cold micro-brew—not an import, a Victory pilsner from Downingtown, Pennsylvania—the pulsing green dot had ceased to pulse. In fact, it had suddenly dropped off radar altogether, as if the lecherous sonofabitch was a UAP, an unidentified aerial phenomenon with cloaking technology.

The double bill of *Casablanca* and *Galaxy Quest* that followed was either a prophylactic measure or wishful thinking. At any rate, it managed to keep Krimmer relatively calm until after eleven, when the pulsing green dot was miraculously pulsing its way back to Arlington and he felt it safe to sleep, even though he wasn't convinced that Mortenson had struck out. He could have hit a solo home run and decided against staying the night. Timmy was always up early, so if the presumptive snake had hung around, he wouldn't be able to hide out in bed all morning and get his beauty sleep.

As the little *phone* icon on his computer screen kept spinning, Krimmer whipsawed between hope and despair. When Samantha finally did click on, she was wearing a ratty T-shirt that would have done Robert proud and no jewelry, but her makeup and her hair were perfect, occasioning a little pang of guilt that he was still lounging around in his bathrobe. At least he had already swiped through the digital versions of the Sunday *Washington Post* and the *New York Times* and had downloaded the crossword puzzle.

"I didn't wake you or anything." It was a statement, not a question. He didn't want to make it obvious that he was fishing.

"No, I got to bed early," Samantha said without further elaboration.

"Maybe you sent me an email or a text and I missed it?" Krimmer suggested.

Samantha dismissed the possibility with a one-eyed squint, disdainfully capped with a frown. "You didn't miss anything, Jake."

"Oh."

By the time the squint spread to both eyes, the frown was in danger of becoming another of her increasingly frequent scowls. "You don't have to worry, Jake, I already checked the maps. The polar vortex and the jet stream are getting ready to do their thing. Norman's finally got off their big, fat duff and announced a tornado watch. It won't be long until the radar signatures start popping up, or someone will see a twister, and the watch will become a warning. You can start checking the Weather Channel around four o'clock here in Washington."

"That's really good news, Sam," Krimmer said, happy to still be Jake, not Krims. "I knew you'd nail it."

"It's not good news for my grandma."

"You alerted her, right?"

"Last night. Before my date," she added, unnecessarily and painfully.

"Look, I wasn't calling about Oklahoma," he said.

She tugged at her naked ear, as if wondering if she'd heard him right. "Is that so?"

"Weren't we going to get together today?" Krimmer asked.

"Oh, yeah. That seemed to be what you had in mind."

"I still do."

"Did I agree?"

"That's why I wondered if you'd tried to reach me."

Samantha drew herself up straight in the chair. "Do you really think it's wise, Jake?"

"To have brunch?"

"To have brunch. To talk. To relitigate our arrangement. That's what you're angling for, isn't it? I thought it was just dandy, the way we had worked everything out."

It was funny how little things, like *just dandy,* gave him optimism. "Surely you don't mean that, Sam."

"What's gotten into you, Jake? It's as though you've been possessed these last couple days. What's going on with the stalker?"

"Why do you think it's got anything to do with her?"

"I know you too well, I guess. There isn't a lot that gets you this way—so excited, so on edge. If it's not weird weather or an attractive lady, what is it?"

"It could be one of those cute Thermian chicks that's causing me trouble," he joked. Then, not caring whether she thought he was fishing, "I missed you, watching our favorite movie by myself last night, after dinner. *Galaxy Quest* is not the same without you."

Samantha passed up the opportunity to commiserate. "Or it could be me, I suppose," she said without any discernable irony.

Why didn't I think of that? He could jump on it and agree, but it would only seem unbearably phony. He owed her for his lack of candor. "You're right, Sam. The stalker does have something to do with it." He paused, considering how much he was ready to reveal. "I didn't want to worry you," he said, preparing to skirt the truth, "but she's actually a consultant."

"A consultant? Really? Why would that worry me?"

"She wants to take a look at our business model."

"Oh," Samantha said, clearly surprised. "I guess that could make me worry. Do I get to hear more?"

"Yes, you definitely do at some point. It's all very preliminary right now. I've got to work some things out first."

Samantha eyed him skeptically. "Can you at least tell me what kind of things?"

Krimmer knew he was on a slippery slope. "The kind of things we started to talk about at Tout Va Bien."

"Whether I'm happy at work?"

"Whether we both are."

"I thought she was a *business* consultant," Samantha said.

"She is," Krimmer affirmed, "but one of her fundamental principles is that business and personal issues are not as separate and distinct as we might like them to be."

"Oh," Samantha repeated, not surprised this time. Reflective. "You didn't seem to pay much attention when I said the same thing at Tout Va Bien."

"That's not true, Sam. I've always kind of thought that way. How do you think we got ourselves into this stupid arrangement?"

She looked at him quizzically, *stupid* and *arrangement* not being words he often linked together.

"So what do you say?" Krimmer asked, not altogether sorry that it had slipped out that way. "Maybe we can talk more about it over brunch."

Samantha went back tugging at her ear. "Can you wait until eleven?"

"Why eleven?"

"That's as early as Timmy can get a Happy Meal."

"Oh." Of course, McDonald's. "Sure," he said, trying to sound upbeat. So much for any visions of Bloody Marys and smoked salmon.

Samantha wasn't buying what he was selling. "I don't want to hear any more about it, Jake," she warned.

As soon as he and Sam finished nailing down the details, Krimmer called his parents. They'd left a message yesterday. *The weather is so beautiful, if your social calendar isn't fully booked, why not come out for lunch or dinner or just a drink, if that's all the time you can spare? You pick the day, even Monday, do you remember it's a holiday? Indigenous Peoples' Day, you work so hard? And please feel free to bring a friend.* Why not? They'd probably be delirious about Rita.

His father answered the phone.

"Hey, got your email."

"So, any chance we'll see you today?" Jake Sr. asked. "We could watch some football."

"Not today, Dad. Maybe tomorrow."

"Is that our son?" he heard his mother call out off-camera.

"The one and only."

"Hi, Jake," his mother said, bustling her way into the frame.

"Hi, Mom. No, I can't come out today. I told Dad maybe tomorrow."

"Well, you'd better call first," his father said. "I was planning to get started on something tomorrow."

"Another project? A toolshed maybe? At last?"

"You might call it that."

His mother gave her husband an inquiring look, as if she were checking with him. "Your father's decided to write his memoirs." She might have well as said he'd decided to write the grocery list, she said it so casually.

Whatever, it seemed to make Jake Sr. grumpy. "Well, not exactly my memoirs. I'm not sure I'm going to write a book or anything."

"What are you going to write?"

"I want to set the record straight about a few things I've done in my life, that's all."

"What kind of things?" Krimmer asked, wondering if he might have an inkling, thanks to Rita.

"Just things."

His mother decided to close ranks. "Don't be so nosy, Jake. He'll tell you when he's ready."

"You're the one who brought it up."

"Just don't be so nosy."

"I'll look forward to it, anyway," Krimmer said, deciding any mutual confessions could wait.

"Well, I hope you've got something nice planned for today, Jake," his mother said, just managing to finesse an outright question, the way she always did when she desperately wanted to know more about what was going on with his social life. "It's such a beautiful day for this time of year."

"I've got a couple of things on the calendar, Mom."

"Oh, what kind of things?" she asked brightly—very brightly.

"Just things," he said with a wink.

Filial duty complete, Krimmer retreated to his man cave—the family room if there had been a family in the house. His sanctuary was bigger than a den but somewhat smaller than downtown Union Station, with entrances from both the compact kitchen and the vaulted-ceiling living room, with its mid-century modern leather-upholstered couch, antique, rust-red Heriz carpet, and tens of thousands of dollars of color-saturated, emerging-artist abstract canvasses scattered strategically around the neutral, off-white walls.

The man cave was dominated by a brand new, ninety-six-inch, ultra-High-Definition TV with a curvilinear screen, fully loaded with Dolby Digital Max Stadium Surround Sound. This ultra-advanced megagadget was taking some getting used to, particularly if he was watching sports, which was just about all Krimmer ever did anyway, except for checking out weird weather or making the occasional foray over to MSNBC or Fox to see what the rascals were up to lately. He'd swear that in addition to all the other gizmos, they had sneaked a teleporter into the set, the way the TV didn't just put you in the middle of the action, but it made you part of the action—almost as much as Rita's VOCS glasses. He'd flinch at the crushing impact of the 350-pound defensive end, futilely cover his ears at the shrill, piercing sound of the zebe's whistle—the black-and-white-striped-shirted officials were always calling roughing the passer or helmet-to-helmet contact—and shake violently as the stadium erupted with the cheers of eighty-thousand fans.

Never, ever, would he want to watch porn.

Early Sunday morning was a veritable wasteland—not even a replay of a tournament on the Golf Channel or an exploding talking head. Krimmer switched channels to see if Mother Nature was cooperating with his outstanding big bet. Norman may have been slow to declare the Apocalypse was nigh, but the Weather Channel was already on the case. One of their crack storm-chasing teams, two young guys in the ubiquitous jeans and T-shirts with the bills of their baseball caps turned rakishly sideways, and the indispensable golly-gal blonde, no baseball cap required as long as her top was one size too small, were yukking it up by the side of a two-lane country road.

The tall, skinny guy had the mike. "You might be wondering what we're doing out here on such a beautiful day, surrounded by farm fields as far as the eye can see," he said, grinning in the direction of his companions instead of the camera.

"Yeah, what the . . ." Just in time, the short, stocky one pretended to remember they were on TV. He flashed a dopey smile. "Yeah, just what are we doing?"

"Let's let Linda answer that," the first one said, handing over the microphone to the blonde.

"Golly," she squealed. "Do I have to?"

"Hey, you want to be part of the team, don't you?"

"Oke . . . Oke . . ." she stuttered as she tried to hit the right note.

"C'mon, belt it out, Linda."

"Oke . . . Oke-la . . ." she started again and stopped, looking bewildered.

"Remember the wind, Linda, the wind," the skinny guy prompted.

"And the wind will be wicked out here in the sticks, bro, don't you doubt it," the short, stocky one improvised, apparently relishing the thought. "That's why we brought out the big dog."

The scene shifted to the opposite side of the road, and the three of them started extolling the features of their new Subjugator-3, an armor-plated vehicle that looked like it had been built on the frame of an Abrams tank, with six fat wheels instead of treads, a short-range weather antenna, a satellite dish, and a remote-controlled panoramic camera, all mounted where the turret would have been. They took turns avowing it was a big improvement over Subjugator-2, which had embarked on an unplanned flight in a previous EF5 and suffered greatly for it. Four hydraulically powered anchoring spikes, with 12-gauge shotgun slugs to lead the way, were ready to blast into the ground at a moment's notice, ensuring that what was down stayed down.

The ragtag crew was particularly proud of how every aspect of their adventures would be captured and uploaded live for instant thrills, not just for posterity. A dashboard cam would record the nitty-gritty of the chase, the camera on the roof would show the big picture, and a third camera, mounted inside just below the rearview mirror, would record a group selfie, memorializing every word of meteorological wisdom as well as the inevitable shrieks and hollers. As for intrepid jaunts outside, there was a handheld minicam.

As Krimmer continued to watch, he became increasingly uneasy about these combat-ready gladiators, with their cocky attitude and bristling equipment and infinite capacity for heedlessness. The placid landscape in the background might not have been the template for "America the Beautiful," with its purple mountain majesties and amber waves of grain, but it was a pretty good approximation for so early in the winter growing season on the Great Plains. The field that unrolled behind them was so perfectly flat and endless that Krimmer imagined he could see the curve of the horizon, and the rich brown earth was speckled with the first impossibly green, knee-high shoots of winter wheat. In the distance, the sloping roof of an iconic, bright red barn was visible, and beyond that, a cluster of trees marked the location of a town. This particular slice of God's creation was locked helplessly in the embrace of an intense blue, cloudless sky that gave no hint of the devastation to come.

Krimmer stared mutely at this tranquil scene for another second or two until it began to look to him a lot like Florida. At that point, he slammed down the remote and headed for a shower and a shave.

CHAPTER 15

MCDONALD'S WAS NO TOUT VA BIEN. FOR ONE THING, THE CORNER banquette was a hard, bright orange, molded plastic bench—definitely not conducive to intimate conversation. For another, the choice of beverage was severely limited—similarly not conducive. For a third, although Krimmer didn't miss the efficiency-challenged minimum-wage workers who in the old days manned the counter and the kitchen, this next-generation Mickey D's had all the charm and vibe of an ancient automat, circa the Great Depression, thanks to its impersonal, electronic ordering terminals and the little boxes inset on the wall where the food was delivered. It didn't help that on Sunday mornings—prime time for kids—the warden was tricked out as Ronald McDonald. With his bloated, bright red smile and striped shirt and leggings, the clown couldn't quite deliver the downcast Piaf ambiance that genuinely *was* conducive to intimate conversation, even though his painted-on teardrops made it look like his mascara was running weepily, too, just like that of the chanteuse.

"My, you're getting considerate in your old age, Jake," Samantha said, as she dragged her darling blond hell-raiser of a son down the aisle. They were only ten minutes late. Sam was dressed for yet another unusually warm day, in shorts and a brightly patterned, sleeveless blouse, showing off her curvy legs and defiant lacrosse scar to perfection. Timmy was wearing shorts, too, along with a T-shirt featuring an ugly, slime-green gnome who may or may not have been giving the world the finger.

"What did I do now?" Krimmer asked, fearing the worst.

"No, I'm not kidding. This is really a great spot to keep an eye on him while he goes off and plays." The adjoining McUniverse had replaced the now defunct PlayPlace, a public health official's nightmare of yet more ugly plastic—giant, multicolored, twisted tubing snaking in, over, and around a jungle gym—the former source of numerous athletic injuries and an incubator for germs of all varieties, making it a bonanza for the Trial Lawyers Association in fifty-one of America's fifty states. McUniverse, on the other hand, was designed to be an educational experience about space travel, chockablock with video consoles and virtual-reality booths, and a full-scale model of the command center of the rocket ship for the long-ballyhooed manned mission to Mars, permanently consigned to the future.

"That's why I grabbed this table," Krimmer said, delighted with his foresight, as accidental as it may have been. But there was nothing unintentional about his adding, "Also, I remembered Timmy wanted to be an astronaut," without mentioning he once had, too. That ship had sailed, just like the cocktail-newbie.

"So maybe this consultant is already changing you for the better," Samantha said, still smiling at Krimmer as she eyed the seating arrangements and settled Timmy into a chair opposite him.

"She works fast," Krimmer deadpanned.

Samantha glanced back to check if there was a free terminal. "Let me enter our order first," she said. "Want anything?"

"I'll just drink my coffee, thanks."

You had to give it to the robots: they were fast, too. The screen on one of the box-doors on the wall was blinking *Timmy* in less than two minutes, signaling their food was ready. When the two of them returned, Samantha spread out the feast: coffee and a salad for herself, and for her son, four little puck-like patties of chicken—grilled, not fried—some apple slices, a yogurt drink, and a rubber statue about three inches high of the aforementioned repellent, slime-green gnome, this time with arms raised and fists clenched. Sam also produced a cardboard basket of french fries that she handed over to Krimmer. "Hold onto these," she said, as she seated herself more or less next to him, around the molded plastic corner and well within knee length. *An auspicious echo of Tout Va Bien?*

"Doesn't he . . .?" Krimmer asked.

"Only if he eats some of his chicken."

He looked at the fries longingly. Timmy must have noticed. "Can I have some now?" the boy asked, politeness-free.

Samantha shook her head, putting Krimmer in an awkward spot.

Timmy was relentless. "Can I have some fries?"

"Hasn't Mommy taught you to always say *please*?"

"Please, Krims?"

"You know you have to eat some chicken before you can have them," Krimmer said, to Sam as much as to Timmy. He was rewarded with a satisfied smile from the one, a malevolent, slime-green glare from the other.

Krimmer resorted to friendliness. "So you want to be an astronaut, is that true, Timmy?"

His pint-sized adversary was not so easily deterred. Timmy took a long swig of his yogurt drink before asking for a third time, "Can I have my fries, now. Please."

Samantha finally took pity on Krimmer. "That's enough, Timmy," she said sternly. "You know the rules. Now answer Krims's question."

"What question?"

"I understand you want to be an astronaut when you grow up."

Even Krimmer had to be impressed by the boy's remarkable certainty. "I don't want to be, I will be," he said, as if going off into space were no more daunting than his previous career aspiration as a fireman, or taking the controls of the rocket ship in the McUniverse.

"That's the spirit," Krimmer said. He pointed to the hideous-looking toy sitting on the table. "So who's that?"

"Grubman," it sounded like, as Timmy tried to answer at the same time as he chomped down on one of the chicken pucks slathered with ketchup.

"Grubman?" Krimmer looked at Sam for confirmation.

"Grubman, Jake," Sam said with a trace of impatience, as if she hadn't noticed how well he was handling the situation. "That's the movie we're going to see at noon."

"Oh, that doesn't give us much time to talk."

Her smile was no longer quite so satisfied. "The theatre's right next door. That's why I chose this spot to meet."

Based on Krimmer's admittedly limited experience, six-year-olds tend to either wolf down their meal or sit there picking at it. Thankfully, Timmy was hungry but not too hungry. He went off to play in the neighboring galaxy without finishing his fries.

"Well, where were we, Sam?" It was eleven thirty and so far, it had all been about the kid.

"The other night, you mean?" she asked, distracted by Timmy, who was running headlong for the rocket ship.

It took Krimmer a moment to reassure himself that she was referring to Tout Va Bien, not any enlightening experience she might have had with Mortenson in his laboratory. He was determined not to bring up the "experiment," no matter what. He didn't have standing, as the attorney would say, until there was some closure about modifying the status of their arrangement going forward—or not.

"I thought you were the one who was keeping track," Samantha said, keeping one eye on Timmy and the other on Krimmer.

"I was. I am." Krimmer was at a loss about how to broach the subject of her happiness, professional as well as personal, without sounding like a human resources clone.

Samantha, on the other hand, seemed to have no such problem. "You were worried that I don't like what I do," she said. "Somehow the conversation with your parents made you more sensitive to other people's feelings."

"*Your* feelings, Sam."

"Yes, my feelings," she said, as she sipped her coffee.

"Well, are you?" he asked as he helped himself to one of Timmy's fries.

"Am I what? And by the way, you should ask him first if you can have one," she snapped.

"You're right," Krimmer said, pushing the container away. "What I was asking was, are you feeling OK about everything?"

"What everything?" she asked, now zeroing in.

"Your work," Krimmer said earnestly, thinking he was circling back to the starting point.

"Oh."

"Well, isn't that what you said?"

"I guess."

The drip, drip, drip is like water torture. "I asked you where we were, and you said that I seemed worried that you didn't like what you do? Is that right?"

Samantha looked at him long and hard before responding, although contrary to her usual athletic instincts, she didn't so much tackle the question as dissect it. "I think you have to distinguish what we do from the circumstances that allow us to do it," she said, knotting her forehead as if she were only now beginning to appreciate the distinction herself.

"You mean distinguish trading Financial Transmission Rights from all the weird weather."

She skipped a beat, then confessed, "From anthropogenic climate change."

"I never heard you call it that before," he said, sitting up straight.

"Frankly, I didn't think it would play well at the office."

"So you agree with my parents, is that it, Sam? You agree that there's something a bit unethical about what we do."

"Like I told you the other night, there's certainly something exploitative."

"Oh, Lord. I didn't expect to hear that from you."

"Sorry, Jake. I thought we'd always been honest with one another."

"But you never mentioned climate change, not once. Was that honest?"

"There's a difference between something you say and something you think it wise to keep to yourself," Samantha reflected, as she fiddled with her paper cup, twisting it one way, then the other. "You can keep your mouth shut and still be honest."

"Hah! Since when?"

Out of the corner of his eye, Krimmer saw that his sudden outburst had gotten the clown's attention. Ronald McDonald was now watching them, not quite as gnomely as Timmy had, but suspiciously for sure.

Samantha started to slide away, then seemed to change her mind and leaned forward instead, looking right at him, into him even. "OK, you want honest? I'll give you honest," she said, subdued enough to put Ronald at ease. "When you first hired me, it took me a few months to fully understand the business model. My education and experience is all in science, not finance. Having to spend every day on the lookout for so-called 'weird weather' was depressing enough, but when I figured out that we were also screwing the utilities' customers with—what's it called, 'congestion pricing'?—I wasn't feeling very good about anything."

"It's generally accepted accounting—" he started to say.

She cut him off. "Hey, at least we had already embarked on our little fling and I was enjoying that part. Silly me, I was even thinking it might lead to bigger and better things, so despite my reservations—about the business, not about you—I was in no hurry to bail out."

"I'm grateful for that," he said in all seriousness.

Samantha wasn't having any of it. "You're grateful because I'm so valuable to you. You've made that clear."

"No, not just because of that. Because . . ." Krimmer searched for the right word but didn't find it. "Because I'm very fond of you."

Back in Oklahoma, when the weather got too cold for lacrosse, she must have wrestled. Samantha's stare pinned him hard against the unforgiving plastic bench. "I suppose I should be grateful that I've been upgraded to *fond*," she said, her tone equally unforgiving. "I gather things are not going well with your new girlfriend."

"I told you, she's not my new girlfriend," Krimmer said.

"Oh, right, she's a consultant. Check."

Krimmer was surprised by how bitter she sounded, but also encouraged. His good feeling didn't last long.

"Pardon my disbelief," Samantha said with exaggerated deference. "It's hard to imagine Jake Krimmer listening to anybody."

Despite his earlier resolve, he struck back the only way he knew how. "I didn't ask you how it's going with your new boyfriend, did I?"

It was Samantha's turn to sit up straight. "There is no new boyfriend," she said evenly.

"What's the matter? You didn't have a good time last night?" He was starting to raise his voice.

"What business of that is yours?" she asked with an annoying sense of calm.

"I know it's not my business," he went on, ratcheting up the volume, not giving a damn about Ronald anymore. "No more than my consultant is your business," he said, truth falling victim to anger.

"Why don't you tell everybody in the restaurant, Jake. I'm sure they'd like to hear more."

In the course of dealing with her maddening equanimity, Krimmer failed to realize that Timmy had returned to the table and was staring at him like he was Jake the Ripper, a comparison that gained verisimilitude when the pint-size astronaut took one of his fries, dipped it in ketchup, and smeared it on Krimmer's baby-blue golf shirt, right across the Liberty Club crest over his heart, so the tiny American flag lost its white stripes and he, Krimmer, actually did look like Jake the Ripper, bloody and incensed. "Goddammit," he muttered with heroic restraint, appealing to Samantha.

Her rebuke was milder than he would have liked. "That's a no-no, Timmy," she said, placing the box of fries out of reach.

"That's a brand new shirt, Sam."

"He was only trying to protect me, Jake."

"You shouldn't yell at my mommy, Krims," Timmy said. "Yelling is a no-no, too."

The kid had a point. "Is everything OK, folks?" Ronald was suddenly hovering behind Timmy, his painted-on smile seriously at odds with the stern stare directed at Timmy's victim.

Krimmer and Samantha locked eyes. "Everything's fine, thanks. Just a little acting out," she said. "You know how children are."

Ronald remained silent for a moment, taking the measure of their détente. "Well, enjoy your meal, folks," he finally said, patting the boy's head.

As the clown waddled away, Samantha's suggestion came as a welcome surprise. "I think it's time to activate Omega 13."

The Omega 13 device was the last, best hope for survival in *Galaxy Quest*. When the rescue button was pressed, physical matter was rearranged and time spooled backward, wiping thirteen seconds off the clock, just long enough to correct a life-altering mistake or two.

Krimmer began cautiously. "I'm sorry about the boyfriend business, Sam."

"It's OK, Jake. I'm sorry about not taking the consultant seriously."

He dabbed at the stain with his handkerchief. "I shouldn't have lost my temper." He hesitated before confessing, "I probably would have done the same thing if it were my mother."

Samantha thanked him with a quick nod and a tiny, fleeting smile. "If we were in a real restaurant, I could get you some club soda," she said.

"It's only a golf shirt. I'll take care of it as soon as I get home."

"Soak it first for an hour or so with some liquid detergent before you wash it," she advised.

"Sounds like a plan."

Samantha checked the time.

"Maybe you two ought to get going," Krimmer said, even as he registered that their knees were now bumping, a haunting replay of the promise of Friday night.

"Maybe we should," she agreed, as she reached down with two hands to retrieve the napkin on her lap. Only one hand emerged to lay the napkin on the table. The other found his leg, squeezing gently. "Want to come with us to the movie, Jake? I could drop Timmy off at a friend's house afterward for a playdate, and we could go out for a drink or something?"

"Yeah, we could go watch the Weather Channel."

"C'mon, Jake," she said with Piaf-like downcast eyes. "You know what I mean."

The stirring in his pants was palpable to him, and perhaps to her as well. But although the Omega 13 device could erase their flare-up, it couldn't take back what she had said earlier, it couldn't change what she believed about the reason for all the weird weather or how she felt about how they exploited it—exploit, that was the word she kept using—exploited the utilities' customers, too. He needed time to think it through when his mind was clearer, when he could see beyond the heartrending images that Rita had bestowed upon him, when he could more fully process the reasons behind the revolt of his crack and sublimely lovely meteorologist and his own escalating doubts about weird weather. "I'm going to need to take a rain check, Sam," he told her, as kindly as he could.

Samantha's face froze; her hand went limp. "All right, I understand," she said after a second or two, her eyes no longer downcast, bravely reining in any disappointment. She rose slowly but purposefully, as if the weight of the world was bearing down on those magnificent shoulders, gathering up the plastic tray with one hand and Timmy with the other.

"See you tomorrow," Krimmer called after her as the two of them started to disappear toward the door.

"Tuesday."

"Oh, right. Indigenous Peoples' Day. Forgot again."

But they were back before he knew what hit him. "By the way, I meant to tell you," Samantha said with a casual smile, as if by chance she had just happened to think of it. "Jared is a very funny guy, once you get to know him better."

It cost him dearly, but he smiled, too. "Yeah, that's why I keep him around," Krimmer replied. And then when she was about to disappear again, he said just loud enough so she could hear, or maybe not, "Don't forget to hold the popcorn."

CHAPTER 16

KRIMMER TOOK THE LONG WAY HOME FROM MCDONALD'S: THE SCENIC route for a muddled state of mind. As his mysteriously reenergized Corvette inched along in the farmers' market traffic around Dupont Circle—the underpass was still flooded from the last storm—he had to wonder what the hell had just happened. *How could I have passed on Samantha's not-so-subtle invitation?* He knew the answer, of course. Rita had called it, right from the beginning. His happiness wasn't just related to his acceptance of climate change, it was inextricably entwined with it—at least, if his happiness was going to involve Samantha. Until he resolved his doubts, he could no more jump in bed with her than he could wish her away, professionally or personally.

Rita had blown through seven of her ten grieves, so she should have no trouble finishing up with him by midnight tomorrow, as she had promised. Assuming conversion was a linear progression, and that he was a hard case but not intractable, he ought to be more than halfway home to becoming a climate-change believer. *And maybe I am, considering that instead of kicking back and celebrating a very profitable day, with another likely in the offing, I'm agitating about what I did to earn those profits and at what moral cost.* He couldn't scrub any of those searing VOCS images from his mind, or erase his parents' heartfelt confessions, or even completely suppress the low-grade tinnitus of the oyster marching band. Whether or not any of it was truly the "terror of the ordinary," if the projections of the Nimbus came to pass, it would bring terror to many ordinary lives.

On the other hand, as the bumper stickers say, stuff happens. He didn't have to invoke menacing global forces to rationalize the destruction of his mother's rose bed. And VOCS aside, the future wasn't just malleable, it was impenetrable. He had read enough about the kind of sheep entrails that the high priests of impending disaster employed for their auguries. Rita had that one pegged, too. For all their data and presumably good intentions, everything was based on probabilities, and even Samantha had an occasional off day. At some level, buying into man-made climate change was more a matter of faith than of proof, little different than being convinced you could beat the stock market or believing in God. The only downside for a climate-change atheist was the risk of being wrong: hell right here on Earth, rather than having to wait.

Krimmer arrived home just in time for the one-o'clock kickoff. His mood didn't improve much when he tried to focus on the football game. The Commanders' inept, slow-footed quarterback looked like he was still playing for the Redskins—the team's name in the pre-PC dark ages—and not at the Little Big Horn, either. Under most circumstances, Krimmer could tolerate a blowout, even root for one, in the hope that it would lead to the forcible removal of the head coach. The guy was an old-school blockhead who had stubbornly failed to adapt to the new realities of the post-CTE NFL, where sheer brutality had been sidelined in favor of speed and deception—kind of like Rita's MO, now that he thought about it. But today, Krimmer felt compelled to yell his support, not because he cared so much about the outcome of the game, but because yelling helped him keep regret at bay for not going with Samantha and Timmy to see *Grubman*, among other stupid things he'd done or not done lately.

When Mortenson's number flashed on the screen, Krimmer hesitated, then clicked.

"Hey, Jakester, want company?"

"Do I have a choice?"

"Sure, if you want to suffer alone."

"How do you know I'm suffering, Jared?" Krimmer asked, alert to the possibility that this was the attorney's roundabout way of broaching the issue hanging over the future of their friendship—i.e. last night's experiment.

Even Jared wasn't that insensitive, at least not when he was inviting himself over. "You're watching the Commanders, aren't you?" he said with a chuckle.

"What's wrong with your TV? Why would you want to watch these bozos on a ninety-six-inch screen?"

"Hey, size matters."

As he waited for his self-styled company, Krimmer kept clicking over to the Weather Channel, but they currently seemed more interested in the old news coming out of Florida than any new developments in the Great Plains. That would change in an instant once they got the word that the tornado watch had been upgraded to a warning, or received an excited call from Subjugator-3. He wondered exactly where in Oklahoma Samantha's grandmother lived. He had the impression it was a small town, not a major city. Maybe Rita could check it out for him. *Then again, maybe I should leave well enough alone for now.*

The bell rang just before the second-half kickoff. "Sorry I'm late, but I hadda stop off for supplies," Mortenson said, as he set a six-pack of Bud Light on the kitchen counter. "You have nuts?"

"Pistachios."

"Ugh, shells. Too much work, pal."

"How about some chips and dip?"

"Blue cheese, I hope."

"Let me ask you something, Jared. Did it ever occur to you to bring the kind of beer *I* might like to drink?"

"Sorry, Jakester, no fancy microbrews at the Speedway."

There were two recliners in the media room, as Krimmer referred to his man cave when guests were present, even a shameless moocher like Mortenson. Dark brown, motorized behemoths, the controls were built right into the six-inch wide armrests, along with foldout trays, cup holders, and a universal remote. The overstuffed upholstery bulged like fat jelly rolls to support ergonomically sensitive body parts like the neck, spine, and lower back, and the entire apparatus was covered from nose to tail with the indestructible hide of the Nauga.

"I bet you could have some fun on one of these babies," Mortenson said, as he pulled back on the joystick to get horizontal. He cracked open his first can and asked, "You try it out with your new girlfriend yet?"

"How many times do I have to tell you, Jared?" Krimmer asked, thinking this might be the opening gambit about last night.

"Oh, yeah, I forgot," Mortenson said noncommittally, as if he hadn't really. "Maybe I should get one for myself," he said, patting the top of the armrest. "It might have helped with my experiment," he added with what could have only been premeditated casualness.

Krimmer knew Jared was dying for him to ask, so he didn't. "Would that mean you'd stop inviting yourself over?"

Mortenson smirked, but his only follow-up was motoring back to a safer position to swallow his beer.

There were no secrets in Washington, not for very long anyway, so Mortenson had to assume that by now Krimmer knew the identity of his experiment. What the attorney didn't know was how Krimmer would react when he confessed. Neither did Krimmer. That depended on his state of mind and the nature of the confession, not to mention how it was served up. With Jared, it could be anything from a simple admission or denial to an elaborate excuse or rationalization. If he'd scored, he might even want to do a little boasting. Whatever the case, for friendship's sake, as well as for the future of their business relationship, Mortenson was smart enough to know it would be better to clear the air.

Before Krimmer could dwell any more on the delicacy of his pal's situation—assuming there was a situation, assuming Jared was still his pal—the Commanders' running back gained seven yards on first down.

"Hey, we've finally got something going here," Mortenson yelped. He checked his phone and tapped the screen a couple times. "I just got five to two on SlamJam that they get a field goal on this drive—whaddaya think?" SlamJam was the latest sports betting app, with a carnival of exotic, real-time wagers and parlays and prop bets—shorthand for *dubious propositions* not tied to the outcome of the game. Gamblers could put money on just about anything that might happen, even in the next few seconds, like whether it was going to be pass or a run, or how many yards the play would gain, or whether the head coach might throw the challenge flag.

"You know I only bet on weird weather, Jared."

"And on golf," Mortenson reminded him.

"Maybe not anymore."

"I don't get it, what's the fun in betting on weird weather when your sexy meteorologist's got all the answers?"

Krimmer kept his cool. "At least she gives it to me straight, unlike some other people I know."

On the next play, the Commanders' running back was hit as soon as he took the handoff. The zebe threw a flag for offside, but that didn't help the runner. He crumpled to the ground, clutching his knee, and the network went to an injury time-out.

"Good time to check on Oklahoma." Krimmer switched over to the Weather Channel.

"Hey, I've got money on this," Mortenson protested.

"You've got money on Oklahoma, too. I win, you win."

To Krimmer's disappointment, the Weather Channel still had Florida on its mind, even though power had been mostly restored throughout the state and life was returning to normal.

"Can you tell us what it was like when the thunderstorms hit?" the cute brunette reporter was asking an excessively tanned, white-haired lady who had no business wearing shorts, particularly the lime green ones that clashed so well with her aqua top.

The elderly woman's lips were moving long before any sound emerged. "It was loud, and it was wet."

"That's how you would describe it? Loud and wet."

The woman thought some more. "And wild."

"Wild," the reporter repeated enthusiastically as she turned back to the camera. "It was wild during the thunderstorms . . ."

The woman tugged at her sleeve. "And weird," she said with a look of surprise, as if she had just thought of it.

Mortenson howled with laughter. "Friend of yours, huh?"

"At least the old lady's still alive."

"Barely."

"Sometimes that's all that's important, Jared," Krimmer said, as he programmed the TV to record the Weather Channel for the remainder of the day, then switched back to football just in time to see the Commanders' running back being helped off the field with what looked like a torn ACL, the law of unintended consequences at work now that heat-seeking defenders aimed for the legs rather than the head.

Unfortunately, the injury failed to inspire his teammates. After two more desultory running plays, the Commanders' kicker shanked the punt for a net gain of fifteen yards on the change of possession. The rest of the game pretty much went the same way, although Krimmer was beyond yelling. It was Mortenson, who lost several more real-time bets on SlamJam, as well as his big bet against the point spread, who ended up hoarse.

"The second game looks like it's going to suck, too. How about some golf instead?" Mortenson asked. "They're playing out in Vegas."

Krimmer was getting tired of waiting for his pal to strap on some *cojones* and address the sore subject directly. He leveled his gaze like he was sighting a rifle. "How about you tell me first what's going on."

Mortenson froze in place—a wary deer that had just spotted something two-legged and orange moving slowly through the trees. "It doesn't sound like your mood is any better than your golf game," he said, the bowl of dip in one hand, a waiting potato chip in the other, lightly clasped between his thumb and forefinger, his pinkie extended daintily as though he were holding a delicate porcelain cup. "You're not mad at me or anything, are you?"

"Do I have any reason to be?"

Mortenson was capable of a modicum of motion after all. Or maybe it was actual emotion the way his forehead twitched—guilty as charged. "You know, Samantha told me she thought you'd figured it out."

"Why would I care, Jared?" Krimmer said sarcastically, thinking that was sure to provoke a complete report.

The attorney seemed to think otherwise. "You don't have to worry," he said, plunging the chip into the bowl and emerging with a healthy scoop, half of which eventually made it to his mouth. "I swear nothing happened, or I'd tell you."

"I don't doubt you would," Krimmer said, although by now he was contemplating precisely the opposite. It had occurred to him that if Mortenson wasn't simply regarding Samantha as a one-night stand, he'd fall back on his lawyer-like slippery ways. "We can switch to golf, but I have to check on my position first," Krimmer told him, flipping back to the Weather Channel.

"Our position," Mortenson reminded him.

Oklahoma was an hour behind DC, and it was getting to the time of day when bad things happened—or good things, depending on your point of view. The studio weather gal was standing in front of a map of the entire US, pointing to the ominous cluster of dingbats—bolts of bright yellow lightning superimposed over screaming-red funnel clouds—hovering over the eastern part of the state. Sam's prediction had come true on schedule. A tornado warning was now in effect.

"Hey, this is the big one you were telling me about yesterday at the club, right?" the lawyer asked. "How much we got riding on it?"

"A couple hundred g's."

"That's all? You wuss, you. What's the matter, you don't trust your honey anymore?"

"Right now, I'm not trusting anybody."

"What are you saying?" Mortenson asked, sounding surprised that the issue wasn't settled. "Didn't I already tell you nothing happened?"

Any further discussion was cut short by breaking news from the Great Plains. "We're going live now to our mobile unit and conditions on the ground."

The studio disappeared. Likewise, this morning's tranquil landscape of the rich brown earth stretching out to meet the bright blue sky. The screen filled with a jiggling image from Subjugator-3's dashboard cam. The storm chasers were barreling down a two-lane asphalt highway, heading directly toward a very ugly, very dark cloud that squatted low over the ground. A red pickup truck a couple hundred yards ahead had stopped and was now executing a three-point turn.

"Hey, this could be the big one," shouted the skinny guy who was driving. "Let's get a beauty shot for our fans."

Whether it was his new state-of-the-art TV or his Nimbus-induced heightened sensitivity, or both, Krimmer wasn't sure. But he'd never seen a tornado quite like this before. The panoramic camera on

Subjugator-3's roof had a wide-angle view and hi-res optics. On the giant TV's curvilinear screen, every detail of the monster storm was astonishingly clear, and thanks to the surround-sound speakers, it was frighteningly loud as well, so loud that every distant rumble, every gust of wind, he not only heard but also felt in every bone in his body.

The low-hanging, battleship-gray cloud looked like it had been forcibly ripped from the sky, leaving a jagged blue hole in the fluffier, paler clouds above. Alive with motion, it had whirled itself into a perfect circle, the well-defined edge rotating rapidly in a counterclockwise direction. The seething mass was as turbulent as a miniature nebula, with wisps of water vapor spinning and eddying into fantastical abstract formations. As soon as they condensed into droplets, centrifugal force flung them wildly into space, splattering the lens of the camera. A horizontal strip of eerie, yellow light gaped hungrily between the menacing underside of the thick, black disk and the waiting earth below, shrouded in darkness.

"I'm going to stop," the driver shouted. "It looks like she's getting ready to put on a show."

"Aw, it's just a baby," the other guy, the short, stocky one said.

"Baby, hell. I'm going to stop and go outside and have a look."

"Oh golly. No, don't—stay inside," the blonde begged.

The driver's voice rang out above the dull roar of the wind, interspersed with claps of thunder. "Look, she's gonna blow."

The center of the bottom of the disk began to swell, then bulge out, giving birth to a slender, cone-shaped vortex that hung beneath its monster mother for an instant, as though catching its breath. Slowly and relentlessly, it expanded and swirled downward to form a thick, dark-gray column: impending doom made visible.

"Holy Christmas," Krimmer exclaimed under his breath. *Was Sam's grandmother in the path of that monster?*

"Uncircumcised," Mortenson noted.

"It's wedging, it's wedging," one of the storm chasers cried like a frightened little boy, as the top of the column grew wider and the bottom sharpened to a point, creating the classic funnel shape.

"My ears are popping," shouted his buddy.

Someone yelled, "Here comes the rain," and someone else, "Lightning, did I see lightning?"

"Oh, my God," the frantic girl shrieked as the funnel began to scour the ground, sending up a shower of black bits of unknown origin into the churning void.

"Hey, what's that? Some poor guy's house?"

"Nah, I think a vacuum cleaner bag just exploded."

"Golly, let's get out of here before we're next."

Whether Subjugator-3 was next or not was left up in the air, perhaps even literally. The screen went black for a second or two, then the face of the now-frazzled weather gal popped back on. "We seem to be having communications problems with our team in the field. We'll get back to them as soon as we can."

"Can we check out the golf while we're waiting?" Mortenson asked, as the Weather Channel went to a commercial break.

Krimmer stared dumbly at the screen for a moment or two, then clicked away without further protest. He didn't want to watch anymore either, even if and when they got the signal back. It wasn't just that the tornado was wreaking havoc. What bothered him more was that the tornado had seemed so eager to do so, almost as eager as the storm chasers were about the prospect of witnessing a catastrophe. *Didn't they have any grandmothers of their own?*

By now, Mortenson must have sensed—correctly—that on a scale of one to ten, ten being the unfolding tragedy in Oklahoma, his offenses were relatively minor, a middling five or six that might easily be forgiven. As the scene switched to the peaceful, desert golf course, he said over the hushed tones of the announcer, "Hey, I'm sorry I didn't fess up about that other thing from the get-go."

"What other thing?" Krimmer asked, still distracted by the thought that the tornado was a sentient being, capable of choosing whom to destroy and whom to spare.

"My experiment."

"It's OK, Jared," Krimmer told him less than truthfully. "All things considered I suppose it's understandable." He didn't want to discuss it any further, any more than he wanted to revisit ground zero of what was looking more and more like a weird-weather bonanza. He was grateful to be able to shut his eyes and will himself to doze off, not to regain consciousness until the golf tournament was over and the announcers were doing the wrap-up.

"Good morning, sunshine," Mortenson was saying. "You missed quite a show."

"The golf?"

"The tornado, the big one. Hope you don't mind I didn't wake you, but I did keep checking. They haven't officially classified it as an EF5, but the weather bunny seemed to think they would. Some places have already received five inches of rain, and now they're worried about a dam just upstream of the power plant. If that goes, we're going to be in fat city. Want me to switch back to the Weather Channel?"

"Thanks, Jared. I DVRed everything anyway," Krimmer said. His little nap hadn't changed his mind about anything, neither the lawyer's perfidy nor not wanting to see a further update from Oklahoma. "Holy Christmas," he muttered at the time and the score on the screen, "it's after six." The second football game was turning into a blowout, too, and Mortenson had decided it wasn't his lucky day, so he didn't have a bet. That meant that there were no more sports worth watching until after eight, other than the usual headbutting on *60 Minutes*. "I guess I'm more tired than I knew," Krimmer yawned, hoping that Jared would take the hint and leave.

Instead, Mortenson leaned back in the recliner and contentedly clasped his hands across his belly. Having survived a dicey situation of his own making, he seemed to feel the need to reclaim his place in buddy-buddy territory with a rambling monologue, totally out of character for a basically unsentimental guy. "You know, Jake, sitting here with you and this fantastic new TV of yours, it makes me understand how weird weather impacts every part of our great and glorious country. Here we are on a balmy Sunday afternoon in Washington with the air conditioner humming in October, if you can believe it, although we probably could just open the windows for some fresh air and still be comfortable.

"Not so in Miami, where they're still having nightmares about thunderstorms because there, air-conditioning is as necessary for life as oxygen. Meanwhile, those pros who were out on the golf course today are probably praying that the PGA will drop Las Vegas from the tour permanently. I mean, a hundred and ten in the shade and they have to drink half a bottle of water before every swing. Then, of course, you've got all the shit going down in Oklahoma, not that little baby tornado you saw but the big boy, the one that's going to make us a bundle, even if you were a wuss and didn't max out your FTRs. It brings it all home, makes me appreciate how you and me, pal, we're really at the center of things." He reached for his beer and raised it in salute. "Here's to us and weird weather, wherever we might find it."

Krimmer just stared at him uncomprehendingly, wondering what had set him off. "Is that your valedictory speech?" he asked.

Mortenson stared back for a second, processing the message. "Yeah, I guess it's time to run," he said, draining the last of the six-pack of Bud Light and getting to his feet.

"What's with you, Jared? You're not going to stay and watch *Sunday Night Football?*" Krimmer asked. "We could order in pizza and you could buy."

"Nah, I'll see you for the game tomorrow night. It's been a long weekend already. I gotta catch up on my sleep." As soon as the words escaped his lips, or more likely before, the attorney must have realized they might leave the wrong impression. "I mean I don't want to overstay my welcome."

"Just like last night, I guess."

Mortenson looked sheepish, but he had nothing more to say. Krimmer acknowledged to his inner skeptic that Jared might be telling the truth and was too embarrassed by his failure to score with Sam to make a full confession. But Krimmer also sensed his old pal was still hiding something. He couldn't help but suspect that Samantha had confided in Jared—told him her doubts, her concerns about the ethics of their business, her insecurities about exploiting the looming threat of climate change to the planet and its inhabitants. Maybe she even told him about his, Jake's, growing doubts and concerns, too. That might have gotten the lawyer worried and would help explain his prolonged and loquacious paean to weird weather—his impassioned defense of the status quo.

For Mortenson, women came and went, but the money to be made from Krimmer's fees would not be easy to replace. Funny, Krimmer reflected, and ironic, too. *For me, it just might be the other way around.*

CHAPTER 17

KRIMMER WOKE UP IN STAGES, CLAWING HIS WAY BACK TO CONSCIOUS-ness. First, the stirring of brain function, then the perception of light, finally the acknowledgment of sound. The sun was streaming in unhindered through the curtainless windows, egging on his smartphone, which was making a racket out of all proportion to its size. Groggy, he reached over to the bedside table, hoping against hope it was Samantha returning last night's bevy of panicky, apologetic calls, texts, and emails, the by-product of his post-Mortenson meltdown. Instead, it was a speeding freight train he was holding in his hand, bearing down on him with a thunderous roar and an eerie, high-pitched whistle. He managed to derail it with a savage shake that mercifully flipped up and snapped open the supersized screen. "Rita?" he asked, still rubbing his eyes.

"Good morning, Jake," she replied, much too cheerfully. "How do you like my new ringtone?"

The ponytail was gone along with the chauffer's cap. She was wearing a plain white T-shirt and sitting behind a featureless white desk in front of a neutral gray background. Her streaky blonde hair fell casually around her shoulders, framing her all-American face, sparkling like a gemstone against her nondescript surroundings. At least she couldn't see the dull, confused look on his own face. Krimmer always shut off the camera before he went to bed, for emergencies just like this, when he had to take the call before he could throw on some clothes.

"I programmed your phone last night," Rita explained with a mischievous, gap-toothed smile. "I thought you might want to relive yesterday's big triumph."

The only thing Krimmer could think to ask was, "Where are you?"

"I'm at work, of course, on the clock. No holidays for those of us trying to save the planet."

Krimmer shook his head to try and focus. "What triumph are you talking about, Rita?" He wasn't remembering any triumphs yesterday, only stalemates.

"Your baby, the EF5? Don't tell me you didn't recognize the howling wind and warning sirens. Who would have guessed that you would have latched on to the deadliest storm in the Great Plains since the Moore disaster, back in '13?" She clucked appreciatively. "I'll wager those goldarned Okies are going to need all the power you can send their way these next few days."

The memory of the horrifying images from Oklahoma cleared the cobwebs. How did Rita know about his so-called triumph? "No way the Nimbus has a line into G&B," Krimmer almost shouted, unaccountably ashamed.

"You're right; we didn't have to try to crack the firewall of your dark pool. When Samantha's upset, she emails her grandmother for advice. She tells her everything."

"Samantha," Krimmer repeated dumbly. He couldn't recall who he was more upset with, Samantha or Mortenson or himself. It didn't matter that he had no conceivable reason to be angry with Sam as a meteorologist, or no right to blame her as a woman, except as a jealous man.

"Is she OK?" he asked. "Samantha's grandmother?"

"She's fine, but apparently it was a close call," Rita said. "So how did the rest of your day go?"

"You don't know?" Krimmer snapped, now fully awake and in possession of all his faculties, including instant replay. "The Nimbus isn't omniscient?"

"Heavens no," she chirped. "This is supposed to be our last day together, isn't it? And I'm still not sure how the game is going—how you're feeling about climate change."

Krimmer wasn't sure either, but he certainly wasn't feeling very good about weird weather. As he waited until midnight for Samantha to get back to him, he could no longer avoid turning on the Weather Channel. Rita wasn't exaggerating about the severity of the devastation in northeastern Oklahoma. The first tornado was just the prelim to the main event. The EF5 touched down an hour or so later, a half-mile outside of Broken Arrow, Tulsa's largest suburb. It roared south along Route 351 toward Muskogee for about fifteen miles, taking a deadly detour to Careyville, a formerly prosperous and picturesque city of about eighteen thousand inhabitants, twenty of whom didn't make it through to hear the all-clear siren. Some 200 others required medical attention, along with—deservedly so—the three storm chasers who'd had to crawl on their hands and knees out of Subjugator-3 as it lay upside down in a drainage ditch, as mortified and helpless as a turtle on its back.

The funnel cloud responsible for the Catastrophe of Careyville, as the media immediately dubbed it, stayed on the ground for more than forty minutes, with wind speeds as strong as 210 miles per hour. At its peak, it cut a path almost a mile wide. It also reproduced itself like some deranged amoeba, dividing and throwing off baby tornadoes with abandon—at least that was what the weather gal claimed, calling it an instance of *meteorological mitosis* in a comical attempt to sound learned. If that's what really happened, or if the storm was just a multi-vortex horror show, it hardly mattered. The collective destruction was immense and unchallengeable.

An elementary school and a high school were flattened, as were more than a thousand homes. The hospital was heavily damaged, and patients had to be relocated to Tulsa and Muskogee. The dam held for five inches of rain, but not for five and a half. Construction debris, vehicles, personal possessions, and bodies that weren't blown away were washed downstream, making search and rescue efforts exceptionally difficult and dangerous. By the end of Day One, property damage was estimated at $3 billion, including one of Great Plains Gas & Electric's power plants and a horrendous chunk of their infrastructure. When Krimmer briefly tore his eyes away from the war zone to log on to G&B and check his FTRs, it was like an old-fashioned slot machine spinning nothing but cherries and bars.

So why was he less than ecstatic this morning? After all, hadn't he told Sam that those EF5s pay the rent and then some? Unfortunately, that reminded him of her snippy reply, accusing him of being clueless about Timmy. "Did she say anything about McDonald's in her email?"

"She did mention that the two of you had a good talk, despite a little misunderstanding with Timmy."

"Oh."

"But she said you really seemed to be trying."

"Oh."

Rita's next revelation seemed to come out of nowhere, even though he should have been expecting it. "Samantha wasn't happy you were blaming her, Jake. She's not the one who suggested an experiment."

Krimmer had only thought he was fully awake before. His entire central nervous system was suddenly flashing red, just like the display in his office when all the power lines were congested. "Holy Christmas, Rita. You know about *that*, too?"

"Like I said, Samantha tells her grandmother everything."

"Yeah, but—"

"Too much oversharing?"

"So where does *everything* stand?" Krimmer heard himself asking. *Pleading was more like it.* He wasn't sure he wanted to hear the answer, much less the details, but not knowing was agony. "How does she feel about the so-called experiment?"

"You know our bargain, Jake. I open the kimono a little more every time I see some progress. You are coming around, aren't you?"

"Sure, sure, I'm almost there."

Rita looked thoughtful. "That's all you have to say?"

"Please, Rita, you gotta tell me more."

Rita's response was characteristically opaque. "There's not much more to tell. I had the impression all the results weren't in."

"What, is it an election? Is Samantha's putting it to a vote? Me or Mortenson?"

"You should be happy she isn't."

He turned his head aside, hoping to deflect the next salvo. "You mean because of Timmy? Is that what you're thinking?"

"Is that what *you* are thinking, Jake?"

After all the hints from both Rita and Samantha, he'd have to be pretty stupid if he weren't.

It had all the earmarks of another stalemate, until Rita's face lit up. "Hey, wouldn't it be better if we discussed this in person? It's a holiday and the weather's still so summery, what do you say about a picnic? Just you and me."

His central nervous system was now processing an auditory warning signal—excessive enthusiasm—suggesting that her sudden inspiration was preplanned. "I thought you were working today."

"I am. It would be a working picnic. Kind of like a business lunch, but more casual."

Krimmer peered out through the sliding glass door. The sheen on the patio table was dew, not frost. It would be a perfect day for a picnic with Samantha. And Timmy. If Sam would only respond.

"In fact, I know just the spot," Rita said, not waiting for his answer. "Plum Cove."

"Plum Cove?" he repeated. "On the Chesapeake? That's where we used to go when I was a kid, before my parents bought the bungalow."

"What a coincidence," she said with a frothy laugh.

"Yeah, right," Krimmer scoffed. "What kind of VOCS spectacular are you planning to cook up? A tsunami of a tidal surge? The last stand of the blue crabs? The inundation of Annapolis?" The Naval Academy was less than ten miles up the coast from Plum Cove.

"Not to worry, Jake, I've given you my best shot. After what you've already seen and heard, I would think a smart guy like you would have all the facts you need to draw the right conclusions."

"You're right, I've had my fill of giant sinkholes and dead oysters."

"Oh, and let's not forget what happened last night."

"I thought it wasn't clear what happened."

"I'm talking about Oklahoma, not Sam."

"I wouldn't exactly call Careyville the terror of the ordinary, Rita."

"But it is now. Isn't that the point?"

Was it? It was getting to seem that way.

"I've got some other business I need to take care of this morning," she said, "but I can meet you there at say . . . two?"

"I'll be starving."

"One thirty then. I need to get things ready."

Why was he so hesitant? Most likely because she was so insistent. If he didn't need more convincing about climate change, what did she think he needed? "I don't know, Rita. I gotta get home early. Jared always comes over to watch *Monday Night Football.*"

"I said a picnic, Jake, not a twelve-course tasting menu."

"Well . . . my parents have been begging me to come out for a visit. They'd be very disappointed not to see me. You do know that I am an only child, their only kid," he added, making sure it sounded meaningful.

"Your parents would be very disappointed, too, if you didn't come around to their way of thinking," she retorted. "Besides, I'm sure they'd be happy to know you were spending the day with someone who's helping you do just that." She added blithely, "Someone who can also help make their fondest hope come true, that you'll finally find *the one?*"

"I don't think you're exactly what they have in mind."

Rita shrugged off the put-down with a cocktail-newbie flip of her hair. Her voice became huskier, too, cementing the impression. "You didn't presume to think I meant li'l old me, did you?"

Krimmer had seen this movie before and he was getting tired of it.

"I still have two grieves at my disposal," she coaxed.

Isn't that what I've been angling for, turning the Nimbus into a double agent? Get to the bottom of my problem with Samantha? Isn't that why I agreed to play Rita's little game?

"So what do you say, Romeo?" she asked with another quick flip of her hair. "If you've made as much progress as you say you have, maybe I can take off the kimono altogether."

"So I get to see you in your birthday suit?" he asked, calling her bluff.

Rita's laugh was as bright and tinkling and full of promise as a pocketful of newly minted coins. "This is climate change, Jake, not global warming, and there's always a cool breeze down by the water. Would shorts be acceptable?"

CHAPTER 18

KRIMMER REMEMBERED PLUM COVE AS A SMALL, PRISTINE JEWEL ON THE western shore of Chesapeake Bay, an idyllic, pocket-sized state park that couldn't be farther removed from the honky-tonk sprawl of Ocean City or Virginia Beach. It was less than an hour's drive from his townhouse, depending on traffic and how anxious he was for a welcome change of scenery. The outside temperature was summery indeed—eighty-seven degrees—perfect for speeding down the highway on a weird-weather October morning with the top down, the fresh air whistling over the Corvette's steeply canted windshield, the stampede of horses in the endangered internal-combustion engine roaring sweetly in his ears.

More better yet, the faster Krimmer drove, the less opportunity he had to think, especially because clear thinking had seemed to be in such short supply of late. If he'd been able to get through to Sam this morning—he'd texted three times, called once, and emailed twice—who knows if he would have known what to say? *I might never know what to say, unless I can put the Nimbus to work.*

Of course, to make that happen he'd have to show signs of progress—probably a lot of signs, a lot of progress. Was he really almost there as he'd told Rita, *there* being the three Cs: contrition, capitulation, and conversion? Could change that consequential—more *Cs*—happen that fast? Not seventy-two hours had passed since he swiped his mother's roses on the screen and set her little game in motion. Then again, Rita did have some help—an *S* named Samantha. Together, they had ignited the uncontrollable chain reaction that was changing everything in his life and thoroughly muddling what was left of his once formidable brain.

If he hadn't initially fallen for the indigo eyes of the cocktail newbie, he would have just laughed off her screwy game of grieves. But when the weirdness started with the oysters, and then his father's confession about the ACEA, the attraction faded but the doubts—plural—started to creep in. Doubts about his business model, doubts about weird weather, doubts about the wisdom of his arrangement with Samantha, doubts that only grew stronger when he discovered Sam had more than enough doubts of her own. In turn, her doubts, together with her simmering suspicions about his stalker-cum-consultant, opened the door for Mortenson to barge into the picture at the most inopportune moment, when Rita's Nimbus tricks were beginning to make Krimmer's own doubts evolve into tentative convictions. Convictions that the way he made his money was indeed exploitative, that the planet was truly threatened by climate change, that Samantha really was *the one*. So now as those tentative convictions were gradually hardening into certainties, he was dealing with a self-righteous weirdo from the datasphere, a discontented meteorologist, an irresolute and inconstant ex-lover, a treacherous best friend, and no clear plan of action—just an inchoate idea that it was time to do something, anything, to make things right for all concerned.

Krimmer willed his mind to focus and his mood to brighten as he exited the highway. *Buck up, boyo, you were always the happiest when spending the day on the Chesapeake.* He hadn't been down this way in years, so he followed his GPS through the maze of local roads that meandered toward the Bay. Last week's gale-force winds had left their mark, forcing him to navigate around the scattered debris from a partially demolished strip mall, but the damage was nothing compared to the toll on the countryside from a three-decades-long heedless construction boom. Ticky-tacky subdivisions sprouted up monotonously in the old farm fields, like row after row of corn, although that wasn't the only comparison that came to mind. Krimmer couldn't get the image of the FEMA trailers out of his head. If Rita's projections about storm surges were accurate, the residents of these death-wish developments might feel right at home when they were relocated to the National Mall.

Eventually the landscape began to look more familiar, and as he rounded the last curve in the dead end that led down to the water, he spotted Rita standing by the side of the road in front of a tall chain-link fence topped with razor wire. An old-fashioned wicker picnic basket with a blanket folded on top sat on the sandy soil next to her, and a big, floppy straw hat framed her face like a halo. She had swapped the white T-shirt for a bright pink, short-sleeved tennis top, and the khaki shorts were more than acceptable, showing off her slim, shapely legs—*as if it mattered anymore.*

"You beat me," Krimmer said, as he sprang out of the Corvette.

"Always," Rita replied, tugging down the brim of her hat as though she was trying to hide her grin. Her eyes were already hidden behind an enormous pair of pitch-black sunglasses. The almond-shaped lenses swept up and around her face like the wings of a bird preparing to take flight.

"Hey, those shades would make a great new VOCS model," he joked. "They're not so dorky."

"I'll be sure to pass that on to R&D."

Krimmer declined to go there. "So where's your car?" he asked after taking a quick look around.

"A friend dropped me off," Rita said.

That was a little odd, leaving her with no way to get back—other than with him of course—but he should have learned by now that everything about Rita was a little odd, if not flat-out mysterious.

"Well, I guess I can always give you a lift," Krimmer told her.

"I could also catch a ride on a transporter beam," she replied, pointedly wiggling the frame of her sunglasses.

Forget about a bird, or a Thermian for that matter. Lose the pretty face, and she'd be a dead ringer for the drawings of the little gray aliens in all those abduction stories.

"So what happened here?" Krimmer asked, taking his mind off Rita's enigmatic origins long enough to notice that the state park sign was gone. "Is the beach closed for the season?"

"It's not closed—it's been privatized. But don't worry, I have the combination," she said, motioning to the sturdy padlock securing the gate.

"Why am I not surprised?" Krimmer asked as he hoisted the picnic basket onto his shoulder. *At least she won't have to divulge the existence of her secret antigravity device to levitate us over the razor wire.*

"Maryland was going to sell the land a few years ago to help make up for the public-employee pension shortfall," Rita explained as they picked their way down the narrow, unpaved path leading to the beach, an after-storm obstacle course of dried seaweed and shards of driftwood and miniature gullies just large enough to twist an ankle. "But the developer pulled out after Hurricane DuWayne and the sale's been tied up in the courts ever since."

"Yeah, I remember DuWayne well," Krimmer said, struggling to keep his balance as he avoided a smoothly rounded boulder that bubbled up from the sand. "As I recall, that was my first half-million-dollar day."

Rita went on as if she hadn't heard. "The park is gone but the cove is still here," she said, as she skirted a washout. "I'll be surprised if you find it's changed all that much."

"C'mon, Rita, it must have changed. With everything that's going on with the climate, the rising sea levels, the storms?"

"Hah, since when do you believe the climate is changing, Jake Krimmer?" she teased, sounding positively girlish.

"Must have been a slip of the tongue," Krimmer said with a choked-down laugh, even though he had known as he was saying it, it was no mistake. It was more like a rehearsal, to see how comfortable he felt about nurturing that inchoate idea he had on the drive down, to see if he could put it into words.

They found a flat stretch of sand in the lee of a gently rounded dune and laid out the blanket. A pair of jetties, no more than a couple hundred yards apart, with the crescent-shaped beach nestled between them, provided all the confirmation Krimmer needed that Plum Cove had not changed—not in any meaningful way. The two elongated riprap barriers were as indestructible and timeless as the jagged, weathered boulders from which they were constructed. Ten feet wide and projecting seventy or eighty feet into the bay, they were encrusted with tens of thousands of grayish-white barnacles, the size of a dime to the size of a quarter. These rough-hewn, cone-shaped, hard-shelled crustaceans seemed like a permanent fixture, embedded in the surface of the stones and covering them right up to the high tide line.

The Chesapeake itself was equally enduring, clear and blue and inviting all the way to the islands off the Eastern Shore, hovering on the horizon. There was no sign of the massive mahogany-colored stretches of dead water that were becoming typical of late summer and early autumn, algal blooms fed by the agricultural fertilizers and septic-system effluent washed into the bay by the frequent storms. Best of all was the way the scrub-covered dunes rose on all sides to enclose them, with no ticky-tacky houses or mogul mansions or other reminders of civilization intruding. Except for the seagulls and a ghostly memory of his much-younger parents, he and Rita had the beach to themselves.

"So, what do you think, Jake?" Rita asked. They sat cross-legged, and Rita went to work setting out the turkey sandwiches and macaroni salad.

"Well, you called it. Maybe the level of the bay is up a little, but that's the only difference."

"Unlike Cape Cod, we've been lucky so far," Rita acknowledged. "The Chesapeake is less than six inches higher since the year 2000, and the jetties shelter the beach from the worst of the storm surge."

Krimmer nodded as he continued to look around, thinking that even if little had actually changed, Plum Cove did seem smaller, more like a scale model than a real place, an artfully constructed diorama of simpler, more innocent days, when it wasn't so difficult to get his priorities straight, or his head screwed on firmly, and in the correct position.

"It's been a long while since the last time I was here," he said.

"You should know by now. You were six," Rita said as she reached into the basket and produced the wine. "You're the expert—do you want to do the honors?" she asked, handing him the bottle and the waiter's-style corkscrew.

Krimmer demurred politely. "Nah, no expert. I just like the stuff," he said, ignoring her persistent hint about his age. "Chablis, Fourchaume, Premier Cru, 2027," he said, checking the label. "Very nice."

"Drink it while you can, Jake. Between the spring frosts and hailstorms and the rising summer temperatures, it's getting harder and harder to produce fine wine in Burgundy."

Krimmer couldn't resist the pun. "The *terroir* of the ordinary?" he asked, as he started to cut away the foil capsule.

Rita made a face as she dug out two plastic cups. "You can joke all you want, but you do know why screw caps are the next big thing in France, don't you? The bark on the cork trees in Portugal is getting thinner and more porous as the trees do your favorite thing: adapt to increased temperatures."

"Hey, I thought we agreed no more lectures," he said as he methodically lodged the tip of the spiral worm slightly off-center in the cork and began to twist clockwise, half a revolution at a time, giving himself a moment or two to consider how much he wanted to say, and how he wanted to say it. When only the last curl was showing, he positioned the first notch in the lever on the rim of the bottle and pulled up the handle. "Didn't you say it's up to me now to decide what to do?" he asked as he engaged the second notch and withdrew the cork.

Rita held out the cups expectantly, saying nothing as he poured the wine.

Krimmer tasted the Chablis and nodded, then set the bottle down and leaned back on one elbow, a less wobbly position than sitting cross-legged. If he was going to go through with what was miraculously morphing into an actual plan, he'd need all the support he could get. "You know, Rita, I was mulling over things on the drive down from Washington."

"Were you now," she said as she took a sip. "What kind of things?"

"The stuff we've been talking about. Is it climate change or merely weird weather?"

Rita exhibited just the barest hint of surprise. "Oh?" she asked. "Did you reach a conclusion?"

"Not on the drive down."

"Yesterday, perhaps? Sunday?"

"Why Sunday, Rita?" he asked, preoccupied with getting the conclusion right, not the timing.

"At McDonald's? When Samantha finally confessed how she felt about so-called weird weather?"

Of course, he shouldn't have been rattled in the least. The only mystery was the source of the intelligence: Sam's emails or the nosy clown.

"Look, Rita—" He wanted to argue, but how could he? He was realizing she was more right than she'd ever know. What Sam had said wasn't news; he damn well knew it was climate change even before

Rita parachuted into his life—after all, he wasn't stupid all those years, only willfully unseeing. It simply took Samantha and her litany of doubts—doubts about exploiting climate change, doubts about ignoring its dangers, doubts about him—to finally rip away the blindfold.

"Look," he began again, conciliatory beyond any previous ability to be so.

"Yes, Jake?"

Krimmer checked with his old self one final time, making sure that what he was about to say was not some impetuous, last-minute attempt to restore order to his life at any cost. More than anything, he wanted to look forward, not back. "I'm willing to give you that with everything that's going on with the weather, there's got to be some link to long-term climate trends. I won't even completely deny that humans have probably done their part to make it worse. I'll even admit that *weird* may be an understatement, that it may not do it justice—what's happening every day all across the country."

Rita kept still, feeding out as much rope as he needed.

"*Violent, extreme,* maybe even *unnatural* might be better words to describe it," Krimmer said, as the images from Oklahoma flashed through his mind.

Rita finally spoke up. "But you like the alliteration of *weird*. Is that it?" she asked.

"Weird weather is not always bad for you," Krimmer said, temporarily getting sidetracked. "That's why you can sit here on the beach in shorts in October."

"But what if it's *wild* weather? Or *wicked*? They're alliterative, too."

"What does it matter?" Krimmer said, echoing Sam. His voice was suffused with anguish as he snapped back up into a sitting position like a coil spring that had been stretched too far. He hesitated, reassuring himself that he believed with his whole heart what he was about to say, that it wasn't just a ploy to get back in Samantha's good graces—although he'd happily welcome that outcome. "I mean, if it walks like a duck, and quacks like a duck, it's probably a duck, right?"

His personal guide and teacher waited him out.

"You win, Rita. It's climate change," Krimmer said with a rush of confidence, freeing up the dirty little secret he'd been keeping from himself for a while now, even as recently as on the drive down today. He had a flashback to his mother on the deck as he announced, "Anthropogenic climate change. How's that? Man-made."

With great ceremony, Rita slid her sunglasses down her nose so he could take in her eyes over the rims, less indigo than sober gray. Her suggestion of a smile was like a secret handshake, a discreet recognition of their complicity. "I'm glad you've come around," she said.

Krimmer sat there, stunned. Rita had won her little game—where was the elation? "Is that all I get from you?"

She took her time before answering, and when she did, she spoke very slowly and deliberately. "I'm delighted that you're finally acknowledging that the climate is changing because of mankind's selfish and shortsighted actions. And I'm equally delighted to take a measure of credit for your enlightenment. But that's only half the battle."

"Holy Christmas, Rita, are you never satisfied?"

"Look at those jetties, Jake," she said, gesturing towards the water. "The barnacles are so thick on some of those rocks that you can barely see the stone underneath."

"Well, sure. The barnacles are all over the Bay. You have a sailboat, they're a bitch to scrape off."

"The problem is, if you scrape off all the barnacles, the stone doesn't go away, does it, Jake? The jetties would still be able to hold back the storm surge, still be able to resist change."

Krimmer sensed where she was going. "Let me guess. You've done the hard work. You've scraped off all the barnacles from my brain, the barnacles that were preventing me from acknowledging the science and where the world was headed."

Rita waited, secure behind the impenetrable dark lenses.

"But you still worry that once you're out of my life, I might resist doing anything about my newfound belief," Krimmer said as he took a big gulp of wine. "Basically, you're saying I'm as obstinate as a stone, is that it?"

"No, I'm simply saying that you're still who you were, you haven't changed. You're the same person who could never find it within yourself to make an emotional commitment."

"You mean to Samantha."

"Or to—" She stopped abruptly to rephrase what she was thinking. "Or to anyone else . . . except maybe your parents."

Krimmer thought he had a good idea who she'd left out, but that didn't seem to be the most important consideration right now. "Don't you see, Rita? Samantha helped convince me, so Samantha can help prevent the barnacles from growing back."

"I do see that, Jake, and I'm glad you do too. But we have a little problem now, don't we?"

We sure do. If there ever was a time to flip the Nimbus, this was it. "What happened after McDonald's, Rita? That's what I need to know."

"Samantha and Timmy went to see *Grubman.*"

"C'mon, it's time to take off the kimono, like you promised. Is Sam still as confused by everything as I am?"

"That's what I meant when I said all the results weren't in."

"But what about today?"

"There were no more emails to her grandmother."

"Can't we find out what she's doing at least? You have two grieves left. I'm just asking you to use your powers to finish the job you started. You told me that my happiness is part of the package, how I win." He threw up his arms in frustration. "All I want is to understand Sam's state of mind. So I can get us both to a better place."

Rita shook her head. "The Nimbus doesn't take sides, Jake. There's no guarantee that it will help. What if you find out something you don't want to know?"

"I stopped worrying about that long ago. Besides, then I'll be aware of what I have to deal with."

Rita took her sweet time thinking about it. "Well, I suppose it wouldn't hurt," she finally said, although it wasn't clear she meant it. She set down her wine and retrieved her phone from the wicker basket, flipping the screen up and opening it to its maximum width, twelve inches, then going to work on the keys. "Voilà," she said, after her fingers finished their complex, syncopated dance.

A giant sign with the picture of a panda bear was suspended from a lamppost, dominating the crowd of parents and children milling around it, and exhorting them to shop, eat, and relax at Panda Plaza. It was easy to spot Sam and Timmy, walking hand in hand, because only Sam was walking. Timmy was scuttling in one direction, then another, pulling and jerking on Sam's arm to get away, then bouncing back like a hyperactive Ping-Pong ball. "It looks like they're having an outing, too," Rita said. "At the zoo."

Krimmer took the phone from Rita and examined the scene more closely. It was only a black-and-white image, and the resolution was too grainy to be sure, but why would Sam have such a big smile on her face, having to drag Timmy along through the crush of people like a tugboat towing a recalcitrant barge?

"There's no sound."

"It's not magic, Jake. It's a security camera."

"How is this helpful?"

"Well, after your brunch, Samantha apparently wasn't so despondent that she had to dig a hole and crawl in."

At that moment, Timmy did break loose and tear down the path, narrowly avoiding a toddler in a stroller, pulled clear by the mom just in time.

"You'll see. Like my mother always said, the kid's going to go ass over teakettle."

In fact, Timmy did go airborne, but right side up. He flapped his arms like a pair of wings and took off, crash landing onto a man walking toward them, a tall, broad-shouldered man with short-cropped graying hair. The boy wrapped himself around the stranger's neck and hung on for dear life. Given the less-than-perfect picture quality, it took Krimmer a moment or two to realize why the stranger didn't seem the least bit surprised or perturbed. He was no stranger. There was no need to check for a pulsing green dot on Immer to be sure.

"Fucking Mortenson," he said. "The sonofabitch swore nothing happened Saturday night."

"Maybe nothing did," Rita said. "But McDonald's happened Sunday, and now it's Monday afternoon."

Krimmer wasn't sure if she was hinting or just being a smartass. He handed back the phone. He didn't wait to see if Sam gave Jared a kiss. "You tried to warn me. You knew all along, didn't you, Rita? In fact, you had it all set up, didn't you."

"I'll never tell."

Krimmer cocked his chin, a manful display of stubborn pride. "Sorry you had to waste a grieve. Now you only have one left," he told her.

Rita finally granted him the broad and nonjudgmental smile that she had refused him all day. "Something tells me it wasn't wasted, Jake."

CHAPTER 19

"SO WHAT ARE YOU GOING TO DO NEXT?" RITA ASKED AS SHE POURED the last drops of Chablis.

Krimmer was stretched out on the blanket, his eyes half closed, trying hard to screen out everything but the lingering warmth of the October sun and the soothing sound of the bay lapping up against the rock-sheltered beach. "Before or after I strangle Mortenson?" he grumbled.

Rita had set aside the floppy straw hat to let the gentle breeze riffle through her hair, but that was the extent of her relaxation. "You need a plan, Jake," she said.

"My plan is to take a little nap. Then strangle Mortenson."

"Do you really think that'll help you win back Samantha?"

"I'm not convinced I've lost her."

"You just can't go on blaming Mortenson."

"No, he did exactly what I would have done in his position."

Rita didn't raise an eyebrow. "You can't blame Samantha, either. She just wanted Timmy to have a good time at the zoo. And he does seem to like your lawyer friend."

"I don't blame either one of them. I blame myself."

"You can't put the genie back in the bottle," Rita told him. "You've got to deal with it."

"Is there more wine?"

"If you'd sit up, you'd see your glass is half full."

"No pun intended, I'm sure," Krimmer muttered. He hauled himself up, sitting cross-legged like her, and found his cup and took a healthy swallow. "I'm going to deal with it by strangling Mortenson," he said.

Rita and Krimmer managed to get through the next five minutes without further mention of either Sam or Timmy, although it was obvious to him by now that his irreplaceable meteorologist and her troubled, troubling son were central to Rita's mission today. But before she was ready to venture deeper into that emotional equivalent of the Bermuda Triangle, where relationships went missing without warning, she seemed to feel she had more work to do to make sure he knew what was at stake.

"My job won't be finished until I know you truly care about what your children and grandchildren are actually going to live through," she said.

Krimmer pointed out the obvious. "You must have forgotten. I don't have any kids."

Rita brushed aside a lock of hair and leaned toward him until she was only inches away. He could smell the fruity, wet-stone aroma of Chablis on her breath. "I didn't forget," she said. "You will."

From that distance, there was no reflection in the lenses of her glasses, only dark, depthless pools, from whose murky bottoms rose the spectral dome of the Jefferson Memorial.

"I sense you're surprised, Jake," she said as she sat up straight again.

"Not surprised," he said with a nervous catch in his voice. "Just a little anxious if the Nimbus knows something that I don't."

"Oh, no shotguns or positive pregnancy tests right at this moment," she said. "Just understand that Timmy and all the other children in that generation, born and unborn, are the ones who are going to have to deal with the world we leave them. If you believe we're fighting for the good of the planet, you've got to want to fight for *them*, because they are the future."

"I hope they can discover something that gets out ketchup stains."

Rita looked like she was about to spank him. "Are you really a selfish, heartless bastard about kids, Jake, or do you just pretend to be?"

"There you go again," Krimmer said with Reaganesque condescension.

But he knew he deserved her rebuke. Mortenson clearly had no problem relating to Timmy. It looked like Jared had figured out that Samantha's son was the shortcut to Samantha. *So what's my excuse for letting Timmy become a roadblock?*

"Maybe I'm moving too fast, Jake. Is that it?" Rita asked. "Maybe you need to be reminded what it's like to be a six-year-old little boy."

Her tone immediately put Krimmer on notice. She sounded scripted.

"I mean, here we are, back in Plum Cove where you spent so many happy days. Have you forgotten what it was like when your entire world was safe and secure, when everything was right, and you could do no wrong?" She paused, then asked, "That's true, isn't it? You could do no wrong?"

"Why do I sense there's a Nimbus moment coming up?"

Rita laughed. "Because you know I'd never let my last grieve go to waste," she said, as she slipped a memory stick into her smartphone and started tapping away at the keyboard. "Do you recall that big sandcastle you built?" she asked. "It was almost as tall as you were," she reminded him, as her fingers fluttered and danced until she found what she was looking for.

"Maybe," Krimmer said evasively. "I built a lot of sandcastles."

"I was thinking of one in particular," Rita said as she handed him the phone. "Have a look at the United States Capitol."

"Another of my parents' videos, right?"

"It's on pause so you can see all the marvelous details. You were quite the little architect."

Krimmer stared at the big folded-out screen. A scrawny towhead peered back at him. His laughably boxy, plaid bathing trunks were in danger of sliding down his bottom as he crouched at the edge of the water, a half-dozen other kids watching in open-mouthed admiration, waiting for the little boy to put the finishing touch on his masterpiece. He had shaped a mountain of sand into an oblong box almost three feet in length and half again as high, bumped out on either end and grooved to simulate the columned chambers of the House and Senate. Between them, the famous Capitol steps, broader than in real life, swept down to the beach. On top, square in the middle, several buckets and cups of different diameters, each smaller than the next, had been used to mold the tiered dome, inset with sticks to suggest more columns.

"I particularly admire the way you rounded it off and finished it with that spiky cylinder. That's the bronze Statue of Freedom at the top, right?"

"As I recall, it was a piece of the tail of a horseshoe crab."

"I remember horseshoe crabs," Rita said, sighing for effect. "Before they almost went extinct, their blood, naturally bright blue in color, was used to detect endotoxins that cause septic shock and death."

Krimmer mugged for the long-ago camera, dropping his jaw at the extent of her learning.

"The video's date-stamped the Fourth of July," she went on, undeterred. "Your father said it was an omen and predicted a bright future for you in politics."

"I sure fooled my dad," he said. "My political career ended as vice president of the junior class at Columbia."

"I wouldn't be so pessimistic. I'd say you still have time."

"Is that part of the plan?" .

"That's for you to decide, Jake."

Krimmer took a sip of wine. "So, what's the deal?" he asked, as he set down his plastic cup and handed back the phone. "This isn't much of a grieve, Rita. What does it have to do with climate change?"

"Don't you listen to anything I say, Jake? This grieve's not for the planet; we've settled that issue. This grieve is for *you*."

Krimmer plucked a stray pebble from the sand. "For a moment there, I did feel like a kid," he confessed, staring down at the small, flat stone he had unearthed. "But I'm thinking you may have picked the wrong sandcastle."

"Why's that, Jake?" she asked politely. Unnecessarily too, he suspected.

"I know what will happen if you play the video. I just remembered what comes next," he said, cocking his arm and launching the stone toward the water. It was one of those childhood incidents that was better forgotten, not because it was so hurtful, but so unexpected, so uncalled-for, less major trauma than a lingering bruise from a sneak punch on an otherwise unblemished day.

Rita nodded sympathetically and swiped the screen, holding it up for both of them to see. His six-year-old self sprang to life. There he was, skipping around his prized creation, warning away the other excited six-year-olds who were edging closer, admiring his true-to-life details from all sides, straightening a column here and there, plumbing the statue that crowned the dome, tugging at the hem of his father's bathing trunks, his embarrassingly tinny, "Look Mommy, look Daddy," barely audible over the gentle, rhythmic swooshing of the incoming swells that splashed around their feet.

"Stop the world, I want to get off," Krimmer joked, prompting Rita to hold up a cautionary finger.

The punch line was immediate. Out of nowhere, a rogue wave

crashed against the beach, upending the unsuspecting boy and engulfing his perfect little world. When the wave receded, there was a pregnant silence, and then his mother's soothing words from off-camera were drowned out by the uncontrollable sobs of the boy, sitting on his bottom and staring at the devastation. The Capitol was still standing, but a sizeable piece had been lopped off from one of the wings, and a substantial chunk was missing from the side of the dome. It looked like a half-eaten wedding cake.

"At last, something I can understand," Krimmer said, as Rita paused the video. "The sandcastle, the Capitol, whatever, is symbolic of the country, right—or maybe the world? And that wave that no one saw coming, not even my father who happened to know about it or should have, even though he sat on his hands all those years, that's climate change. But he didn't bother to tell me about it or do anything to protect my creation. So in comes the wave and smashes the sand castle, just like if we don't do something about climate change, everything's going to go to hell in a handbasket—America, the world, everything destroyed—is that it?"

Rita shrugged as she retrieved her cup of wine and drained it. "Well, that's an interesting interpretation," she said, "but I keep telling you, this grieve's about you, not the country or the planet. How did *you feel* about what happened?"

"How do you think I felt? I was crying my eyes out, wasn't I?" Krimmer said, as he scrabbled around again, searching for another stone.

"And then what?"

"I'm supposed to remember? I got a hug, a candy bar?" he asked, apprehensively fiddling with the flat rock in his hand. There was something else, another image lurking just beyond the ragged edge of memory.

Krimmer shied away as Rita reached over to ruffle his hair, a fond acknowledgment that he had never grown up. A quick tap on the screen and the sobbing boy was hoisted in the air, nestled in the strong, tanned arms of his father, who was trying to whisper in his ear. But rather than calming the boy, it seemed to heighten his agitation. He squirmed and beat his tiny fists against his father's face, shouting, "Let me down, let me down," until his father did just that, dropping his son the last foot—frustration or a forceful life lesson?— resulting in a hard, butt-first landing. As the camera zoomed in, instead of crying more, the boy jumped up and brushed away the remainder of his tears, compressing his lips into a thin, unswerving line. Pushing aside his astonished playmates and ignoring his parents' pleas to stop, he began kicking and stomping his wounded creation until it was no longer merely wounded. It lay in ruins.

The screen faded and went to black, no longer a window to the past but a dark mirror for Krimmer's psyche. It was beyond weird, more like some kind of hallucinatory time travel, seeing himself on the video while he sat there on the exact same beach, not twenty yards from the exact same spot, reliving one of those harsh, dimly realized epiphanies of childhood that was only fully registering now, many years after the fact. "So what am I supposed to make of that?" he demanded. "I was a kid, all right? I was angry and upset. I threw a tantrum. I didn't know any better."

"Why couldn't you just leave it alone, Jake? Maybe the other children would have fixed it up. Maybe the other children would have wanted to play with it after you left. That's what your parents were telling you, isn't it?"

"Sure, that's what they were telling me," he said, skimming the flat rock toward the water. "But maybe I felt it was mine. Maybe I didn't want anyone else to have what I created. Maybe I felt betrayed . . . resentful . . . selfish. What does it matter? I did what I did."

"Did your parents punish you?"

"I think I lost TV privileges for a week, but I'm sure my sentence got commuted to a couple of days."

"Really?"

"No, not really," he said, resigned to tell the truth. "My parents were fair but strict. I served out the time. For my own good, they insisted."

"Was it?"

"For my own good?" Krimmer asked, now reflective. "I don't know. I'm not sure I ever fully learned the lesson." He paused, then added, "Whatever the lesson was supposed to be."

Rita smiled as if she had already known. When Krimmer didn't say anything else, she asked far too innocently, "Make you think of anybody you know, Jake?"

Krimmer balled up his fist and rubbed at his forehead. "Not really," he said when his skin was good and red.

"You're sure of that?"

"I don't know. Maybe."

Rita peered at him intently behind her swept-wing prop, although when she eventually spoke, she sounded less like an alien than an oracle, the roundabout, riddling way she completed the lesson.

"If you don't remember the past, Jake, how are you ever going to remember the future?"

Krimmer erupted in frustration. "Will you please say what you mean, for once?"

Rita look skyward, as if she were searching for guidance, then came back to earth. "You know what Confucius had to say."

"He said a lot of things."

"'Know thyself.'"

CHAPTER 20

"THIS TRAFFIC SUCKS." KRIMMER COULD NO LONGER CONTAIN HIS frustration as he slumped down in his seat, glaring at the endless line of brake lights ahead of them on I-495. "Who decided to take the long way back to Georgetown?"

"The Nimbus," Rita replied unapologetically as she inched the Corvette forward in second gear. They were heading west, and the sun was getting lower in the sky, so she was still wearing her spacey sunglasses. Krimmer made do with flipping down the visor and squinting when he wasn't glaring.

"More proof that the Nimbus is not all-knowing."

"There's a bad accident on the Eleventh Street Bridge. The direct route would take us an hour longer."

"It could have given us a little warning," Krimmer groused. "We could've packed up sooner."

"Enlightenment keeps to its own schedule, Jake. Isn't that what you learned back at Plum Cove?"

In truth, it was just as much his fault as hers that they were late in leaving. After the double bill of *Zoo Parade* and *Godzilla Goes to*

Washington, he was in no mood to think about holiday traffic, or how to handle his customary *Monday Night Football* date with Mortenson. More than anything, he needed a minute or two of silent and soulful communion after her oracular pronouncement—*Confucius? Hah! Since when?* He damned well knew "Know thyself" was Greek, from the Temple of Apollo at Delphi. He also damned well knew what she was driving at. *OK, so I was a little brat, too. My dad was right to drop me on my butt.*

By and by, Rita had produced a six-pack of brownies and they had devoured them, pretty much in silence. She glanced over at him from time to time, while he reserved his stare for the narrow strip of sand that marked high tide, impatient for the water to recede and take with it the disquieting images of the ghost of Krimmer past—all the ghosts, actually: past, present, and future.

When they finally retreated up the rutted path, Krimmer followed a dozen feet behind, cautiously watching his step and shifting the picnic basket from side to side, trying to keep his balance. He still was a little uneasy about how quickly his conversion had progressed—or more accurately, how quickly his self-deception and denial had been revealed. But final confirmation that things were headed in the right direction was right in front of him; the lure of the cocktail-party newbie was no more. Every time he did look up, he looked right back down again. For all it mattered now, Rita's legs were thick and straight as tree trunks, saplings at any rate, and her bottom as flat as the proverbial pancake and about as beguiling.

The late-afternoon air was getting chilly. As they closed the top of the Corvette, Rita had insisted on driving.

"You drank most of the wine," she explained.

"I didn't notice. My apologies."

"You don't have to look so alarmed. I can handle a stick," she said as she stowed her floppy beach hat in the cargo area behind the seats to get it out of the way.

"It never entered my mind that you couldn't." Krimmer had never been a passenger in his own car, but compared with his seismic shift this afternoon, letting Rita drive didn't seem all that momentous. In fact, once they got out on the open road, she handled the transmission and the gas pedal like a symphony conductor working every section of the orchestra, giving each of the seven forward speeds and a sizable majority of the 755 horses their opportunity to shine. More better yet, it kept her fully occupied and conversation-light until they ran into nightmarish traffic, when having little else to do, she reverted to being the schoolmarm from hell.

"While we're just sitting here, let's try to make our time productive. We never did get around to talking about your plan."

"Didn't I tell you? I've decided that strangulation is too good for Mortenson."

Rita was not perturbed. "It's not going to be easy for you, you know. There are some difficult decisions ahead."

"Like what? Whether to propose to Sam?"

"Oh, you've made that decision already," she said cheekily, as she seized the opportunity to power ahead by several car-lengths.

Have I? I suppose I have. Nonetheless, there was no conceivable way it could have been uploaded to the Nimbus. "Did it ever occur to you that you might be getting a little ahead of yourself, Rita?" he said, retroactively piqued. "That this is not all as cut-and-dried as you seem to believe?"

She had to brake hard as traffic came to a standstill. "It's true for many of my clients," she said, as she turned to face him. "They're the last ones to realize what's happened to them." The little gap between her two front teeth peeked out between her lips. "The real question, Jake, is whether Samantha will have you."

He decided to ask, even though he wasn't anxious for the answer. "Did Sam have anything to say about it to her grandmother?"

Rita stared at him, forever it seemed, the color of her eyes masked by the dark lenses, as if she was unsure what she should tell him, or if she should tell him anything at all. "There are no emails on that particular subject."

"Holy Christmas, Rita," Krimmer said, exhaling. "You had me going there for a minute."

"Cheer up Jake," she said. "You should be glad I haven't heard anything. If Samantha were that upset with you, she'd have unburdened herself already, or have an email ready to go to you in her draft folder." The car behind them honked. The line was moving again, and Rita turned back to the wheel. "Besides, I know how you can improve your odds."

"I bet you do."

"Sam's not going to be satisfied with a bunch of *kumbaya* talk, and neither am I. Now that you've come over from the dark side, it's time for action," Rita said airily, as she stepped on the gas pedal. "Let's start with changing your business model."

"Oh, that's really helpful," Krimmer scoffed, although by now, he was well aware that had to be part of the package. Still, it was supposed to be his decision. "It's not my business that's causing climate change, Rita."

"No, but you know as well as I do, it's making Samantha unhappy," Rita said, as they rolled forward several dozen precious yards. "It's like a sugar-teat. While it satisfies your material needs, it undermines your ideals, just like real sugar decays tooth enamel."

They stopped short again, and Rita turned on him with a vengeance. "You have a lot of invaluable experience and knowledge, Jake. You could work with the ISOs as a consultant. You could make the grid more efficient, instead of profiting from their troubles."

"You mean profiteering," he reminded her.

"You and Sam could work together. You'd be an unbeatable team."

The SUV ahead of them put on a burst of speed, causing Rita to switch gears, first literally, then figuratively. "When you go public, your parents will be supportive, of course, but you're going to get a lot of heat from your old friends and cronies. They're going to say you're deluded, you're nuts."

"About closing down my business or marrying Sam?"

"Oh, they'll be envious about Samantha. Especially you-know-who."

The thought of Mortenson's reaction made the enormity of the changes loom even larger. Telling Jared would give him *mucho* satisfaction, but it would also be *mucho* tricky. Krimmer's business was Mortenson's sugar-teat, too.

The sun was getting ready to set, and now they were fully entangled in the spaghetti bowl of approach roads to the Woodrow Wilson Bridge, spanning the Potomac to Alexandria. Rita must have thought he needed time to sit in the corner and think about everything she had said, because the lesson was suspended while she concerned herself with a renewed flurry of on-again, off-again mini-leaps forward.

"I'm beginning to regret that my aging jalopy doesn't have slow-speed collision avoidance," Krimmer told her after the Corvette slammed to a stop.

"Well, the automatic cutoff system would help when it comes to greenhouse emissions," Rita said, as she slipped off the dark glasses, "but I have to confess, the way this baby was cornering and passing before we hit traffic, all I could think was that this was such a fun car compared to the limo." Her big smile wasn't exactly what he'd call heartfelt. "You're going to miss it, I'm sure."

"Huh?"

"Think about it, Jake. How would it look, you tooling around in a dinosaur?"

Krimmer sat up straight and objected loudly. "I'll close down my business, I'll ask Sam to marry me, but I goddamned well am not going to give up my Corvette."

"Well, I suppose if you're discreet," she allowed.

He lapsed into muttering again. "It would be like Sam giving up Timmy."

Rita gave him a wicked glance. "Unlike this automobile, Timmy's a human being, you know."

"Hey, just joking, Rita."

She didn't seem so sure. "It worries me, Jake. You say the right things, but sometimes I don't have a lot of confidence that you mean them. You're the kind of guy who lets his head get in the way of his heart."

"It runs in the family, doesn't it?" Krimmer reflected.

Rita's amusement was evident. "So how long did you resist admitting to yourself that Samantha was *the one*?" she asked.

"It was simply a business decision, that's all," he said, realizing too late that his knee-jerk answer was tantamount to a confession.

"Case closed," Rita said.

Just then, a sudden surge of movement bought them a good hundred yards. "Hey, maybe the logjam is breaking up," Krimmer said, as he glanced at his watch. "Holy Christmas, it's past six o'clock. I've got to deal with Mortenson."

"Ah, yes," Rita said, as if she'd forgotten about him. "The one remaining complication. Have you thought about what you're going to say to your pal?"

"Yeah. 'Let's have pizza.'"

She gave him a quizzical look.

"I had Chinese Saturday night." When Rita's expression didn't change, he said, "I promise you, I'll think of something that gets the point across without unnecessary violence."

Rita smiled as Krimmer checked the time again.

"When's kickoff?" she asked. "Eight-fifteen?"

"Yeah, but Jared always comes over by seven. He gets indigestion if we eat during the game. I should text him and tell him to hold off."

He pulled out his phone and proceeded to make a series of discoveries, the last borderline bone-chilling. "Looks like he's got Immer on . . . he's left the zoo . . . he exited Rock Creek Parkway onto K Street . . . he must be heading directly for my townhouse."

"He'll have bad traffic, too."

"Not as bad as we have. How about if we drop you off before we get there?"

"I can't imagine why you feel the need to do that."

"I can't either."

"There's an easy-on, easy-off McDonald's in Alexandria."

Krimmer made sure she registered his displeasure. "Wouldn't a gas station do?"

"McDonald's has clean restrooms." The line of cars was at a dead stop again, giving Rita ample opportunity to consult her phone. "This is about to lighten up and we're almost to the bridge, so we should be there in about twenty minutes."

The Nimbus was a little optimistic. Make that twenty-five. Krimmer jumped out of the car as soon as they pulled into the inevitable prime parking spot right by the front door. Thankfully, there was no McUniverse to remind him about things he didn't want to be reminded of, and he didn't have to pee badly enough to go inside. By the time he got around the Corvette's aggressively prognathous hood, Rita was holding the driver's side door open for him, a polite, affecting echo of Saturday morning at the Jefferson Memorial when their little game was just getting started.

"You going to be able to get home OK, Rita?"

"Thanks for asking, but my friend is on the way to pick me up."

Krimmer looked around distractedly, unsure of what to say. It was the conclusion of a weird weekend—oops, make that a *wild* weekend—albeit a chaste one. He was feeling like a teenager standing on the doorstep at the end of a first date. "Well, I guess this is it."

If Rita sensed his agitation, she didn't seem ready to help him out. "Anyway, I can look back and say I did my job."

"You sure did. Too bad you didn't bring champagne. We could have popped the cork and declared mission accomplished."

"Better watch it, Jake," Rita warned. "Some people would say that means just the opposite."

He dropped his eyes. "Sorry I've got to run like this," he said.

Or maybe she was more ready to help than he'd thought. "Hey, at least you didn't *hit* before you ran," she kidded.

Krimmer smiled at the cocktail newbie, a fond farewell to a missed opportunity. "I bet you get a lot of that," he said.

Rita returned the favor with one last gap-toothed grin. "It's an occupational hazard."

Krimmer hesitated, then stuck out his hand. "Well, thanks for everything."

Indigo eyes considered their options, then their owner leaned in and gave him a peck on the cheek. "Breaking up is always so hard to do," she said with a muffled laugh.

Krimmer was already behind the wheel when she tapped on the glass. "Jake, Jake," she was saying.

"What's up?" he asked as he lowered the window.

"Let me know if there's a hiccup."

"There won't be any hiccups, Rita. Like you said, you did your job." He paused and added, "And you can tell your boss you did it well." *Whoever the hell you were working for.* Although, by the end he was starting to think she was almost human.

As he drove off, Krimmer began to consider his game plan. Oh, sure, he was looking forward to *Monday Night Football* with his buddy, almost as much as he was dreaming about a prospective new life of unbridled domesticity and comfortable penury. Considering strangulation was off the table, he decided to give Mortenson just enough rope to hang himself, then tell him the truth about how he felt about his crack meteorologist. That was assuming he could find the right word this time. *Or more better yet, save that consequential word for Sam.*

Krimmer's old-fashioned GPS took him through Alexandria and Arlington to avoid a pileup on Memorial Parkway, and he was across the Key Bridge and in front of his townhouse at seven-fifteen. So was Mortenson's baby-blue Miata. So was Mortenson, leaning up against the fender, keeping an eye on his phone.

"Right on time," the lawyer said by way of greeting, sticking his head through the open window.

"You wouldn't believe the traffic."

Mortenson's fluorescent grin lit up the interior of the car. "What did you expect on a beautiful day like this?" he asked. "Doesn't everybody want to go to the beach one last time this year?"

They hadn't even had the coin toss, and Krimmer knew he was already playing defense. *Talk about unforced errors. How could I forget about Immer?*

"Yeah, I guess it wasn't the smartest time to go visit my parents."

Mortenson's eyes flicked around curiously, as though he wanted to remember what a real sports car looked like—the Miata was a joke and his semi-mythical Bimmer was long gone. "Your parents? I thought they lived over on the Eastern Shore," he said, as he took in the aeronautically inspired dashboard and the stubby gear shift on the center console and the padded leather bucket seats.

Krimmer calculated how long the lawyer might have been tracking him, and how closely. "They do, Jared. After I crossed the bridge, the GPS almost got me lost on the way home, trying to avoid the main roads."

"Well, it was a nice thing to do, Jakester. Going out of your way like that to pay them a visit and give your mom a thrill ride in your fancy souped-up chariot."

Krimmer said something on the order of "Huh?" although less a question than a non-committal, guttural noise.

"You mean it wasn't your mom?" Mortenson shook his head, tut-tutting. "It's terrible getting old, isn't it, the way you keep forgetting things, like turning off Immer."

Just for a moment, Krimmer figured he'd dodged the bullet, that the lawyer was just needling him, per usual. That's when he realized the unsettling corollary. There was only one reason Mortenson would have expected him to turn off Immer: he had gone to the beach with a lady who was RFPT.

Mortenson added a wink to drive home his next innuendo. "Unless you're saying that really is your mom's floppy straw hat back behind the seat."

CHAPTER 21

IT COULD HAVE BEEN THE SUPER BOWL; KRIMMER WOULDN'T HAVE cared. He had declared a state of emotional lockdown, not to be lifted until tomorrow morning in the office when he would see Samantha at last. In the meantime, he was stretched out to the max on his recliner, his legs extended flat out in front of him, his back diverging only ten or fifteen degrees above the horizontal. He was keeping one eye on the TV screen, a second on his bottle of Victory Pils, and his third, the mystical eye in the middle of his forehead that he had heretofore pooh-poohed, firmly focused on the blank white ceiling where he hoped it would find a brief and well-deserved respite. There was nothing like the past few days to convince him that one of his more spacey ex-girlfriends hadn't been kidding about the *Ajna chakra*. The last thing he needed was any more perception beyond ordinary sight.

"Hey, Jakester, it wouldn't hurt to give me a little moral support, would it? I just lost fifty bucks on that Green Bay interception. I had two-to-one that the Bears would score on that drive. Whaddaya think? Should I double down on those losers?"

Krimmer didn't even have the energy to tell Mortenson to go home, now that everything that could be resolved before tomorrow had been resolved, other than the final tally of the lawyer's compulsive wagering on the football game. Jared was the anti-Jake. He had discovered that his recliner was not permanently fixed in the hammock position. The back was straight, and the seat was largely unoccupied, except for the front six inches or so where his butt was precariously perched on the slippery faux leather, the better to tap into SlamJam on his phone to check the odds and place another bet.

"Or maybe I should hedge and put some action on Green Bay."

Krimmer was always partial to his dad's hometown. "I wouldn't do that. Chicago is the better team," he said, his sluggish monotone at odds with his optimistic advice. "You watch, they'll kick a field goal as the clock runs out."

"Your new girlfriend tell you that?" Mortenson quickly corrected himself, the corner of his lip curling up into a rascally smirk. "Your consultant, I mean."

Krimmer didn't bother to argue, especially since that once-intriguing possibility had forever bit the dust, vanquished by the home-grown alternative, gorgeous and brainy and waiting in the wings, or so he fervently hoped. "Rita doesn't predict the future, any more than Samantha does," he explained patiently, as the referee blew the whistle for the two-minute warning. "It's all based on probabilities."

Mortenson lurched up from the recliner as the network went to commercials. "Yeah, well the probability is I'm gonna go broke unless you're right about the Bears."

"I'm thinking that with all the beer you've been drinking, the probability is you have to pee."

"Yeah, that too," Mortenson said, as he wandered off to the bathroom.

Krimmer shut his eyes for a moment, all three of them, happy to at least have cleared the air about girlfriends in general without any compromising revelations. Even though it had been a bloodless exchange, negotiating the truth had proven tricky.

"C'mon, Jakester, fess up. Who is she?" The legal beagle hadn't even waited for Krimmer to hem and haw about the straw hat in the back, much less park the Corvette in the underground garage. He had stuck his head deeper into the car and ostentatiously scratched his five-day growth of beard in case Krimmer missed the point. "You've been holding out on me since Friday. It's looks to me like your new girlfriend is more than ready for prime time."

Strategic subterfuge was quickly forgotten as Confucius came riding to the rescue. "What about *your* new girlfriend?" Krimmer demanded with his best, kick-ass attitude.

"Mine?" Mortenson said, backing off and looking genuinely puzzled.

"Where were you today, Jared?"

"At the zoo," Mortenson said, a statement of fact, not a confession. "With my kids."

"You have kids?" Krimmer asked, incredulous.

Mortenson smiled, a restrained, poignant smile, no porcelain veneers in sight. "C'mon, I told you about them. A boy and a girl, twelve and fourteen. I get visiting privileges one day a month."

"Oh, yeah," Krimmer acknowledged.

"James and Sarah," Mortenson reminded him, just in case.

"I must have forgotten," Krimmer said, not sure what was more telling. That a guy who consistently came across as selfish and callous could have children who he apparently loved, or for whom he at least felt some degree of responsibility, or Krimmer's own willful blanking out about same. In a day full of surprises, both of them were near the top, an unexpected encore to the lesson at Plum Cove. Rita couldn't have planned it better herself.

Mortenson eyed him skeptically. "You seem to be doing that a lot lately, boyo. Forgetting."

"I've got a lot of shit on my mind, that's all."

Skepticism gave way to a sly grin. "That's no way to describe the amazing Okie."

"When did you get to be so perceptive, Jared?"

Now that the matter was out in the open, he still wasn't one hundred percent certain that he believed his learned counselor's defense, denying any culpability. But after they had retreated to the man cave and passed the peace pipe by drinking a beer and passionately debating the merits of the toppings for their pizza—Krimmer's plea for salty anchovies went unheeded—Mortenson did make a plausible case for forgiveness. Samantha had mentioned on Saturday that she planned to take Timmy to the National Zoo, and Jared had suggested he meet them there so that his daughter, who was a babysitter-in-training, could get some on-the-job experience. And oh yes, his son wanted to see the pandas, too. As for Timmy's over-the-top greeting, Krimmer couldn't ask because that wasn't something he would have known about. That wasn't something Sam would have told him, if she had indeed answered even one of his countless texts or calls or emails, which of course she hadn't.

"So now that we've cleared up that little misunderstanding, and Guido's on the way with pizza, can we return to Exhibit A, that big, floppy straw hat?" Mortenson had said. "Why do I suspect you might be two-timing your sublimely lovely meteorologist? I haven't had a chance to send the hat to the laboratory for forensic analysis, but I do believe I espied a blondish filament caught in the warp and woof of the straw."

By then, Krimmer had had ample time to come up with an equally plausible cover story that wouldn't cause his pal to collapse in hysterics: he cleverly expanded on his brainstorm with Samantha. "My consultant left it behind," Krimmer told him straightaway. "She's a blonde."

"Your consultant?"

"Haven't I mentioned her, Rita Ten Grieve? We're doing some strategizing about the future of the company." Krimmer stuck to the broad outline of the facts but omitted certain key, difficult-to-explain details, like VOCS glasses or their little game of grieves or any of his more fatuous speculations about his personal guide and teacher's otherworldly origins. His account also laid the necessary pipe for the disclosure he owed Mortenson about the future of the business, providing he could keep his nerves steady and go through with Rita's plan. *My plan, that is.* "She's helping me understand how the accelerating changes in global weather patterns will impact our operations and profitability."

"What is she, some kind of scientist or something?" Mortenson asked suspiciously.

"More of a computer geek. Remember at the club, I asked you about the Nimbus?"

"What I remember is your lousy golf game and your limo driver. She looked like a real cutie pie."

Krimmer quickly steered him in a different direction. "The Nimbus is a supercomputer that spits out projections about the climate. Not many people have access to it. My consultant does."

"Well, if she's a computer wiz, why did you feel the need to spend the afternoon in the great outdoors with this consultant? I'm not aware of any computers down at the beach."

"No, but there are plenty of barnacles," Krimmer said with an impish grin.

"Barnacles?"

"Yeah, clinging to the rocks." It was as good a time as any, Krimmer thought, to begin to open his own kimono. "We were counting the barnacles to assess firsthand the early effects of climate change on Chesapeake Bay. They're like the canary in the coal mine for a warming ocean. As water temperatures increase, the barnacles dry out and die."

Mortenson squinted. "Wait a second. Did I hear you, of all people, call it climate change?"

"Yeah. That's one of the things Rita's teaching me that I need to wrap my head around."

The lawyer must have intuited that Krimmer's education might mean trouble ahead, because he wasn't anxious to discuss it further. They had watched most of the game in parallel worlds, Krimmer nodding off, Mortenson getting indigestion. Not only was the score unbearably close, but the pizza didn't arrive until midway in the first quarter.

As it turned out, Krimmer could foretell the future, even if he claimed his consultant couldn't. When play resumed after the commercial break, the Green Bay running back was stopped by a wall of tacklers short of the Chicago thirty-yard line, and proceeded to fumble as he recklessly extended his arm trying to gain the first down. The turnover quickly changed the momentum of the game. Not even the Packers' three time-outs could save them as the Bears marched down the field, eating up the clock by keeping the ball on the ground and securing the two-point victory with a chip-shot field goal with one second remaining.

"You sure this Rita babe didn't whisper something in your ear down at the beach?" Mortenson asked after he quit celebrating.

"Sweet nothings about climate change, that's all," Krimmer said.

That flippant remark was enough to convince Mortenson to expand on his suspicions. "I still think that you're getting a little on the side with that tasty, blonde limo driver," he said. "I stopped to hit a few balls on the way to the zoo, and Mike, the caddie master, told me she picked you up after our game, like you had it planned all along."

"You asked Mike to spy on me?" *Talk about chutzpah!*

"He wasn't spying, he was looking. He thought she was kind of cute, too."

Krimmer kept his cool. "I know it's difficult for you, Jared, to recognize when I'm being a serious person, but I can assure you, the limo driver's got nothing to do with anything," he fibbed as he switched over to the Weather Channel.

"What, you don't want to see the post-game wrap-up?"

"I was hoping there might be some wrap-up on Oklahoma."

"Hey, it's old hat, boyo. Over and done with. When you've seen one flattened subdiv, you've seen them all."

"You know, Jared, that's right up there with wishing the daughter in Florida dead."

"Hey, you made your point. Are you ever going to let me forget it?"

But apparently Mortenson was right. The weather gal was happily chattering about the balmy temperatures in the Northeast. Krimmer wasn't sure if he was disappointed or relieved. "You'd think they'd be covering the aftermath of those twisters," he said. "The Catastrophe of Careyville isn't an overstatement."

The attorney sounded like he took offense. "Hey, don't get soft and squishy on me, Jakester. Like I told you the other night, you got a good thing going. What difference does it make what your new not-girlfriend wants you to call it?"

"Didn't you ever listen, Jared? With Rita's help, I'm reexamining my options regarding my *good thing*," Krimmer said, stepping ever closer to the truth.

Mortenson must have thought so, too. His eternal tan darkened further, and there was no sign of a smile, fluorescent or otherwise, as he said, "When did you send me this momentous message, when I was in the can? Should I be worried about making my child support?"

Before Krimmer could reply, the weather gal seamlessly segued to a gloomy countenance and warned the audience that what they were about to see might be disturbing. With that, the studio faded to black, and the camera opened on the grim scene in Careyville, videotaped that afternoon, made grimmer by the unignorable immediacy of the big screen. The young female reporter was standing next to an overturned SUV, her face as shattered, as riven, as fish-belly white as the vehicle itself. The substantial brick house in the background was still reasonably upright, although the windows were smashed, and a giant bite had been taken out of the majestic mansard roof. A lone tree in the front yard was nothing but a deformed skeleton, stripped of all its leaves and any branch less than a couple of inches in diameter. Smoke was rising from somewhere in the distance, while in the foreground, hope was an American flag lashed to a piece of cream-colored PVC pipe propped up in a pile of rubble. Mocking this scene of utter devastation was the enduring emerald greenness of the carefully tended lawn and the bright-blue, cloudless sky.

As the reporter launched into a description of the damage, Mortenson said, "Enough already."

Krimmer watched for another few seconds, then decided he'd had enough, too.

"You know, Jakester, I don't care what you say, I think you must have it bad, the way you're all of a sudden fixated on this shit," the lawyer said, waving his hand at the darkened television, as if the searing image had burned itself into the screen. "I mean, the money for this job is in the bank already, so my advice is to forget about this consultant broad and start looking forward to the next opportunity for weird weather."

Krimmer corrected him. "Climate change."

"Sorry, climate change I mean."

"What do you believe it is, Jared?" Krimmer asked, his eyes searching out Mortenson's. "You're not just humoring me, are you? I mean, we've both called it weird weather ever since we started working together."

The attorney hesitated, then said with a burst of conviction, "Oh, yeah, it's climate change, all right. The science is rock solid."

Krimmer hesitated, as well. "If that's the case, does it worry you at all?"

"What do you mean, *worry me?*"

"What do you think I mean, Jared? Are you concerned that climate change is going to create a situation where it's going to be difficult to lead a normal, productive life? What we consider normal now, at any rate."

The lawyer was silent for several long seconds, forever by his standards. "Not really. I think you and I will be dead by the time we have to worry. Or be in la-la land with Alzheimer's."

Krimmer nodded cautiously, as if he might be in agreement or might not. "What about your children?"

Mortenson looked uncomfortable as he acknowledged the kids could be an issue. "Yeah, I know, it's a bitch," he said. "But somebody will figure out something, I'm sure."

"It's their mother's problem, is that what you're thinking?"

The attorney's only response was a half-hearted shrug. And then, as if he were embarrassed by the whole conversation, he clapped Krimmer on the shoulder and said, "Look, I gotta be going. Got a court date tomorrow and I need to get up early to shave."

There was nothing more Krimmer wanted to say or learn, other than to recommend an emergency intervention by an experienced personal guide and teacher with whom he was well acquainted. Given his proclivities and initial interest, Mortenson might even succumb to her charms.

But his pal's belated guilt trip wasn't quite finished. "About the other thing," he said, as he was about to put one foot out the door. "For the sake of our friendship, I want you to know what I told you yesterday was absolutely true. Nothing happened Saturday night, and nothing happened today, either."

"Haven't I made it clear, Jared? As far as I'm concerned, it's over and done with," Krimmer told him, even as Mortenson's superfluous denial made his doubts resurface.

Mortenson looked down. "I won't kid you that I wasn't hoping for more, but Sam's heart wasn't really in it . . . really," he said.

"How many times do I have to tell you?" Krimmer replied, increasingly unsure whether to believe him. "I don't need to know any more details."

"So we just played a little nibbly-lips, that's all it was. You can't blame me for that."

Krimmer exercised his right to remain silent.

"I mean, what would you have done in my place, boyo?"

Since Mortenson was clearly not paying attention to anything he was saying, or not saying, Krimmer decided to leave him with another demonstration of his predictive powers, a kind of delayed-action zinger. It would give the attorney something to chew over after the fact, assuming he managed to remember it when he heard the next installment of the news tomorrow. "To tell you the truth, Jared, if I'd been in your position, I wouldn't have been satisfied with nibbly-lips. I would've gone ahead and done everything I could to make those sweater puppies sing."

Mortenson's rugged-looking face grew ruggeder as deep cracks spread across his tanned forehead. No question he wasn't sure if he was hearing things: that his buddy would have advised him to go for it with his ex, or his not-ex, but in either case, to attempt to seduce the sublimely lovely meteorologist who, for the past twenty-four hours, had been the object of heated contention.

That was the point that Krimmer put his arm around his mystified pal's shoulder and made it crystal clear what he was saying, if not to Mortenson, surely to himself. "After all, who knows if you'll ever get a second chance?"

CHAPTER 22

TUESDAY MORNING COULD NOT COME TOO QUICKLY. UNTIL IT actually came.

Krimmer had spent the night tossing and turning, reviewing the head-spinning events of the past few days. The exposure of Mortenson's reckless ability to live with himself despite his understanding of the consequences of climate change was a fitting coda to Rita's campaign. Since willful blindness about the fate of the planet or the consequences of his choices was a thing of the past, his challenge was to fit all the diverse pieces together into a coherent picture of the future that he could unequivocally embrace—his business, his parents, Samantha, and most critically, Timmy. It wasn't merely change he was struggling with, but total transformation. It wasn't motivation he lacked, but experience. And it wasn't just a question of uttering the magic words to Sam and having Rita's prediction come true. It was how to articulate it convincingly to her, to explain what their new life might mean for both of them when he wasn't entirely sure of the details himself. It was like trying to complete a jigsaw puzzle with no clear idea of what the finished picture would be.

Krimmer was the first one in the office on Tuesday. Normally after a big payday, business casual would do, or a blazer if he happened to be having lunch at the club. But today he wanted to dress the part. He had chosen his most sincere blue suit, paired with a white shirt with spread collar and French cuffs, and a jazzy tie to help give an upbeat tone to the necessary formalities. The tiny lemon-and-tangerine–colored Japanese parasol pattern just might remind Samantha of *Madama Butterfly*, and the indigo background was for luck.

A little before nine, the jacket was draped over the back of his chair, and Krimmer was finishing up the *WaPo* online crossword and diligently working on his third cup of coffee when he heard the outer door open and the sound of high heels clipping across the hardwood floor. Then silence. An unbearably long minute or so later, he was about to get up and check out her cubicle, when he sensed that Samantha was already standing in the doorway. "Can I see you, Krims?" she was asking.

"Sure, what's up, Sam?" he asked, startled but controlled as he spun around his chair to face her, his back to the desk. He kept his tone just the way he had rehearsed it in his mind, pleasant, plainspoken, without a hint of suggestiveness—*Sam* instead of *Doc*. "How's your grandmother? She come through the storms OK?"

Samantha started to say something but stopped short, as if her train of thought had been interrupted. "Yes, thank you, she's OK," she said as she stepped inside his cubicle and picked up where she'd left off, "but we need to talk."

She was dressed to the nines again, this time in a classic, understated, taupe pantsuit. She was also holding out a plain white number-ten envelope—no stamp, no address, just his name. "What's this?" he asked.

"My letter of resignation."

No battle plan survives the first shot. That wasn't Confucius or Columbia either, but the dictum of some smart Prussian on the German

General Staff that got drummed into him at Harvard Business School. Unfortunately, Krimmer had spent so much time and energy gearing up for the big moment that he was caught flatfooted when the first shot turned out to be an ambush. His emergency contingency plan was to snatch the envelope and sail it over the cubicle wall like a Frisbee.

Samantha watched it disappear. "That's not going to change anything, Jake."

Krimmer clutched the arms of his chair, mad at himself for his impetuous reaction when, just like with Mortenson, the situation called for playing clever defense. "How many times did I try to call you, how many texts and emails did I send?" he asked in a steady voice. "Sunday night, yesterday morning?"

"I know, I saw them all," she said, as sympathetic as he was calm.

"I felt bad about how we left it Sunday."

"I'm sorry to hear that."

"Why didn't you get back to me?"

"I was busy."

"All day yesterday?"

"I had a hot date," she said with a regretful smile that came and went in an instant. "With Timmy."

Krimmer thought better of mentioning he knew all about it. "Please," he said, with a sweeping gesture in the direction of the sofa. "Please sit down and let's discuss everything like two adults."

"What's to discuss?" Samantha asked, her eyes widening as if she knew him better, as if she were surprised by his suspicious equanimity. "I'm giving you notice," she said as she carefully lowered herself to the cushions, her hands going to her lap, smoothing the folds of fabric. "Two weeks and I'm out of your life."

"You mean out of the company."

"That, too."

"Look, Sam, you know I can't go on without you."

"You mean the company can't."

"How can you possibly walk away from such a lucrative job?"

"I knew that's the first thing you'd ask." She skipped a beat and said, "I already have an offer. In nonprofit." She skipped another, and added, "Money isn't everything."

"I never said it was," Krimmer cried.

"You never said a lot of things," Samantha said as the brief, regretful smile returned.

He squeezed his eyes shut in frustration. "I knew you were interviewing last Friday. That's why you were dressed to kill."

"Today, too. I'm having lunch with my new boss."

"It's my own fault," he said, as he regained his composure. "I should have locked you up with a contract."

"You did."

"I mean a different kind of contract."

"Yes, in hindsight you probably should have," Samantha said tonelessly, as if she were only being polite.

"I know you won't believe it, but when I came in this morning, I was getting ready to tell you something very important."

"Is that why *you* are all dressed up?"

Krimmer paused, standing and gathering himself for what he hoped would be a sprint to the finish line. "I was getting ready to tell you that I'd decided we ought to end our arrangement. Throw it out the window."

Instead, it was just another stumble. "That's what I've done, Jake. End our arrangement."

"No, I mean that our relationship was too artificial, too restrictive, the way we'd set it up, not to see each other outside the office."

"Problem solved. Now we don't have to see each other at all."

"That's not the way I thought we could solve the problem."

"That's the way I've solved it."

Krimmer made a motion to go over and throw his arms around her, to tell her he loved her, but as so often happens in the fog of battle, timidity—masked as prudence—prevailed. Instead, he sat and turned to stare out the window. The expensive view of the National Mall might as well have been filled with FEMA trailers, the way it failed to provide its customary high. Clumsy he was, clumsy in the way he was trying to express his feelings. Whatever he said, Samantha would interpret it as just the opposite of what he meant. She seemed so adamant, so unyielding, that for a moment he lost sight of his objective, spinning back around and crying out in frustration, "What happened? What did I say, what did I do?"

"Nothing you said, Jake. Nothing you did."

"What then?"

"Goddamnit, it was what *I* said, Jake," Samantha cried, hiding her face in her hands. "What *I* did."

"Sam . . ." Krimmer said, now levitating from the chair and discarding his earlier faintheartedness as though it were "the coat which fitted him when a boy." He approached her warily.

"Don't you touch me," she warned.

"Sam, Sam, what is it?" he asked tenderly, backing off until he felt the sharp, hard oak of the desktop pressing against his butt, and he could safely perch there like a man on a ledge, his fingers closing around the solid wooden surface on either side, bracing himself, contemplating whether he should jump. "You can tell me," he said, now almost whispering, as if somehow his uncharacteristic deference could dissipate the harsh haze of silence.

They remained motionless for the longest while, together but apart. When Samantha at last spoke, she spoke not to him, but to some less-judgmental third party sitting off to the side on the couch, visible only to her. As Krimmer listened and did his best to comfort her, he desperately wanted to be optimistic. The personal and the professional and the moral were so bound together in her mind, three strands so tightly intertwined, that it seemed all he had to do was grab them like a lifeline, and everything would work out fine.

"It's not right, Jake, what's happening. The earth is dying, people are dying, that elderly lady in Florida is already dead, and for what? So we can squeeze out more barrels of oil, more tons of coal, more cubic feet of natural gas to keep us going? Where do you think we're headed, Jake? Do you have any idea what will happen if we don't stop now?"

"I know, Sam. It's not right," he agreed, could have agreed all day in fact, but she still didn't seem to be listening.

"I tried to tell you Friday night at Tout Va Bien, Jake. I tried to tell you again at brunch on Sunday."

"I heard you, Sam, I really did."

But she apparently didn't. "For God's sake, I threw myself at you, I threw myself at you at McDonald's—at *McDonald's* of all places— even as I was telling you how I hated what we did here."

"You never said *hate*, Sam," he said, daring to take a tentative step forward.

"Don't you see, I was afraid to say hate, Jake? I was afraid to say it. I was afraid you would hate me." She wiped her eyes with the back of her hand as if she were crying. Her words sputtered out one by one, like an engine running out of fuel. "I'm ... so ... ashamed ... of ... myself."

"Sam ..."

"What we're doing here is just plain wrong. It's making matters worse, not better."

"Sam ... Sam," he repeated mindlessly, taking another step toward her. "I know, I know."

"If you know so goddamned much, Jake," she said, "why don't you do something about it?" A single tear rolled down her cheek.

And that was the precise moment when he felt he had no choice but to do what he was here to do, to bring the lessons of the past three days to a successful and appropriate conclusion. In a dreamlike state, he knelt down and took her hands in his as he heard himself say, "Look, Sam, I know this is not when or where or how it's usually done, but ... Samantha Richards, will you marry me?" only to watch in bemusement as the law of gravity was temporarily suspended by the force of atmospheric resistance, allowing that question, corny and old-fashioned perhaps but no longer hazardous, to hang in the air interminably between them, as insubstantial yet as momentous as her letter of resignation a few minutes before.

Except Samantha just didn't snatch it away. She incinerated it. "You want to marry me?" she hooted, a wicked impersonation. "Hah! Since when?"

"Since forever," Krimmer said, standing, fighting off his instinct to retreat. "That's how long it took to admit it to myself."

He finally did back away to the desk, back to the safety of the ledge, hoping to relieve the pressure on both of them. Samantha just sat there for a moment, motionless and silent, as if disbelief had given way to shock, as if she were stunned by the inexcusably presumptuous proposal, made in such a halting and hackneyed manner, at such an inappropriate time and place. When she rose from the sofa, her eyes were dry, Southwest desert–dry, and she quickly closed the distance between them. "You really want to marry me?" she asked skeptically, as she stopped just short of the magical, invisible boundary where their polarity would suddenly switch, making it impossible to escape each other's arms.

"I do," Krimmer said, fully awake and alert.

"Are you sure it's not just because it's the only way you can keep me here?"

"There's something else I need to tell you," Krimmer said, clutching at the hard oak desktop, gathering himself one more time. "Whether you marry me or not, I'm closing down the business."

Samantha's reaction was swift and unforgiving. "I don't believe it."

"Maybe you don't, but it's going to happen. I've got a nice chunk of money set aside, enough for both of us to get by at least for a couple years." Once he started, it just poured out. "As for the future, I thought that maybe we could hire ourselves out as consultants. We could do the same kind of forecasting we're doing now, but for the power companies and the Independent System Operators. The money that speculators like us would have siphoned off, they can use to keep down their customers' electricity bills."

"I don't believe it," she repeated, but softer this time. "You've got it all worked out."

"That's a good thing, right?"

Samantha turned away from him, her eyes drawn to the window, her incredulity waning, replaced by a strained calm, as if she, too, had found something to hold on to tightly. "What brought about this change of heart, Jake?" she asked in an expressionless voice.

Krimmer was encouraged by the look of her magnificent shoulders, not slumped, but not drawn up in defiance either—thoughtful and confident, as square to the world as Jefferson's statue. "It's not a change of heart, Sam. It's just a change of perspective," he said.

"And where did you get this change of perspective? Did your so-called consultant work a miracle, or was she really your new girlfriend all along and she dumped you?"

"I'm telling you the truth, Sam. There never was a new girlfriend, only the consultant, and she did work a miracle, but let's not talk about it now. I'll tell you everything when we have more time, I promise. Please, let's just talk about us."

Just as Krimmer was beginning to think he had done enough to win her over, that she was seriously weighing the possibility of getting to yes, Samantha whirled around and leveled him with a blindsiding accusation. "That's not the way I heard it."

"I'm sorry?" Krimmer said meekly, as the lifeline parted and the precious ring buoy began to drift away.

"I said that's not the way I heard it from Jared."

"Jared?" Krimmer asked, struggling to keep his temper. "What's Jared got to do with it? What did he tell you?"

"He said your new girlfriend was a blonde in her twenties."

That wasn't interference on Mortenson's part, that was betrayal. "Anything else?" he asked, calm and dispassionate on the surface, on fire inside.

"She drove you to the golf club Saturday morning, and your game was off, like something was on your mind or you'd been up all night. Or maybe both."

"Is that so."

"She picked you up after golf, and you spent the whole afternoon with her yesterday, at the beach. He said you were behaving strangely when you two watched the football game, saying things that just didn't make sense, about him, and me, and about the business. He thought she had some kind of hold on you."

"Did he tell you what kind of things?"

Samantha shook her head. "He said he'd told me too much already."

"And when did Jared make this report?" Krimmer asked, still outwardly cool to the touch.

"Last night. He called me on the way home, after he left you."

"Jared called you last night, as soon as he left my house?"

"He was only trying to help, Jake."

Krimmer had no problem with Samantha's jealousy. It was his jealousy that was consuming him. His jaw thrust forward, a closed, apelike face. "He wasn't trying to help, he was trying to sabotage my plans, that's what he was trying to do," Krimmer said, starting to raise his voice. "He just wants to get into your . . . your pantsuit," he said, catching himself just in time from being cruder.

"That's not it at all. I had a long talk with Jared Saturday night, about how you and I were going through a rough patch at the office. I thought he might be able to give me some perspective."

Krimmer could no longer control himself. "You had a long talk with Jared *about me* on Saturday night?"

"I was upset," Samantha said defensively. "I was trying to make sense of what happened between us at Tout Va Bien."

"Are you sure this long talk wasn't yesterday, when you went to the zoo?"

Samantha recoiled as if he had given her a hard slap. "No," she said, her voice a little wobbly. "Saturday night when we went to the basketball game."

He pressed his advantage. "The basketball game? That was your rain check with Jared on Saturday night?"

Samantha recovered quickly. "With Jared and Timmy. Why not? After our dinner at Tout Va Bien I was going to bow out. But then he told me he'd be able to get courtside seats at the Wizards game and locker room passes for himself and Timmy."

Krimmer knew he ought to be happy that it was just a basketball game, with Timmy along as a third wheel, and not some champagne-soaked, sunset liaison à deux, but it galled him, nonetheless. "So you went for Timmy's sake, is that it?"

"Timmy is a kid, Jake," Sam said with a mix of impatience and disbelief. "A six-year-old kid. Do you know what it meant to him to go back into the locker room and see all his heroes?"

"I guess that explains Timmy's enthusiasm when he saw Jared at the zoo," Krimmer said. "Leaping up on him that way like he was his daddy." He saw the pain in her eyes as he went in for the knockout. She was too dazed to even ask how he knew. "Do you know how I felt when you went out with Mortenson behind my back?"

Somehow, Samantha found enough reserves to strike back like a cornered prizefighter. "Behind your back? Since when do you own me?"

"You went out behind my back so Timmy could see some seven-foot freaks standing around in their jock straps?"

"You really don't like Timmy, do you." It wasn't a question.

He couldn't help himself. "Not at this very moment. He seems to have successfully inserted himself between us in our relationship."

"You really think it was only because of Timmy that I went out with Jared?"

"I certainly hope so. I would like to think that you had better taste in men than a sleazeball like Mortenson."

"Well, I happen to like basketball, too."

"Sure, and I bet you were really annoyed you couldn't go back into the locker room and check out the merchandise yourself. I bet you couldn't wait to start playing nibbly-lips with Jared."

"He mentioned that's what he told you," Samantha said, the words as sharply pointed and cold as icicles.

"Fuck Jared and anything he said. He doesn't know from shit."

Sam tilted up her chin as if she were daring him to throw another punch. "How do you know I didn't?"

So there it was, laid out like a dead body waiting to be embalmed, so it could never naturally go to dust, so it always would be something that would be held between them. Krimmer's fingers clenched into a fist before he became conscious of what he was doing. "Oh, Christ," he said, throwing his hands up and open and letting out an agonized, death rattle of a gasp, even as he realized that he had managed to transform the lifeline into a gallows rope. "Omega 13? Please?"

Samantha seemed shocked into silence.

"Please?" he repeated.

"OK," she said.

"I want to marry you, Sam. I want to close the business and I want both of us to devote our intelligence and our energies to the fate of this small planet that we call our home. We can't stop climate change by ourselves, but we can start changing attitudes so it can be stopped, or at least mitigated."

Samantha didn't say anything immediately, but when she spoke, she too had calmed herself. "What about Timmy? Where does he fit into your plans?"

"With us."

"*Between* us?"

"I said *with* us, why can't you believe me?"

It took a while before she answered, a *while* that may have been only a second or two but felt like an hour. "Why would I believe you? Timmy always seems to be an afterthought. Or worse," she added.

"He's not an afterthought, he's the future," Krimmer said passionately, but perhaps she'd had enough passion at that point. When Samantha didn't react, Krimmer said, "You should be happy I'm focused on *you*."

"It took you long enough," she snapped, but not without a note of triumph.

As Krimmer took a half-step forward, Samantha stepped back, crossing her arms over her breasts in the classic hands-off position.

He threw his arms open anyway. "C'mon, Sam, what do you say? A new start for all of us."

"All of us?"

"Right, Sam. All of us. Timmy, too."

Samantha's stare was alternately hardening and softening, as if she was trapped on a rickety emotional seesaw, as if she couldn't make up her mind. "OK, I'll give it some thought," she finally said.

"What about your letter of resignation?"

"What does that matter if you're going to close the business?"

Krimmer's arms slumped to his sides as he stared back at her, but only hard. Soft would never hold back the pressure building behind his eyes. "Is that all you have to say, Sam?"

She thought about it for a moment before answering, echoing another old in-joke from a different movie, not *Galaxy Quest* this time, but an affectionate trope they often shared after one of their moony, dream-fueled, celebratory-drink sessions had led to something else. So what if it verged on a cliché—it still had the power to sting. "We'll always have . . ."

"Don't say it. Please?"

But she did anyway, as if she might be resigned to having nothing more.

CHAPTER 23

How frustrating. Krimmer had no idea how to get in touch with Rita. He'd meant to ask, but in the bittersweet rush to say good-bye it slipped his mind. Not that he had ever expected he would be in further need of Rita's services. Then again, he'd never expected Sam to walk in and resign. He was hoping that at worst, she'd just make a point of hesitating a bit when he popped the question, double-checking that she could believe her ears.

How perfect. Even though he took the precaution to type *Find Rita Ten Grieve* into Google, the AI chatbot must have been doing its Big Brother thing behind the scenes, translating *Grieve* into *grief* and giv-ing him a one-touch option to initiate an emergency call to a mental health counselor. He made sure Bing was in manual mode, although the results were no more satisfying. It found a couple of Ritas with similar-sounding last names, but he doubted his Rita would have spent much time in New Mexico or Biloxi. All he could do was wait for the Nimbus to get on the case.

How embarrassing. "Hey, chief." Robert was standing in the entrance to the cubicle with a peculiar look on his face. "I found this on the floor. It has your name on it."

Krimmer grabbed the unopened envelope. *Quants have no sense of humor.* On the back, over the seal, was the blazing red imprint of Samantha's lipstick. In the lonely white space between the remnants of her kiss, she had written *off.*

How calm. The weather, all across the country. Nevertheless, he decided against telling Sam to leave early. She could just as easily do her thinking in the office as anywhere. Besides, he might be able to overhear whether or not she cancelled lunch.

How stupid. He liked Timmy, he truly did. The problem was that he too easily lost his cool *about* Timmy, whenever he thought Timmy was getting in the way of his relationship with Sam. It was a failure of expression, not an insufficiency of intention. He needed to just accept the kid for what he was: a devilish six-year-old. Not so different than he'd been at that age, as Rita had taken great pains to demonstrate at Plum Cove and the Jefferson Memorial. *A devilish six-year-old who stands to inherit whatever planet we leave him.*

How long. The morning, as he was hiding out. At five minutes to twelve he was standing at the entrance to the Athenaeum dining room. The door opened for lunch at noon. There were no oysters on the menu and both he and Marcus avoided mentioning the not-so-imaginary waiter.

How alone. On the short walk up Pennsylvania Avenue back to his office, he paid no attention to the once-delightful June-in-October scenery crowding the sidewalk. The prospect of an afternoon filled with more silence from the neighboring cubicle—or worse, an unwanted answer—weighed him down beyond any human tolerance or understanding, as though the dome of high pressure responsible for all the sunny weather had collapsed into an earthbound singularity and was sitting squarely on top of his head.

How inept. Samantha loved Timmy; Jake loved Sam. Was it really that difficult to convince Sam that he was anxious to complete the circle—*let's never think of it as a triangle again*—and love Timmy too, unreservedly, without qualification, the same way his parents had loved him when he behaved like a brat at Plum Cove, and probably a hundred other times as well? "*La commedia è stupenda!*" That was *La Bohème*, not *Casablanca*, but Sam would recognize it all the same.

How scared. There was no sense just hanging around, waiting for the proverbial feces to hit the fan. Sam's cubicle was empty—she hadn't cancelled lunch after all, and it looked like a long one. The weather was still balmy. The Corvette was parked in the basement garage. He should have taken his parents up on their invitation sooner. *Maybe talking it over with them will help me sort things out.* It was an hour-and-a-half drive from downtown Washington, past Annapolis, and across the Chesapeake Bay Bridge to his parents' bungalow on the Eastern Shore, but he could be there by three-thirty. Somehow he made it by three—too fast, apparently, to have the time to figure out how he was going to delicately broach the purpose of his visit.

As soon as pulled into the gravel driveway, Ben loped toward the car sounding the alarm, a stentorian bark followed by a hellhound growl, culminating in the ritual impaling of a wet nose in Krimmer's crotch.

"Jake," his mother cried out. "What are you doing here?" She and his father were sitting on the deck, reading.

"Hey, son," his father looked down and waved, setting aside his book. "What brings you out our way?"

Krimmer took the short flight of stairs two at a time. His mother pouted theatrically as he bent down to kiss her cheek. "We were hoping you'd come yesterday," she said, a mild reproof in the grander scheme of things. "We thought that's what you'd promised."

"Hey, that doesn't matter, Susie Q. He's here now and that's what counts."

"Have you had lunch?"

"How about a cold beer?"

"I made some tuna salad this morning."

"And get rid of that ridiculous tie while you're at it."

Krimmer smiled and raised his hands in abject, filial surrender. "Hey, it's such a beautiful October day, I thought I'd take a drive."

His mother started to pout again. "That's the only reason you came?"

Krimmer's smile widened into a boyish grin as he sat down next to her, leaning forward, hands clasped, forearms resting his on his knees, giving him an unimpeded view. "Nah, Mom, I just wanted to be able to see the look on your face when I told you the news."

"Uh-oh," his father joked.

He had to start somewhere, so he just blurted it out, putting a positive slant on the whole situation before either one of them could say any more. "I intend to marry Samantha."

His mother looked so ecstatic, and his father so pleased, that he immediately felt guilty about having to add an itsy-bitsy caveat. "There's just a minor issue that I have to deal with first."

His mom's expression went from ecstasy to alarm as she looked over at his dad.

"What's that, son?" Jake Sr. asked gravely.

"Well..." Krimmer's eyes darted back and forth between the two of them. "Samantha hasn't actually agreed to marry me yet."

His mother sounded personally offended. "And why not?"

"Well..." All Krimmer's resolution and good intentions vanished. How was he going to tell these two people, who loved him most in all the world, that his own beloved wasn't convinced he adequately loved her six-year-old son? "Well... I haven't exactly asked her." To keep it reasonably truthful, he thought to add, "Not in the right way, anyway."

"So what you're saying," Jake Sr. said, in his best inveigling courtroom-baritone manner, "is that you're *planning* to ask Samantha to marry you."

"Yes, that's what I'm saying, Dad," Krimmer said, relieved to escape that linguistical cul-de-sac. He needed to find a different way into the delicate discussion, although it was soon apparent that the approach he chose next had its own shortcomings. "As soon as I close down my business."

"Oh," his father said.

Give his mother credit for her big smile. "*Oh* is right. Now there's some news."

"You're not in any trouble, are you, Jake?"

"Trouble? You mean like money trouble? No, business has been fine. Don't you watch the news on TV? Climate change is wreaking havoc with the weather."

His mother immediately picked up on his casual confession. "Did I hear you say climate change?"

Judging by the sudden frown, his father was still focused on the finances. He didn't look convinced.

"Don't worry, Dad. I've got plenty of money, and I plan to keep making more. There'll always be enough to help you guys, I promise."

Krimmer turned to his mother. "And yes, I did say climate change. It's a long story."

Jake Sr. stood up abruptly. "Well, we certainly want to hear it, and I mean all of it," he said. "As for the economics of your decision, let's not worry about that now. Whatever you do, it's unlikely that you'll maintain your present income, but your first priority must be Samantha, and . . . and . . ."

His mother was happy to finish the sentence, lest her husband might be losing his nerve about rooting for his posterity. "And any children you and Samantha might have, that's what he means," she said sweetly.

"Actually, Susan, I was trying to think of the name of Samantha's son. You remember, he came with her the time Jake brought her out to meet us."

"Timmy, Dad."

"That's right, Timmy. A very nice boy."

Krimmer was quick to second the motion. "Yes, a really good kid," he said.

"Well then, why don't we all go inside and hear more about it?"

When his parents sold the big house in Chevy Chase, sentiment had motivated them to keep as much of their furniture and artwork as they could squeeze into the bungalow. For Krimmer, sitting in the living room of their former summer cottage was like being transported back to the home where he grew up. The major difference was that instead of the tree-shaded, hermetically sealed atmosphere of the suburbs, the sliding doors and windows were flung wide open to admit the gentle Chesapeake breeze and the insistent midafternoon sun, bouncing off the lush blueness of the bay. It was an invigorating tonic of cleansing light and oxygenated air that he would need for what was surely going to be an interesting conversation—interesting in the sense of the ancient Chinese curse, "May you live in interesting times."

They arranged themselves around the coffee table, Krimmer taking tenuous possession of one of the high-backed wing chairs, jacket and tie cast off, shirtsleeves rolled up. His parents sat side by side opposite him on the richly upholstered couch, as Ben dozed at their feet. The two men drank beer from freezer-chilled mugs, while his mother sipped iced tea. It was all so homey and familial that Krimmer gradually relaxed, settling deeper into the cushions as he expanded on his decision to shutter his firm and exit the morally problematic business of speculating in Financial Transmission Rights.

His explanation was notable for what he downplayed or judiciously omitted as much as for what he actually said. He saw no need to dwell on Samantha's long-concealed feelings about the ethics of exploiting weird weather, as influential as they had been. And he certainly didn't want to open up a host of unanswerable questions by mentioning the intercession of some climate-obsessed, Nimbus-wielding, indigo-eyed guardian angel from the datasphere who had bludgeoned him with the terror of the ordinary. Nor was he overly specific about his new career path. Despite his dad's protestations to the contrary, he knew his parents would be concerned about the future of their monthly check. In short, he did everything he could not to muddle up what sounded like a well-thought-out, purely rational decision, his visceral reaction to the Catastrophe of Careyville excepted, as it was too raw to leave out entirely. After all, that was what they would expect of their son, what they would have done themselves: stick to the facts but leaven them with tenderness and sensitivity.

Still, the more Krimmer explained, the more he avoided getting to the heart of the matter. He knew it would be difficult for them to understand or forgive him for always thinking first of his own needs, even if they were misguided, and shortchanging Samantha's and Timmy's. Especially Timmy's. The problem with not telling them the ugly truth was that they were so goddamned solicitous, so understanding about everything else. He explained how living with weird weather every day had made him increasingly suspicious that there was an overarching pattern to all the seemingly random climatological events, a singular cause. They nodded. He related how he had researched the opinions of the scientists and discovered that, aside from a few wing nuts on the fossil-fuel payroll, they were unanimous—the planet was heating up, and dangerously so. They agreed. He described the depth of his horror, his actual physical distress, when he saw the devastation of the EF5 in Oklahoma on his big-screen TV. They commiserated. He reported the projections of what could happen right here in Washington if no action was taken, tugging at their hearts as well as their memories with the example of the Jefferson Memorial. They shuddered. He sympathized about his mother's roses. They held each other's hand more tightly. He freely used the dreaded words—climate change. They smiled.

What made it worse was, thanks to Rita, he was privy to their thinking. He knew, although his parents weren't aware he knew, that long ago they had come to the same conclusions. Surely his mother would've liked to give him a couple of jabs about all those years of making money from other people's misery. And he couldn't believe his father didn't want to speak up and take credit for his deviously ineffective attack on the ACEA before the Court. Although they made it clear that they agreed with his newfound conviction, they seemed determined to pass up every opportunity to chide him for coming late to the party, or to skeptically question him about the startling suddenness of his conversion, or to interrogate him more about his bumbling revelation about marrying Sam. Instead, they sacrificed their egos for his, and simply offered him their encouragement and support as he prepared to leave, the matter of the obstacle of Timmy still left unbroached.

"I think you've come to the right decision, son," his father said. "I know it wasn't easy."

"And don't you worry about the money one bit," his mother echoed. "The money will take care of itself."

His dad threw his arm around Krimmer's shoulder. "It's a terrible pickle we've gotten into in this country, too many of us denying that it's us humans who are causing the climate to change. I know you're going to figure out a way to make it better."

His mom gave him a long hug. "We're very proud of you, Jake, and I'm sure Samantha is proud of you, too."

"Yes, we want to be the first to know that it's official, that you're engaged."

Sitting in the usual traffic on the drive back home to Georgetown, Krimmer realized that his parents had given him exactly what he had come for: a role model to emulate. Sure, they hadn't been totally candid about their long-held beliefs, but that was only so he could be the hero for a day, so he could demonstrate to them that he was their grown-up son of whom they could be unquestionably, unequivocally proud. Nor was it lost on him that it was the same role model they had always tried to provide throughout the years.

So why was he feeling so let down rather than energized? Why was he wondering if it was a wasted visit? Why was he left with the gnawing fear that they had set the bar so high, he might never be able to measure up?

CHAPTER 24

KRIMMER DIDN'T EVEN HAVE TIME TO PUT HIS KEYCARD BACK IN HIS wallet. The minute he opened the door every monitor in the townhouse was beeping. The screen in the vestibule read *Private Caller*. It had to be Sam or Rita, it didn't matter which. Either one meant progress, or at least Krimmer hoped and prayed it did. He raced to his bedroom and clicked the *accept* icon on his laptop before the call could transfer over to his smartphone. "Oh, it's you," he said when a photo of the Jefferson Memorial, the island green version, popped up on the screen.

"You sound disappointed," Rita replied.

Krimmer was alarmed that he was panting. "No, I just got in," he told her.

"I know. I've been tracking the pings from your phone."

"Why didn't you call earlier?"

"I saw you were with your parents. I didn't want to interrupt while you were telling them the good news."

He rushed out the bad news, part of it anyway. "Sam quit this morning."

"That doesn't matter if you're closing down the business, does it?"

"Why close the business if she won't marry me?" he asked plaintively.

"I'm not going to answer that, Jake."

"Bad joke," Krimmer said quickly. "I didn't know how else to tell you."

"Aah—" Rita said, and then, "What's odd is, when I got an alert from the Nimbus that you had Googled me, I checked Samantha's Facebook page, expecting to see a happy surprise. There was no mention of any problems."

"Technically, she's thinking it over."

"Technically, you screwed up, is that correct? It was Timmy again, wasn't it."

"No . . . yes . . . maybe."

"Are you expecting me to choose?"

"Look, Rita, she has another job lined up."

"Oh, she told you."

"She must have been interviewing all along."

"Why wouldn't she be exploring alternative career paths, considering how she felt about your business model?"

Rita's lack of surprise was a painful tell. "You were holding out on me, weren't you? You always knew."

"I admit I did my due diligence before taking the assignment," she said. "Did you really think I was a miracle worker? That I could actually convince you, Jake Krimmer, about the catastrophic peril of climate change in just three days? I always knew I would need Samantha's help."

"You could have warned me."

"About what?" she asked. "That the way to your head was through your heart? Why do you suppose I was under such pressure to wrap up your case?"

"You owe me, Rita."

"You owe *me*, Jake. Until now I've had a perfect record," she said as she switched on her camera. She was sitting in front of the same neutral gray wall as yesterday morning, but instead of a T-shirt she was wearing one of those time-honored little black dresses with a straight neckline, leaving her arms and shoulders bare. Her deep-set indigo eyes were framed by a flurry of blond tendrils teased out in all directions. A double string of pearls rounded out the classic look. "Oh, my God, all that hard work down the drain," she said with a theatrical sigh.

Krimmer started to feel sorry for her, too. "I don't know what gets into me," he said apologetically. "I just say things that come out sounding wrong. And even if they sound right, Sam's measuring it against all the other things I've said in the past." He paused to take a deep breath. "Look, Rita, you gotta help."

"I'm juggling a lot of clients these days," she replied, sounding distracted.

"Isn't there something you can do? Can't the Nimbus convince Sam I mean what I say?"

"The Nimbus isn't a mind-control machine, Jake. Besides, I've already used up your allotment of grieves."

"Can't you get a mulligan, a make-up?"

"And what would I do with it? You're still convinced that it's climate change, right? And you know for a fact that you were just as much the little brat as Timmy. What's left to do?"

"Have a drink?" He thought about it some more. "Have several drinks? Drink the whole bottle?"

"Doesn't sound like the worst idea," Rita agreed.

"Why don't you come over?" he asked, a purely innocent proposal. "I could use some company."

But Rita, too, was measuring him against all the things he'd said in the past. "Fat chance, Romeo," she snapped. "I'm not your fallback position."

"Honestly, I didn't mean it that way."

But she didn't seem to be listening. "Sometimes I wish I had tried to convert Mortenson instead of you."

That declaration was at once so humorous and patently offensive that Krimmer was unable to resist. "Hah! Since when?"

Rita waited until he settled down. "Look, Jake, I don't want to keep you company. I want to stick a 5 Iron up your butt and call it a spine so you can fight for yourself. I want you to get back in there and convince Sam."

"How am I going to convince her?" he asked. "How many times can I try?" And then he added a mindless afterthought, "I guess I'll never be the man my father is."

For some reason that seemed to get her full attention. "What's that, Jake?"

"What's what?" he asked.

"What about your father?"

"What about him?"

"Why did you say you could never be like him?"

"I said that?"

"Words to that effect."

"If I did say it, I don't know why," Krimmer told her, not altogether truthfully. He was thinking back to the visit with his parents that afternoon and remembering his reaction on the way home. "Maybe because my dad could convince anybody of anything. He always figured out how to make things come out all right. Even when it was a question of *not* saying something, like he did when he deliberately blew up the ACEA case."

There was a ponder-filled pause on Rita's end. "So what was his advice when you told your parents you were having a problem convincing Samantha to marry you?" she asked thoughtfully.

"I didn't exactly tell them I was having a problem convincing her," Krimmer confessed. "I couldn't bring myself to explain the reason why."

"I see..." Rita said, dragging out the words as a splash of color slowly spread up her pale, spectral cheeks. If an idea was starting to register, it was less like an incandescent light bulb instantly clicking on than one of those squiggly fluorescents that take a couple seconds to reach full power. "You know what, Jake? I'm starting to think I should come over after all. How about your place in half an hour, say six thirty?"

"What about Sam? Don't you want to talk to both of us?"

"Does Samantha know about me?"

"Well, not exactly . . ."

"Then it doesn't matter. Something tells me that Samantha's not the issue, Jake."

Fashionably late wasn't Rita's MO. The doorbell rang precisely at the appointed time. Krimmer checked the camera and buzzed her in. He was waiting for her at the bottom of the short flight of stairs that led to the stylish living room. Her eyes darted around, hastily taking in how he had enlivened the staid Federal bones of his townhouse with a more modern sensibility. "So where's the TV?" she wanted to know, acting like everything else was no big deal.

Chagrined, he didn't object. "Follow me."

As he led her into the media room, Rita took one look at the two recliners and asked, "Isn't there a place to sit?"

Crushed was more like it. "I'll take care of it," he said. "How about a drink?"

Rita scowled at the bottle of beer clutched tightly in his hand. "Help yourself. I have a client dinner."

When Krimmer returned with a straight-backed chair from the dining table, she was scrolling through something on her smartphone. "So what exactly happened with Samantha?" Rita asked, as she promptly sat down.

Krimmer balanced on the edge of the recliner, like Mortenson nervous about the outcome of his bets. "Sam quit," he said, taking a swig straight from the bottle.

"You already told me that," Rita said, not looking up, still scrolling.

"Sam said she hated what she was doing. She said she felt ashamed."

"If anything, that should have worked in your favor. Why don't you take it from the top, Jake," Rita suggested, as she finished reading whatever she was reading.

She listened intently as Krimmer replayed the morning's scene. Rita only glanced at her watch once, and that was when he was going on at great length about how emotional Sam was about the incident at McDonald's—the throwing-herself-at-him part, not the ketchup-on-the-shirt part. In fact, he was almost as successful in avoiding dealing with the Timmy factor as he had been with his parents, only saying that he'd assured Sam that it was going to be a new start for all of them.

When he was done, Rita had only one question. "Did you ever come right out and tell Samantha you loved her, Jake?"

"Not in so many words, I guess. But there's no way I didn't make it clear."

It turned out she had two questions. "What about Timmy? Did you ever tell her you were prepared to love him, too?"

Krimmer was not so quick to answer this time. In fact, the sound that eventually emerged from his mouth was not composed of actual words but was more like an extended interval of voicelessness, a monosyllabic utterance that rhymed with *duh.*

It further turned out that the second question had two parts. "Or did you think that assuring Sam that the way Timmy had successfully inserted himself into your relationship *with* you, not *between* you, was the same thing as saying you loved him?"

"How did you—?"

"I checked Samantha's email while you were getting the chair. Lucky for you, I forgot to cancel the open line."

Krimmer didn't want to ask but did, leaning forward to better hear her answer. "What else did she tell her grandmother?"

"That you never came straight out and said Timmy would be your son, too."

"Maybe not in so many words," he repeated, shrinking back quickly. "But I certainly tried hard to leave that impression."

Rita gave him the full treatment—a hard, intense, indigo stare. But instead of a vitriolic denunciation, she surprised him with an apology. "I think that I'm as much to blame as you, Jake," she said, as grave and somber as a judge delivering an opinion from the bench. "I misread the situation from the beginning."

Krimmer was baffled by this sudden reversal. "What are you talking about, Rita?"

"All the hints I dropped. All the research I did to set up those last two grieves at Plum Cove." She just shook her head.

"You mean about Timmy?"

"I thought he was the problem, and he was, and maybe still is, from Samantha's perspective. Not that Timmy isn't part of your issue, too," she went on to say, "but he's not the core of your problem."

"Can you please explain that to Sam," he said flippantly.

"It's your father, Jake."

Krimmer's head jerked, more shudder than shake. "My father? What the hell are you talking about?"

"I finally started to understand when you said you couldn't bear to tell your parents about being unable to convince Samantha to marry you because of your attitude toward her son. It was clear you were afraid they'd think you didn't measure up."

It wasn't the first time he wondered if she was a mind reader. He'd used the same words in his note-to-self on the way home from his parents, *measure up.*

"Not so much your mom," she continued. "It's always the father that sons worry about."

So she's not a judge, she's a psychoanalyst, but I'm not the one who's crazy. "You're nuts, Rita," he said, "Why would I be afraid to tell my dad? If there's anyone in the world I love and respect, it's him."

Rita continued rendering her decision, or her diagnosis, or whatever the hell it was. "Maybe too much so. You think your dad's set such a high standard that you worry you'll never be able to achieve it yourself. So in self-defense, you avoid trying."

"I don't know how you figure that," Krimmer scoffed.

"Think back on how you've handled your life, Jake. Some sons who feel the way you do would run away as fast as they could and never turn around. Others would do their best to follow in their father's footsteps."

"That's what I've done," Krimmer contended.

"Yes, you've followed him, all right, but like a shadow," Rita said. "You make the same moves, but always at a safe distance."

When he didn't question or object, she continued undeterred. "Same college, Columbia—but different majors, English and government. Same university for graduate work, Harvard—but different schools. Choosing to jump into the same big-time Washington cesspool, but different career paths—finance, not law. I think you want to be like him, but different enough so there can be never a direct comparison, except how much money you earn, and that's where you've done everything and anything to be the winner."

Krimmer remained silent and motionless, tending to his smoldering resistance, even as he remembered his mother's words when his parents were arguing about the importance of his monthly contribution—"*I think it's one of the few ways our son knows how to show his love.*"

Rita flashed a forbearing, gap-toothed smile, her first of the evening. "Why were you so upset when you learned that your father deliberately blew the ACEA case in the Supreme Court?" she asked. "Was it because you were worried how it was going to affect your business? Or was it because you thought you could never do what he had done: put principle over profits and push back against climate change?"

Krimmer slouched deeper into the bulging folds of the recliner, as if teenage posture were an effective preventive for self-examination.

Rita challenged him one last time. "Don't you see? That's why you're disappointed in yourself, Jake Jr. That's why you were so ashamed about not convincing Samantha," she told him. "It's not the next generation—it's not Timmy that's holding you back from what you want."

What finally came down from high was less a verdict than a summation. "You're afraid, Jake," she said. "You're afraid you don't have what it takes to be Timmy's dad."

CHAPTER 25

RITA'S HARSH JUDGMENT ROUSED KRIMMER FROM HIS TEMPORARY stupor. "That's truly bullshit." He sat straight up. Actually he was thinking just the opposite, that perhaps she'd nailed it, giving voice to a thought that had been lurking at the edge of understanding, shielded by yet another instance of willful blindness. Even so, it was unclear how it would help him do anything about the situation with Sam.

"Do you really think it's bullshit?" Rita asked, indigo eyes sparkling merry blue. "Perhaps you need another grieve, Jake."

"So I get a mulligan after all?" he joked, trying to keep up the pretense of denial.

"An eleventh grieve is permissible in exceptional circumstances," she assured him, "especially when your personal guide and teacher has screwed things up so royally." She shook her head again. "But thank heavens, she knows how to fix it."

Rita took the phone in one hand, the remote in the other, and began orchestrating a duet for the Nimbus and the TV. In a matter of seconds, the outsized television screen was filled with the fuzzy color image of a dapper, middle-aged man with receding, slicked-back hair, a scraggly toothbrush of a mustache, and dark, imposing eyebrows. Dressed in a plain gray suit and maroon tie, he was sitting behind an uncluttered, nondescript desk with only an old-fashioned, push-button telephone for company and a stylized image of the earth looming behind him on the wall.

"You'll have to excuse the picture quality on your fancy toy," Rita said. "It's early videotape."

The man's serious but friendly face looked vaguely familiar to Krimmer, like that of a distant relative he couldn't quite place. On the giant TV the blurriness was magnified, adding to the impression of a kindly, long-lost uncle reemerging from the mists of time. "So who is this guy, anyway?" Krimmer asked.

"Would you believe a ghost from the past, Jake?"

"And the point is?"

Rita pressed her finger to her lips as the unknown man came to life. He spoke directly to the camera with a soothing baritone voice and measured cadence.

> *Good evening. A unique day in American history is ending, a day set aside for a nationwide outpouring of mankind seeking its own survival, a day dedicated to enlisting all the citizens of a bountiful country in a common cause of saving life from the deadly by-products of that bounty: befouled skies, the filthy waters, the littered earth.*

"OK, I know I've seen him on TV before."

"Maybe old clips from the Kennedy assassination?"

"The moon landings—that's it."

"Walter Cronkite," Rita said, nodding her agreement as she paused the video. "When he was the anchorman for the *CBS Evening News*, he was the most trusted man in America. The night in 1968 when he came back from Vietnam and declared that America was mired in a stalemate, President Johnson reportedly said that if he'd lost Cronkite, he'd lost the country."

Krimmer drew back, increasingly suspicious. "So what's this, another Nimbus trick, Rita? Bring him back from the dead and put words in his mouth to convince everybody about the threat of climate change? How's that going to help me resolve things with Sam?"

"First of all, Cronkite's not talking about climate change. He's talking about the first time we felt it necessary to save the planet. Earth Day, April 22, 1970. That was when America learned to spell *environment*. As for how it will help you with Samantha, there will be a quiz after we finish watching."

Rita continued in schoolmarm mode. "This is the original footage, Jake, from a CBS News special broadcast that evening. Back then, nobody knew that the endgame was climate change. It was all about smog and pollution and garbage. There were demonstrations all across the country. *Teach-ins,* they were called."

She clicked the remote. "Sadly, it wasn't our finest hour," she said, as Cronkite resumed his opening remarks.

> *By one measurement, Earth Day failed. It did not unite. It did not attract that broad cross section of America that its sponsors wanted. Not quite. Its demonstrators were predominantly young, predominantly white, predominantly anti-Nixon. Often its protests appeared frivolous, its protestors curiously carefree. Yet the gravity of the message of Earth Day still came through: act or die.*

Krimmer noticed that Rita was watching him closely; having been sandbagged more than once, he adopted a poker face.

"We begin our report in Denver," the anchorman was saying as the scene shifted to a male correspondent standing in front of the tangle of pipes and smokestacks of an oil refinery.

"A place for purple mountain majesty, a place where on a clear day, the legend said, you could see forever," the reporter said, ominously adding, "The clear days are fewer now," as high schoolers pedaled by on bikes to protest the smog produced by automobiles.

"Here's Philadelphia," Rita said, tapping her phone. The picture changed to a second correspondent, also a man, in the midst of a crowd of students. A young woman with long, flowing hair was playing the guitar and singing in a gentle, reedy voice about the perils of pollution, rhyming sulfur dioxide with carbon monoxide.

"A song from the worldwide hit musical Hair," *said the reporter. "It was one of the first hints suggesting that young people were beginning to care as much about the environment as they do about the peace movements and civil rights. Their dream for the age of Aquarius was to 'let the sunshine in, let the sunshine in.'"*

"The whole program was an hour long," Rita said. "I'm just going to jump around to give you an idea of how serious Earth Day was, how heartfelt the emotions, how committed the kids were."

And they were all kids: mostly white, middle-class, long-haired college students, with the notable exception of Mrs. Willard Hopper's sixth-grade class in Council Bluffs, Iowa, who were taking an early morning nature walk. The student demonstrators were picketing the GE stockholders meeting in Minneapolis, collecting trash at Albion College in Michigan, conducting a die-in at Logan Airport in Boston, holding a Mexican fiesta–style rally in Albuquerque, marching on the Department of the Interior in Washington, releasing hundreds of black balloons during an ecology fair at Stanford University, and organizing more conventional demonstrations at Caltech and UCLA, and in the Chicago Loop and New York's Union Square.

"I can see why it was a bust," Krimmer said. "Bicycles, folk songs, tramping through the woods, picking up litter. It seems more like a party than a protest. How's that going to convince anyone? What did the powers that be have to say?"

Rita permitted herself an amused smile. "This should sound familiar," she said. "The White House issued a statement that all the events around the country should be 'a beginning of a new and sustained public commitment to the environment,' but somehow Nixon could never get around to officially recognizing Earth Day or even Save the Environment Week. It just didn't measure up in importance to two of his more recent proclamations, National Boating Week and National Archery Week." Rita tapped away at her phone as she continued, "But he did send out his minions. Here's what his top environmental advisor had to say when a reporter asked if there was any sense of urgency about the environment."

Very definitely we are not dragging our feet. Of course, the administration and the president has to speak for more than one interest. He has to represent all the interests of the American people here and abroad. And there are a vast number of competing claims upon federal programs.

"You do know who those competing interests included," Rita said with undisguised irony. "The same fossil fuel polluters that you deal with every day."

"The more things change . . ." Krimmer mused.

"That's right, Jake—the more they stay the same. I can't resist showing you this next one, too. The organizers chose April 22 because it didn't conflict with college exams or spring break, and it was the original date of Arbor Day, which had been celebrated for years. But the wing nuts—they weren't called wing nuts in those days, but that's what they were—the wing nuts noticed that it was significant for another reason." A few more taps and Cronkite once again appeared, a true professional, somehow managing to deliver this part of his report with a straight face.

> *Some quarters saw more than coincidence in the fact that Earth Day occurred on the one-hundredth anniversary of the birth of Lenin, the father of Soviet communism. A high school in Boca Raton, Florida, postponed its activities until tomorrow. And the comptroller general of Georgia sent out sixteen-hundred dollars' worth of telegrams warning that Earth Day might be a communist plot.*

Rita paused the video again. "Sound familiar? Ever hear anybody say anything like that about climate change?"

Krimmer's lip curled thoughtfully, the precursor to a tentative nod. The parallels were clear, but he still wasn't sure where she was heading. "What's the point of showing me a failure, Rita?" he asked. "Aren't you afraid it will discourage me?"

"Earth Day wasn't a total failure, Jake. It's still observed every year."

"Sure, in elementary schools all over America. Kids are still taking those nature walks and picking up trash."

"I like to think of it as an object lesson for how difficult it is to do what you know in your heart needs to be done. How easy it is for people to miss the point that the future of the planet is at stake."

With that, she restarted the video, and it was a different Cronkite who now filled the screen. As he finished watching the final segment from the field and turned to the camera, the grim set of his jaw signaled that his demeanor had undergone a profound change. He was no longer the avuncular reporter and anchorman, but the stern, skeptical conscience of the editorial board. As he began to speak, he seemed just the least bit uncomfortable, shifting his body sideways and forward as if he wanted to make sure he was on absolutely firm ground. The tics and tricks he customarily used to punctuate his delivery—the subtle shake of the head, the decisive nod, the raised eyebrow, the staccato phrasing, the powerful pause—all were more pronounced than usual. His deep voice was respectful and contained, but that did not prevent him conveying the impression that he was hurling what he had to say at the unseen audience, accusing them of missing the point about what was at stake. Every time he threw down those three scathing words like a gauntlet— *missed the point*—he followed them up with the briefest of silences to let them penetrate, and his face seemed to grow a little grimmer.

The hoopla of Earth Day is over. The problems remain. Only time will tell if these demonstrations accomplished anything. Now, let's summarize the points that were brought home today to a lot of people who have missed the points so far.

For instance, the politicians who see this as a "safe" crusade. They seem to have missed the point that it will involve treading on more special interests than ever in our history. For the first time, they may even have to come out against motherhood.

For instance, those in industry who see the crisis as only the hysterical creation of do-gooders. They've missed the point if they haven't heard the unanimous voice of the scientists warning that halfway measures and business as usual cannot possibly pull us back from the edge of the precipice.

For instance, the too-silent majority. The greatest disappointment today was the degree of nonparticipation across the country, and especially the absence of adults. And the young people who did participate were in a skylark mood, which contrasted rudely with the messages of apocalypse.

Those who ignored Earth Day, well that's one thing. Those who ignore the crisis of our planet, that's quite another. The indifferent have missed the point, that to clean up the air and earth and water in the few years science says is left to us means personal involvement, and may mean personal sacrifice the likes of which Americans have never been asked to make in time of peace.

That's what today's message really means. And those who marched today, and those who slept, and those who scorned, are in this thing together.

What is at stake, and what is in question, is survival.

As soon as Cronkite finished delivering his impassioned warning, Rita paused the video again. She stared at Krimmer and waited.

"You could have just as easily substituted climate change for Earth Day and broadcast it last night," he admitted. "It's as timeless as Jefferson's words chiseled in marble."

Rita nodded sympathetically. "The problem is, saving the planet was never meant to be just a one-hour TV special," she said. "What happened next—a lot of lip service for change—was the failure of an entire generation. An especially puzzling failure considering these are the same kids that marched for civil rights and ending the Vietnam War. They wanted to make a difference, and they did for a while. And then they stopped, even though the threat to Earth is much greater now than we knew then. They put their career aspirations before their ideals. They 'sold out,' as it was called back then." She paused, then added, "But now your generation has another chance."

All this while she had continued to stare at him, although for once, her eyes had not morphed into a different color. They remained their natural, enigmatic shade of indigo, forever trapped between true blue belief and purple hope.

Krimmer shifted self-consciously on the edge of the recliner. "That's all well and good, Rita, but how does this make me feel better about myself—that I can ever be the kind of dad my father is?"

"You really are some kind of straight man, Jake," Rita said with a glorious, full-blown smile. She reached for the phone one last time. "Let's go to the videotape again, and New York."

The balding, middle-aged CBS correspondent was standing beside a typical demonstrator, a long-haired, scruffy-looking, fidgety young man who was shuffling from one foot to the other, his eyes darting around as if on the lookout for an escape route. "Among the thousands of persons jammed into Union Square for the rally today, was the student coordinator for the Earth Day observance for Columbia University, Jake Krimmer," the reporter announced. "So tell me, Jake, will this concern about the future of the planet pass? Or is it just a fad?" he asked, pinning the microphone up against the young man's lips, as if, more than anything, he was trying to get him to hold still. "Is your generation going to find something else to protest about next year?"

Jake Jr. managed to recover his composure in time to catch his father's expression as nervousness resolved into contempt. His old man was no longer camera-shy. "With all due respect," Jake Sr. said in a hoarse and impassioned voice, as though he had been saying the same thing all day to anyone who would listen, "I think that's one of the stupidest questions I've ever heard. I don't see how this can pass. The problem is here, it's now, and it's real and if we don't do something about it, it's just going to get worse for all of us, and for a very long time."

The reporter nodded solemnly but rather than withdraw the microphone he continued to wave it gently, inviting further elaboration. As the camera zoomed in for a close-up, Jake Sr.'s jaw hardened and he quietly but staunchly reaffirmed his position with a confidence born of youth and inexperience. "There will be no going back, I promise you. We wouldn't just be selling out our generation, selling out ourselves. We'd be selling out the planet."

Rita froze the image. Krimmer stared at the screen, dazed. He wasn't seeing his father's resolute face; he was seeing only a black void, a void so deep and disturbing and unfathomable that if he were ever to fall into it himself, he might never touch bottom.

When Rita felt he'd had enough time to fully absorb the lesson, she said, "I trust you're not missing the point, too, Jake." As if she wasn't completely certain, she continued, "That afternoon when you learned how your father had deliberately sabotaged the ACEA case before the Supreme Court, do you remember what your mother said to your dad about how long it took him to come over from the dark side?"

Krimmer replayed the scene in his mind as Rita reprised the haunting words, even to the forgiving intonation. "Nobody's perfect, Jake Krimmer."

EPILOGUE

"Where's Timmy?" Samantha asked. Her eyes popped open and she leapt up from her chair. Dozing in the warmth of the August-in-May sunshine on the Krimmers' deck, she had apparently forgotten there was no need to be anxious.

"He's down on the beach, having a swimming lesson," Jake Sr. said.

"No, I'm not, Mommy. The water's too cold." The happy shriek in her ear, not to mention the gentle pat on her bottom, made her jump. Jake Jr. and Timmy had snuck up behind her.

"Look what I found," Timmy said excitedly. He was holding an oyster shell.

"Not dead yet," Krimmer noted, as Ben, rousted out of his slumber by the genial chorus, ambled over.

"It was Krims who really found it," Timmy said, as he offered his mother his prize. "But he gave it to me."

Samantha carefully inspected the shell, turning it over and over in her hand.

"I wish I could say the same for your roses, Mom," Krimmer said, scratching behind Ben's ear to ward off any overenthusiastic display of affection.

"Well, if my roses are the worst casualty of climate change, we'll all be very lucky."

"It's beautiful," Sam said as she handed the shell back to Timmy with the pearly side up. "You take good care of it, OK?"

"I told him that the oyster shell was nice and hard. And it was up to him and his friends to keep it that way," Krimmer said as he tousled Timmy's hair. "We're going to make a little presentation for show-and-tell, aren't we, son?"

Timmy nodded enthusiastically; Sam just smiled.

"I never would have believed it," his mother exclaimed. "The way he treats that boy. You must be a very good influence on him, Samantha."

"It's really not me," Samantha said, launching one eyebrow off into space, all the way up to the datasphere. "I'm just the beneficiary of the terror of the ordinary."

Krimmer's parents traded glances, tacitly agreeing not to pry. He had told them about his "consultant," but he didn't dwell on the particulars or go into any details, other than to say she was the one who had alerted him about his father's appearance on the Cronkite special. With Samantha, he had, by necessity, been a lot more forthcoming.

As soon as Rita had left for her client dinner, Krimmer had hopped into the Corvette. Ten minutes later he appeared in the vestibule of Sam's row house, unannounced. Thankfully, she took one look at his hangdog face on the video monitor and, saying nothing, buzzed him in. When Timmy answered the door in his PJs, Krimmer picked him up and threw him over his shoulder, tickling his ribs and making him squeal in delight. Once again, Sam said nothing, but she did hang her head, along with clasping her hands and closing her eyes. She looked like she was praying. After the two of them put the little boy to bed, Krimmer, armed with his newfound self-awareness, confessed everything. Well, almost everything. There was no sense in mentioning how it all got started by the alluring eyes of a cocktail-party newbie.

As he related the ten grieves Rita had employed to work her miracle, Samantha was naturally skeptical, but Krimmer was sensing that the eleventh grieve might do the trick. He gave her his best imitation of Cronkite's rousing delivery and ended with a heartfelt replay of his dad's cameo appearance, confessing how it made him realize that, among other points he'd habitually missed—like the existential threat of climate change and that she'd always been *the one*—he'd missed the point about himself.

Rita's diagnosis of his hang-up about fatherhood was not only true, but also correctable, he swore. It was going to take some time and effort on his part, but now that he "knew himself" the path was clear. If he could overcome his willful blindness and stubborn denial about how he was profiteering at the expense of the planet, he could certainly learn to be a good dad, and love a boy who wasn't all that different than he was at that age. With that fervent pledge, and with a clear, straightforward articulation of the question at hand—no dreamlike state this time—Krimmer told Samantha he loved her and asked her to marry him.

Sam responded the way he'd hoped she would the first time, a short but brutal blank stare while she confirmed that her brain and ears were in agreement, and that she was, too, followed by a smile that encompassed all of them, even Timmy safe in bed. But before she formally accepted, she told him in no uncertain terms that she'd take him at his word for now, but that he'd be on probation until he demonstrated to her satisfaction that he was a good citizen of the planet and a loving dad. She warned him that she'd toss the four-carat diamond he promised her into the Potomac like a cheap cubic zirconium, and the wedding ring with it, if he ever backtracked on his vows—and not just the marriage vows, either, although them, too.

"And don't you think I wouldn't," Samantha had said, pointing proudly to the scar on her shoulder, coming clean at last about her injury. "It started with lacrosse, but I blew it out completely when I threw a frying pan at my first husband for fooling around with another woman."

As they lay in bed afterward, the most intimate moment came when he told her how disappointed he was about how he'd behaved, how ashamed both personally and professionally, and Sam bestowed on him one of her more rueful smiles. "You can't one-up me on shame, Jake," she said. "Don't you see we're two of a kind? What I did at McDonald's was nothing. How long did I hang around, even though I knew every day I was helping speed up the destruction of the planet? All I could do was hope and pray that things would change between us, even though I knew it would take a miracle."

"And that's what we got," Krimmer said.

"Yes, Rita Ten Grieve."

"And you."

Sam's glistening gaze and grateful, lengthy silence let him know he'd truly been forgiven. "So who was she, really?" she finally asked.

"What's the mystery?"

"Hard-to-place accent? Weird, indigo eyes that are always changing color? Are you sure she wasn't one of those doe-eyed kids in those tacky paintings from the 1960s, all grown up and come to life? You know, the ones you always see in flea markets? Or how about those spooky extraterrestrials in all the abduction stories? The way everyone describes them, they have big, dark eyes, too."

"It never would have occurred to me," he'd fibbed.

As for his parents, once they recovered from their surprise—they suspected he hadn't been entirely truthful the day he'd come to visit—they were ecstatic about the news. While Samantha and his mother barricaded themselves in the kitchen to make wedding plans, and Timmy watched *Galaxy Quest* on his iPad for the umpteenth time,

Krimmer and his dad had sat down together to take in the Cronkite special on YouTube. Mysteriously, his father didn't remember being interviewed, although he swore he had been down at Union Square on Earth Day 1970, and that indeed, he was the student coordinator for Columbia. Whether he was just getting forgetful or the Nimbus had struck again, it didn't matter. Seeing his younger self—the long-haired, idealistic zealot on the screen—had almost brought tears to his eyes. "I don't understand how I missed the point for so long, too," he said.

Jake Sr.'s lingering regret had led directly to today's positive announcement. "Hey, I think I forgot to tell you," his dad said, as they all lounged on the deck, soaking up the sunshine. "I got word that the *Washington Post* is going to publish my op-ed piece. Going public with the real story of the ACEA is one small thing I can do to get people to pay attention to how screwed up the country is when it comes to our future."

"I hope you weren't too vitriolic," Krimmer said good-naturedly. "Who knows if someday I might want to get into politics, and I'll have to admit you're my father? I have enough enemies already."

"It's not the number of enemies you have that matters, son. It's who they are that counts."

His mother chimed in. "Well, he's already off to a good start, the way he set straight that crazy congressman."

Krimmer and Samantha had led a protest on the Capitol steps two months before, demanding more action on climate change in general, and higher emissions standards for the ACEA in particular. The day before the protest, a freak mid-March snowstorm had deposited six inches of snow on Washington. This serendipitous display of "weird weather"—no longer a dismissive catchword but their rallying cry to call attention to the looming peril for the planet—had inspired the ranking Republican on the House Science Committee to approach the picket line carrying a snowball and yell, "How the hell can the world be getting warmer, if I can make one of these at the same time we're having the cherry blossom festival?"

The news cameras quickly panned over to Krimmer who yelled back at him, "If it makes you feel any better, sir, just call it weird weather, and if you don't believe it's weird enough today, just wait until tomorrow, when it's supposed to be ninety degrees." All the TV networks had broadcast the clip and the video had gone viral on the Internet.

"Politics would be all right," Samantha said, "but I think Jake ought to write a book, first. A lot of people have no idea how these financial wizards take a bite out of the pie before anyone else gets to eat."

His mother enthusiastically agreed. "Now, there's an idea, Jake. You always did want to be a writer when you were in middle school."

"I always wanted to be an astronaut, too, Mom," Krimmer mumbled.

Samantha pretended to shriek. "You did? I thought there were no more secrets between us."

"Hey, the first model Timmy and I built was the NSEA-Protector, wasn't it?" He had to explain to his mom and dad, "That's the spaceship in *Galaxy Quest.*"

"And here I thought you were just trying to turn Timmy into a Questie, too," Sam said as she shook her head in mock disbelief.

"Well, I succeeded, didn't I?" As his smiling parents looked on, Krimmer squatted down and rested his hands on Timmy's shoulders and stared into the boy's very normal eyes. "You . . . are . . . our . . . hope . . . for . . . the . . . future," he said in a halting, high-pitched, nonhuman voice, as though he was gasping for breath in an alien atmosphere.

"Pay no attention, folks," said Samantha. "He's just pretending to be a Thermian using a language synthesizer."

"Hey, you guys going to stay for dinner?" Jake Sr. asked. "I could spring for a couple dozen oysters to start off. We can live on beans for the rest of the month—right, Susie Q?"

"Yes, please do stay."

"Thanks, but we've got to get back early tonight. With the baby on the way, Samantha needs all the beauty sleep she can get." Krimmer glanced as his watch. "As a matter of fact, we ought to get going."

"How are you liking your new minivan?" his father asked as they prepared to leave. "Are you sorry you sold your Corvette?"

"Zero tailpipe emissions, Dad, and I smile every time I pass a gas station."

"Plus, he doesn't get any speeding tickets anymore," Sam pointed out.

"And by the way, I didn't sell the Corvette. I gave it to Mortenson as kind of a severance present." The Corvette and a tutorial about the tenacity of barnacles, both Krimmer's and the Chesapeake's, wrapped up with a parting jab. If size really mattered that much, he'd asked Jared, why were seemingly dull and unremarkable organisms like barnacles endowed with the longest penises, proportionately, in the animal kingdom—as much as eight times their body length?

Samantha seemed to know what he was thinking, and gave him a preemptive nudge in the ribs. "Actually, Jake wanted to see how guilty he could make his old pal feel about helping bring us together," she said. "It violated all of Jared's principles."

"Oh, nonsense, you were always together," his mother said. "It just took a while for my blockheaded son to recognize what was staring him in the face."

Samantha smiled her thanks. "But we do have to go. Timmy's got school and Jake has to catch a morning flight to Miami. He's got a big meeting with Sunshine Energy and the Southeast Power Combine. They need his expertise."

"Don't you mean your expertise, Samantha?" Krimmer's mother said. "My understanding is my son's just the salesman."

"We're a team," Samantha replied, putting her arm around Krimmer's waist.

"That's right, Mom. We're a team."

Timmy wandered over and Krimmer pulled him in *with* the two of them—definitely not between.

"In fact, we're a family," Sam said as Ben nuzzled his way in, too.

Krimmer nodded his wholehearted agreement. But as thankful and content as he was with the way things had worked out, such an extravagant display of togetherness was bound to rouse one last maverick impulse, making the familiar, tried-and-true barb hard to resist.

"Hah!" Krimmer yelped, but before he could finish, Sam had her hand plastered firmly over his mouth.

"Don't even think about it," she said.

Know someone who'd like to hear more about how "weird weather" is the first sign of the existential threat of climate change?

If so, help spread the word.

Recommend to your friends that they read
The Eleventh Grieve.

Recommend this novel to others by posting
a review. Even a quick rating will help!

Many thanks in advance,
Garth Hallberg
garth@garthhallberg.com

AUTHOR'S NOTE

ALTHOUGH THIS IS A WORK OF FICTION, CLIMATE CHANGE IS A FACT. The relentless rise in global temperature is transforming our weather from something to chat and complain about into something to fear.

The Initial Draft of the 2023 National Climate Assessment: The federal government's report on the climate, issued every four years, states in stark terms, "The things Americans value most are at risk. More intense extreme events and long-term climate changes make it harder to maintain safe homes and healthy families, reliable public services, a sustainable economy, thriving ecosystems, and strong communities."

The draft also reports that the United States has warmed 68 percent faster than the planet as a whole over the past fifty years, with average temperatures in the lower 48 states rising 2.5 degrees Fahrenheit, or 1.4 centigrade.

https://www.nytimes.com/2022/11/08/climate/national-climate-assessment.html

The Paris Agreement: Under the auspices of the United Nations, the Paris Agreement of 2015, adopted by almost 200 countries, called for limiting global warming by the end of the century to well below 2.0°C compared to preindustrial levels, and preferably to 1.5°, or 2.7°F.

https://unfccc.int/process-and-meetings/the-paris-agreement/the-paris-agreement

As of 2023, the latest assessment by the Intergovernmental Panel on Climate Change (IPCC), states that Earth has already warmed by 1.1°C, and predicts that we will exceed the 1.5°C threshold around "the first half of the 2030s." Without a radical shift away from fossil fuels, and achieving net zero emissions by 2050, the 2.0°C objective may well be out of reach, and temperatures could be considerably higher than that by the end of the century.

https://www.ipcc.ch/report/ar6/syr/

The US Contribution: Depending on the source, the United States, with less than 5 percent of the world's population, accounts for 12–15 percent of global greenhouse gas emissions, second only to China. On a per-capita basis, the US has the highest emission rate in the world—about two-thirds higher than China.

The Political Situation: The US government's fealty to the Paris Agreement is sporadic at best and appears to depend on the vagaries of our constitutional system of checks and balances, and which party is in power.

In 2017, the Trump administration informed the UN that the US would withdraw as soon as it was eligible to do so. That withdrawal became official on November 4, 2020, a day after the presidential election. On his first day in office, newly elected President Biden signed an executive order to readmit the United States to the agreement.

In December 2021, Biden signed an executive order for the federal government to "lead by example" and to achieve a 65 percent reduction in government emissions by 2030, and to make the US government carbon neutral by 2050. Unfortunately, the government's contribution to US emissions, including the military, is well under 1 percent of the total.

The Biden Administration's attempts to do more to honor the country's greenhouse gas reduction goals have been met by fierce opposition. The most severe blow was the defeat of a $150-billion proposed program to reward electric utilities that switched from burning fossil fuels to renewable energy, and penalize those that didn't. The provision was scratched from Biden's Build Back Better plan because of the objections of a single senator from a coal-producing state.

On a more optimistic note, $370 billion for climate change measures were included in the final version of the bill, the Inflation Reduction Act, passed in August 2022 entirely along party lines. Money is allocated for an array of measures that include spending and tax credits for clean-energy solutions, electric vehicles, and carbon capture and sequestration.

https://earthjustice.org/brief/2022/what-the-inflation-reduction-act-means-for-climate

Public Opinion: The public's response to Biden's climate policies are sharply polarized. According to a 2022 national survey conducted by the Pew Research Center, 49 percent of US adults believe the policies are taking the country in the right direction, versus 47 percent who say it's going in the wrong direction.

This split persists despite general agreement that climate change is making extreme weather events more frequent and severe. Over 70 percent of Americans say their community has experienced such an extreme event in the past year, and well over half of them believe that climate change has contributed "a lot."

https://www.pewresearch.org/science/2022/07/14/americans-divided-over-direction-of-bidens-climate-change-policies/

The Role of the Electrical Power Industry: The largest single emitter of greenhouse gases — principally carbon dioxide and methane — is the electrical power industry, accounting for roughly 25 percent of US greenhouse gas emissions. Electricity is vital to our way of life, but the highly fractionalized industry that produces it is handicapped by outmoded technology and trapped in an economic model that places short-term profit first, failing to reflect the long-term costs imposed on the planet.

The US Environmental Protection Agency (EPA) reports that more than 60 percent of our electricity comes from burning relatively cheap fossil fuels, mostly coal and natural gas. Power plants account for almost as much greenhouse gas emissions as automobiles, trucks, trains, ships, and planes combined. Thus, placing the industry front and center in this novel reflects reality by pointing the finger at one of the major culprits contributing to the problem.

https://www.epa.gov/ghgemissions/sources-greenhouse-gas-emissions

Although some progress has been made in moving the industry to renewable energy, organized opposition remains strong. In the latest blow prior to publication of this novel, the Supreme Court ruled 6–3 that the Clean Air Act, passed under the Obama administration, does not give the EPA broad authority to regulate power plant emissions.

https://www.nytimes.com/2022/06/30/us/epa-carbon-emissions-scotus.html

Technical hurdles are also a problem. Adding new wind farms and solar arrays to the grid often takes years because of the antiquated systems used to connect new sources of electricity to homes and businesses.

https://www.nytimes.com/2023/02/23/climate/renewable-energy-us-electrical-grid.html

The Role of Speculators: Speculators who profit from the industry's dysfunction, like Jake Krimmer, make the problem worse by siphoning off money that could be better used elsewhere. They also directly impact the cost of electricity to consumers. The size of their profits is difficult to gauge, but it's safe to say it approaches billions of dollars per year. Jake is actually a small fry compared to the Wall Street banks and other large independent traders that buy and sell FTRs—electricity Financial Transmission Rights. For a rare glimpse into this arcane world, here are two articles, the first from The New York Times in 2014, the second from Bloomberg Media in 2022.

https://www.nytimes.com/2014/08/15/business/energy-environment/traders-profit-as-power-grid-is-overworked.html?search ResultPosition=1

https://www.bloomberg.com/news/features/2021-11-05/why-is-my-electric-bill-so-high-energy-traders-bets-could-be-the-culprit

Final Thoughts: So what can we do to combat climate change? Reforming the electrical power industry and the parasitic system that feeds off it, as important as that would be, is only one small step. The more overarching mission is to elevate awareness and concern about the problem, and put it front and center in the national political debate to leverage the power of the voting booth. This novel is a modest attempt toward achieving that objective.

While I'm no expert, I have attempted to be true to the facts while creating a work of fiction. Other than the customary fictionalization of people, places, and business entities, the only license I have knowingly taken is to create an eighth Independent System Operator, the "Southeast Power Combine," to better illustrate a hypothetical situation in the disaster-prone state of Florida.

It's impossible to watch the *CBS News* Earth Day television special from 1970 and not draw the parallels between cleaning up the environment and combatting climate change. The young people in that report appear as deeply committed to fighting for cleaner air and water as those of today who advocate for the Green New Deal. Their limited success attests to the difficulty of the challenge we're now facing. Let us strive to do better. As the esteemed journalist, the late Walter Cronkite, says in his impassioned summation when calling for the inevitable sacrifice that will be required, "What is at stake, and what is in question, is survival."

https://www.youtube.com/playlist?list=PL3480E41AA956A42B

Let's not miss the point, too. I urge all readers to watch Cronkite's 1970 broadcast.

Garth Hallberg
Waccabuc, New York
April 2023

ABOUT THE AUTHOR

GARTH HALLBERG HAS HAD A VARIED CAREER AS A NAVAL OFFICER, advertising executive, marketing consultant, and college professor. He lives with his family in a small hamlet forty miles from Manhattan, where they can enjoy both the stimulation of the big city and the quiet pleasures of the surrounding countryside.

Hallberg's approach to fiction is simple—"Write what you don't know you know"—because writing a novel is not only a willful act of imagination but also a journey of discovery.

Made in the USA
Middletown, DE
03 May 2023

29908183R00161